Praise for *All of Me*

"Berry brings the protagonist to life as a smart, good-humored and resilient woman. . . . By turns serious and funny, Berry's tale is, in the end, a hopeful one, with a lovable and soul-searching heroine readers will sympathize with, and root for."
—*Publishers Weekly*

"Readers come to know and like this feisty [heroine], who has much more to give herself and those she loves than she realizes. Women of all races will find this book funny, sad, inspiring, and delightful."
—*Library Journal*

"Berry tackles the subject of weight with humor and tact. . . . Excellent."
—*Booklist*

"More than being about bigotry as found in race, gender and size, *All of Me* is about the importance of knowing who you are and why you're here. . . . This is a book that deserves attention."
—*Dallas Morning News*

"A welcome respite during this season of weight-loss resolutions. . . . If Berry's latest is true to form, it will enjoy the success of her debut effort, *So Good*."
—*Washington Post*

"By exposing one woman's secret battle with the bulge, Berry's fast-paced second novel may be just the stimulant we need to encourage more dialogue among sisters. . . . An entertaining and realistic read . . . peppered with just enough humor. . . . Readers of all shapes and sizes will be inspired."
—*Black Issues Book Review*

continued . . .

Praise for Venise Berry's debut novel
So Good

"Venise Berry has written a wise and funny book about the relationships of three sharp, beautiful sisters. *So Good* is a welcome addition to the growing body of literature that illuminates the inner lives and worldly struggles of contemporary African-American women."
—Charlotte Watson Sherman, author of *Touch*

"Entertaining . . . snappy, real-life characters double-dare you to put the book down."
—Rosalyn McMillan, author of *Blue Collar Blues*

"A sisterly novel . . . colorful . . . a page-turning peek into the lives of three thirtysomething friends struggling to find independence, financial success, and true love." —*Essence*

"Witty and comical. . . . [Berry's] brazen approach to female sensuality and sexuality is quite illuminating. . . . A poised and frank observer of life's adversities." —*Style*

"Humor, wit, and compassion. . . . Berry will undoubtedly be recognized for her contribution to the African-American fiction writers' library shelf, and for *good* reason!" —*Booklist*

"A hip, savvy, contemporary 'girlfriends' tale. . . . features some lively huddle-and-trash scenes that any woman can identify with and surely chuckle over." —*Star Tribune* (Minneapolis)

"A fresh, frank, and utterly absorbing first novel in the tradition of Terry McMillan. . . . Passionate and full of life, Venise Berry's characters spring from the page with unforgettable realism in a novel that's sure to win over the hearts and minds of readers everywhere." —*Crusader Urban News* (Cleveland)

continued . . .

New American Library
Published by New American Library, a division of
Penguin Putnam Inc., 375 Hudson Street,
New York, New York 10014, U.S.A.
Penguin Books Ltd, 27 Wrights Lane,
London W8 5TZ, England
Penguin Books Australia Ltd, Ringwood,
Victoria, Australia
Penguin Books Canada Ltd, 10 Alcorn Avenue,
Toronto, Ontario, Canada M4V 3B2
Penguin Books (N.Z.) Ltd, 182–190 Wairau Road,
Auckland 10, New Zealand

Penguin Books Ltd, Registered Offices:
Harmondsworth, Middlesex, England

Published by New American Library, a division of Penguin Putnam Inc.
Previously published in a Dutton edition.

First New American Library Trade Paperback Printing, April 2001
10 9 8 7 6 5 4 3 2 1

REGISTERED TRADEMARK—MARCA REGISTRADA

LIBRARY OF CONGRESS CATALOGING-IN-PUBLICATION DATA

Berry, Venise T.
All of me : a voluptuous tale / Venise Berry.
p.   cm.
ISBN 0-451-20262-7 (alk. paper)
1. Afro-American women journalists—Fiction. 2. Overweight women—Fiction.   I. Title.

PS3552.E7496 A79 2001
813'.54—dc21   00-048686
CIP

Set in Simoncini Garamond
Designed by Leonard Telesca

Printed in the United States of America

PUBLISHER'S NOTE
This is a work of fiction. Names, characters, places, and incidents either are the product of the author's imagination or are used fictitiously, and any resemblance to actual persons, living or dead, business establishments, events, or locales is entirely coincidental.

BOOKS ARE AVAILABLE AT QUANTITY DISCOUNTS WHEN USED TO PROMOTE PRODUCTS OR SERVICES. FOR INFORMATION PLEASE WRITE TO PREMIUM MARKETING DIVISION, PENGUIN PUTNAM INC., 375 HUDSON STREET, NEW YORK, NEW YORK 10014.

"Have a Good Life"

All of Me

❧

A Voluptuous Tale

Venise Berry

"God Bless"

To Trish
Let's love ourselves
more!

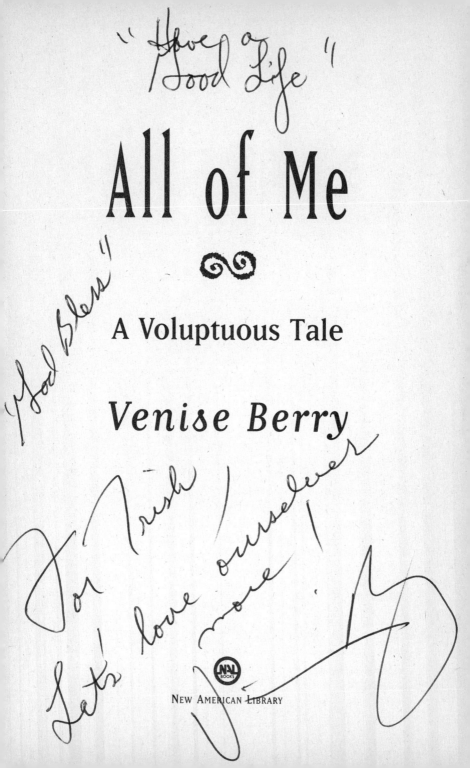

NEW AMERICAN LIBRARY

For the Rubenesque women of the world,
especially my African-American sisters
who have wondered if they're beautiful.

You are!

Acknowledgments

It is impossible to thank everybody who has touched my life in the creation of this important story. But these are some of the folks that I need to acknowledge. Please forgive me for any oversights.

My first thanks must always go to God and my guardian angel, Toni.

My family: Averi, Jean, Virgil, Steve, Raquel, Everett, Gwen, Blanche, Leona, and Maxine.

My sistah-friends: Stephana, Denise, Vanessa, Ayo, Tyna, Poppy, Stephanie, Nancy, Jan, Kelly, Terry, Telester, Pam, Katrina, Deborah, Joyce, Paulette, Joelle, Sharon, and many more.

My brotha-friends: William, Eric, Reverend Blount, Reverend Dial, E. Lynn, Jason, Victor, and many more.

My colleagues in the School of Journalism and Mass Communication at the University of Iowa.

The Des Moines Alumnae Chapter of Delta Sigma Theta Sorority.

The Chicago Alumnae Chapter of Delta Sigma Theta Sorority.

My "always focused," bottom-line agent: Denise Stinson.

My original editor: Michaela Hamilton—Thanks for taking a chance on my talent.

My editor: Elisa Petrini—Your vision and support made this book a reality, and I thank you sincerely!

All of Me

THE MIDDLE
(This Winter)

Crazy People

I'd like to explain how I got to the point in my life where I didn't care if I lived or died, but to tell the truth, I don't really know how it happened. I do know that I feel silly writing in this journal. It was a suggestion from my psychiatrist, Dr. Greeley. He said it might help me organize my thoughts.

My main thought for today is about life. It seems to me that life is a lot like toothpaste. You have to squeeze very gently because once it's out of the tube, it can't be saved.

I tried to explain to Dr. Greeley about Carlin, Mama, LaJune, the job, and the weight. I tried to tell him that I'm not crazy, it's the world that's screwed up, especially for somebody like me. Unfortunately, he was more interested in doping me up than hearing what I had to say. "No drugs!" I had to tell him over and over again. I didn't want them. I didn't need them. I know I'm not crazy, no matter what anybody else thinks!

It took several weeks of telling the good doctor what he wanted to hear: "Yes—I'm sorry I attempted suicide, and no—I don't plan to do it again" before they would finally open the security doors and let me out.

ဢ ဢ ဢ

Serpentine Williamson woke up on New Year's Day in a pale yellow hospital room with a plastic name band fastened to her wrist. As she drifted in and out of consciousness through the night, she only remembered bits and pieces. She could hear the piercing screams of her sister, LaJune, who had found her in the garage.

That memory was mixed with the sound of a high-pitched ambulance siren whirling repeatedly out into the night. Another layer of the memory included the rhythmic crackle of her oxygen mask each time she took a breath.

She still felt the pounding that occurred in her head each time her body was moved. First, from the front seat of her car to the ambulance, next from the ambulance to the emergency room, then, once her vital signs were stable, up to the psychiatric ward on the fifth floor.

Her stomach was queasy and the throbbing pain in her head seemed even more intense as she lifted her body upward. Serpentine pulled off the clear plastic mask and bent over to look for the silver pan.

She didn't see it, so she steadied herself and slid to the floor. She carefully made her way across the room, crawling past the bed, around a metal chair, and finally into the small, sterile bathroom. There wasn't enough time to raise the worn toilet seat, so she shoved her head into the oval opening and threw up a large hunk of lumpy, yellow-green gall. Serpentine squeezed her eyes shut and grimaced when toilet water and vomit splashed back up against her face.

She started to pull her head out, but the vicious churning forced her down again. She pressed her hand hard against her chest until the nausea subsided. Then she slowed her breathing to avoid fully inhaling the smell. She didn't move right away, she couldn't. She sat on the cold, orange, tile floor, leaning her head on the toilet seat and waiting for the next round.

After the second bout, Serpentine slowly lifted herself up from the floor, flushed, and washed out her mouth in the sink. She wet the edge of a towel with cold water and held the cool cotton up to her face, creating a sensation that had to be what the grace of God felt like on judgment day. Then she wiped off the sides of the stool and used the wall to maneuver her way back to the old, metal bed.

Serpentine's first week on the fifth floor went by very slowly. She fought the chills, headaches, and nausea that rotated frequently. After signing a form to disallow visitors or phone calls, she also refused both sessions with her assigned psychiatrist. Serpentine didn't feel like talking. She didn't have anything to say.

It had been a long time since she'd dreamed, but twice that week, Serpentine was awakened by a familiar nightmare from her childhood. She found herself in the middle of a huge spider web with an immense brown spider circling her body. The dark red eyes focused on his task of covering her skin with gooey white thread. She opened her mouth to scream, but there was no sound, and no matter how much she fought the silk binding she couldn't break free.

When the huge spider finally picked her up, Serpentine started to cry. She cringed each time her head bumped up against the creature's round, hairy body. It dragged her kicking and screaming into the same hole where, as a child, she had watched other meals disappear. Then, as the wide jaws opened slowly above her head, she'd force herself to wake up.

During the second week, Serpentine attended her scheduled psychiatrist's appointment, mainly out of boredom. When the door first swung open, she stood and stared at a tall, elderly man with wrinkled knuckles and a thin gold band on his left ring finger.

"Good morning, Serpentine," he said cheerfully. "I'm Dr. Greeley."

Serpentine didn't respond right away. She flopped down in the padded black wingback chair and stared out the window.

"So, can we talk about why you wanted to die?" Dr. Greeley asked with caution.

Serpentine rolled her eyes and continued to focus on the soap-streaked window.

"Serpentine, I need for you to talk to me in order for us to get anywhere," Dr. Greeley added.

She hesitated for a moment watching a newly planted sapling outside dance with the wind. "I just didn't want to be here anymore," she finally replied.

Dr. Greeley scribbled a note on his pad, then continued. "*Why* didn't you want to be here anymore?" he asked. "Can you tell me?"

That question had so many answers, it would take much too long to explain. She absorbed the beauty of the sunshine outside, ignoring the intrusive question. She closed her eyes, thinking how even the sunshine could hurt you, if you stayed in it too long.

"Okay, then let's get to know each other a little bit. I see from your file that your mother and father are Nolita and Kendrick Williamson. They live in Kansas City, Missouri. Is that right?" he asked, stopping to give her a moment to respond.

She glanced in his direction and took a deep, disgusted breath.

"You have a sister, LaJune Thompson who's married to a naval officer, and an aunt, Regina Bentley, both living here in Chicago."

Serpentine frowned. "Where did you get all of that information?" she asked, resenting the invasion of privacy.

"Your sister LaJune checked you in and other family members have called since you were admitted."

"I don't want to talk about them." Serpentine continued with an attitude. She wasn't crazy, but this man and his questions could easily drive her there.

"Well, can we talk about you?" Dr. Greeley paused for a moment.

"It doesn't matter, really," Serpentine mumbled.

"It could help me to help you," Dr. Greeley responded, quickly.

Serpentine crossed her arms over her chest. "I don't need your help," she said.

The tick of the clock grew louder as a painful silence swept the room.

"Maybe we could at least clarify some additional information today," he said, almost pleading for her cooperation. "You're not married, no kids, right?"

Serpentine twisted her head toward him and nodded. He was anal. Probably one of those men who could complete his Christmas shopping for twenty-five relatives on Christmas Eve and still have time for a quick nine holes of golf.

"What about your job? It has to be very exciting to work at a television station. You're a reporter at WXYZ?"

Serpentine rolled her eyes up into her head. "I'm sorry, but I really don't want to do this right now," she moaned. "I think maybe it was a mistake for me to come today."

"Maybe we can try something else," Dr. Greeley said, struggling to break through. "There's something else I'd really like to know."

Serpentine welcomed the disgusted look that took over her face. Why couldn't he just let her go back to her room? She looked him up and down. His marriage was probably domestic incarceration.

"Your name is very unusual. Can you tell me how you got it?"

Serpentine didn't answer right away. She watched as Dr. Greeley waited patiently.

"From my mama," she eventually muttered.

"And how did your mother come to choose such a name?" he came back, quickly.

Serpentine glanced in his direction and slowly lifted her sunken shoulders up to sit straighter in the chair. It was obvious that he wasn't planning to let her go until she told him something.

" 'Serpentine' was a word in a crossword puzzle that my mother was finishing the day her water broke," she explained. "When Mama looked up the word in the dictionary, it was defined as 'coiling, winding, and twisting like a serpent,' and those were characteristics she wanted me to have when it came to life's contradictions."

"Interesting. Do you have those characteristics?"

Serpentine turned and stared out the window again. "I tried," she murmured.

As she watched a dog mark his territory her lips curled slightly. Her name was one of the few things she liked about herself. It was special and it made her special. It had been a long time since she'd had those feelings. Serpentine swallowed hard. Since Dr. Greeley had to know something she would tell him about the concert that changed her life.

"The second semester of my sophomore year of college, I had been dumped by my first love and went into a serious funk for several months. I didn't want to go anywhere, but my cousin Tevan dragged me to an Earth, Wind & Fire concert with him."

Serpentine had gone to Sycamore Mall that morning to find something to wear. It was then that she realized she'd lost weight during her blue funk period. Her regular size fourteen hung off her medium frame like a baggy canvas, but the twelve fit perfectly. A racy red halter dress with black-leather wedged pumps was her final selection. Even though she could barely sit down in the minidress without feeling like something was hanging out, she was so excited, she refused to care.

When Tevan picked her up, he teased her about looking too sexy. She smiled. Tevan knew how to boost her ego, always focusing on the positive. Whenever she complained about anything he'd say, "The more you complain, the more work you have to do here on earth, so the longer God will let you stay."

When they stepped into the Hancher Auditorium, she tossed her head high up in the air and hung on to Tevan's arm. Serpentine enjoyed the attention of men old and young, staring, winking, and grinning. When Tevan wasn't looking, one guy slipped her a piece of paper with his phone number on it and whispered through a heart-carved gold tooth, "When ya call ax for Pretty Boy."

They found their seats in the middle of the sixth row just as the lights went down. Serpentine's eyes searched the darkness until she saw wisps of smoke filling the stage. It smoldered around three gigantic white pyramids; sliding inside and out like a snake stalking its prey. Serpentine shifted forward in her seat just as the music began.

Suddenly bolts of red, green, and yellow light flashed in front of her and nine men ran out onstage, shaking to the funky beat of "Shining Star." The audience leaped to their feet, clapping and whistling. Serpentine reflected on the many shades of brown. Each member was dressed in white. Some wore vests with bell-bottom pants; others had short-sleeved shirts on and wide-brimmed hats, and a few sported clinging blazers that hung open to give sexy bare chests the exposure they deserved.

"Shining Star" was followed by "That's the Way of the World," "Getaway," and "Keep Your Head to the Sky." They kept the jams coming, including Serpentine's favorite, "Reasons." When Maurice White paused onstage to introduce the members of the band, he talked briefly about their new album, *All 'N All.* Suddenly Philip Bailey's falsetto voice began to sing and Serpentine's mouth flew open. She thought she would die, because he was singing her name.

Her face went flush as she closed her eyes and repeated the chorus under her breath. "Gonna tell the story of morning glory, all about the serpentine fire. Surely life's begun, you will as one, battle with the serpentine fire."

It felt good to remember that wonderful moment in her life. It was one of the few times she could remember being truly happy. She had never seen or heard her name anywhere before. It often made her mad as a child that she couldn't find her name on the pre-designed key chains like the other kids. But this more than made up for it. "Serpentine Fire" was her song.

Serpentine couldn't get the melody out of her head that night. She silently hummed the tune all the way back to her dorm room, as she lathered up in a warm shower, while she put on her cotton pajamas, and even when she closed her eyes and summoned sleep.

In the cafeteria the next day, several friends teased her. One asked if she was related to somebody in the group. She lied and said Maurice White was her cousin. A couple wondered if she had heard the song before and she told them that her uncle Philip sang it to her over the phone months ago. She even fibbed to her best friend, Marleen, saying that she'd met Maurice White and Philip Bailey a few years back when they were staying at a hotel in Kansas City, and her name inspired the song.

"I bought the album the next day and collected as much background information on the group as I could. I was so crazy that I spent days researching the album cover," she told Dr. Greeley.

"What kind of research?" he asked.

"It wasn't a normal cover; they had a bunch of symbols on it. I don't remember all of them right now, but the front was focused on the past. There was an Egyptian pyramid that resembled a temple built by King Ramses II called Abu Simbel. Two chiseled warriors sat on each side of the doorway, and above the entrance was an image of a woman holding on to two small children. From inside the open doorway there was an intense beam of light pushing outward. I thought that light held all the answers back then."

Dr. Greeley shifted in his seat. "How?" he asked, softly.

Serpentine tilted her head and thought for a moment. "Because it pulled you inside the cover to reflections of good and bad experiences in life. There were dark, menacing clouds and lightning mixed with angels, and an open book for knowledge. Ten or twelve pedestals each held symbols like the wand of Hermes, a Greek god, who was said to have power over dreams. There was a Buddha seated on a lotus flower, representing meditation and serenity. I also remember an ankh, a Star of David, a menorah, and even a cross."

"So how did all of this change your life?"

Serpentine turned and faced Dr. Greeley. "Maybe it didn't change my life, but it definitely changed my attitude about my life, at least for a little while. You probably can't understand, but that song made me special. It made my name and ultimately my life, unique. The back cover of the album was all about the future. There were a series of modern-looking space station facilities, with five rockets flying upward. And I just knew that's where I was headed—up," Serpentine told him, then suddenly stopped talking.

"Is something wrong?" Dr. Greeley asked, taking note of her abrupt mood change.

"That turned out to be a pretty good year in my life," Serpentine continued, but her heart wasn't in it. "In 1974 I officially adopted 'Fire' as my middle name, then, not long after that, everything fell apart again."

"Do you want to tell me what happened?"

Serpentine shook her head no, and turned and stared out the window again.

Things got a little easier the third week. Serpentine stepped into Dr. Greeley's office with a slightly better attitude. She had counted the bricks on each wall in her room three different times. Every time she came up with a different total: first, 1,456; second, 1,355; and third, 1,460. She couldn't count the bricks again, so she needed something else to concentrate on or she might really go crazy.

Dr. Greeley was on the phone when she entered. She sat down on his faded brown leather couch and intensely surveyed the wall behind his desk. It was typical for someone at his level, with two diplomas, a few certificates, and several gold-and-silver plaques.

"So, Serpentine, are you ready to get started?" Dr. Greeley asked as he hung up the phone. "I thought from the last session we could begin by contrasting happiness and sadness."

"Fine," Serpentine replied, picking at the raw cuticle on her left thumb.

Dr. Greeley waited for her to speak, but when a few silent moments had passed he continued. "Why don't you tell me about something you like to do? Maybe something that makes you happy or even something that makes you sad?" Dr. Greeley's childlike tone annoyed her.

"I like to write," she replied. "I've always liked to write. That's why I went into journalism. I don't really know what makes me happy, because I've been happy so rarely in my life. And sad? Almost everything makes me sad."

"Is that why you attempted suicide?" Dr. Greeley asked, letting the question float out into the air and hang there for a while.

Serpentine tried to organize the jumble of words in her head, with little success.

Dr. Greeley seemed to recognize her difficulty. "So what did you want out of life, Serpentine, that you didn't get?"

She scratched her forehead and glanced at him thoughtfully. "I wanted the world to stop trying to fit me into neatly arranged categories. I wanted this screwed-up society to allow me a little happiness. I wanted the fact that I'm black, a woman, and full-figured to have no impact on my relationships."

Dr. Greeley nodded his head stiffly. "When people try to squeeze you into these categories, how does it make you feel?" he continued.

Serpentine's mother had always told her that no question was a stupid question, but Serpentine had to disagree here. "How do you think I feel?" she screamed at the balding figure in front of her. "I get mad. I get pissed off! I get sick of it! Why do you think I'm in here listening to your bullshit?"

Dr. Greeley waited a moment before he spoke, showing no visible reaction to her outburst. "What could you do differently if people did not see you as black or female or full-figured?"

Serpentine rested her elbow on the edge of the couch and shook her head. "Maybe I could live a normal life for a change," she replied. "Focus on simply being a human being. I could walk into a job interview or a meeting without putting my guard up. I wouldn't have to keep watching for the bias that always appears because of my race or gender or weight."

Serpentine wondered how interested he really was. His sincerity seemed as phony as those people who put plastic on their furniture to keep from using it.

"Can you give me a specific example?" Dr. Greeley asked.

Serpentine took some time to think before she spoke. She felt patronized, but offered the easy example that came to mind, anyway. "I saw this report on television once about a study that had been conducted at Vassar College. For forty days they fattened up a group of rats, then put them on a low-calorie diet. It took twenty-one days for the rats to go from obese back to normal. Then they fattened up the same rats again. The second time it only took fourteen days to get them back up to obese, and when they put the rats back on the same diet, it took forty-six days for them to lose the same pounds."

"And explain how that study relates to you?" Dr. Greeley asked with a wrinkled brow.

Serpentine's eyes shot up into her head. "I'm one of those rats, Doc. I'm caught in that cycle. I go up, then back down again. Only it's not just my weight, it's my family, men, my job. My life is like a never-ending twirly-cup ride at Adventureland making me sick!"

"But doesn't everybody have these same kinds of highs and lows?" he asked soothingly.

Serpentine scowled at his insensitivity. It was impossible to explain her reality as a black female in America to this man. He had no clue. As long as his white privilege was in place so he could wear thousand-dollar designer suits, live in his big house out in the suburbs, and drive his convertible sports car, he was not about to take the blinders off. This world had been good to people like him and their experiences would never connect.

As if unconsciously responding to her changing mood, Dr. Greeley nervously fiddled with the blinds. "Do you prefer that these be open or closed?"

Serpentine twisted her face in disbelief. "Who gives a damn about the blinds!" she screamed. "I thought we were supposed to be talking about me!"

Dr. Greeley shifted uncomfortably in his seat and glanced at the clock on the wall. "You're right, I'm sorry, but our time is up, unfortunately. I'll see you next week," he said quickly, standing up. "I think we covered some important ground today."

Serpentine jumped up from the couch, and rushed out the door without looking back. "I can't believe I'm the one locked up," she fumed.

It took a while for Dr. Greeley to release Serpentine back into the real world. He decided, however, that there would be a stipulation. Because she refused to take the drug he was recommending, she would need to continue outpatient therapy with him twice a week.

The Sand

I'm sitting in the sandbox at a park two blocks from my house. I started walking, not going anywhere in particular, and here's where I stopped. I can't believe how warm it is for February, almost fifty degrees today. I took off my shoes and let my toes burrow into the sandy mound. I've always found it fascinating that the sand readjusts itself into matching footprints beneath me.

The tiny off-white particles sprinkled with small green leaves, rocks, twigs, and dirt remind me of my mother. She's a combination of good and bad, selfishness and love, weakness and determination. And over the years, Mama has tried to shape me into her matching footprints. I love Mama, but I don't want to be like her. I don't want to be "like Mike," either.

ண ண ண

Serpentine wanted to go home, but she was also dreading it. Although she missed her own bed at the beige ranch-style house in Hazel Crest, Nolita was there waiting, and Serpentine wasn't ready to deal with her mother. She cringed, realizing that the suicide attempt would be one more thing for Nolita to disapprove of.

As soon as LaJune stepped into the room, tears shot through Serpentine's eyes, and she hugged her sister tightly. LaJune squeezed back as best she could despite her large, rounded belly that was in the way. When the embraced ended, LaJune made a fist and hit Serpentine's shoulder as hard as she could.

"Owwww," Serpentine yelped, rubbing her arm.

"What the hell is wrong with you? Why didn't you talk to me?" LaJune demanded in an agitated voice.

"I didn't know what to say," she replied, not able to look La-June in the eye.

"We've always been able to talk things out, what do you mean you didn't know what to say?" LaJune continued.

"I'm sorry, June," Serpentine replied. "Can we please just drop it for now?"

"It *will* come back up later," LaJune said, then grabbed her big sister and hugged her again. "If my baby comes out neurotic I'm gonna kill you myself," she joked.

Serpentine picked up her blue tote bag from the floor near the door and the paperwork for her release off the bed. She clutched the papers tightly to her chest, excited about her freedom, and followed LaJune out into the hall.

Several of the nurses and orderlies nodded and briefly waved as they walked toward the exit. Serpentine fixed a crooked smile on her face and tried to be cordial. When they reached the nurses' station the head nurse motioned toward them.

"Excuse me, Ms. Williamson," she called. "But I will need your signatures."

Serpentine walked over to the counter, skimmed the form, and signed. Then she turned to walk away.

"Mrs. Thompson will need to sign for your release, as well," the nurse added, pointing to the paper.

Serpentine whirled back around. "Why does she need to sign?" she asked angrily.

The nurse shifted nervously, as if this were something she didn't enjoy. "Technically, we're releasing you into her custody," she replied.

"What the hell does that mean?" Serpentine yelled. "I'm a grown woman and this ain't prison!"

"But you're still under Dr. Greeley's care. It's hospital policy, insurance reasons. We need to have someone sign you out," the nurse explained.

Serpentine opened her mouth to complain some more, but La-June marched over to the counter and signed the form. "Just let it go, Serpentine," she said. "Arguing about it is like getting your hair done on a rainy day—a waste of time."

The nurse buzzed the security doors open and in just a few minutes they were out of the hospital and headed home.

It was a quiet ride. Serpentine didn't want to talk and LaJune didn't know what to say. As they drove up to the house, Serpentine saw her mother's gray minivan in the driveway and noticed the familiar corrosive knot in her stomach. LaJune turned off the engine and opened her door. Serpentine didn't move. She sat very still.

"You okay?" LaJune asked, pulling her left leg back inside the car.

"I don't know if I'm ready to deal with Mama," Serpentine mumbled.

LaJune frowned. "I don't know why you let her get to you. Can't you ignore her like I do?"

"I try, but I can't seem to get control. Dr. Greeley says she only does what I expect her to do," Serpentine replied.

"When she says something that upsets me, I imagine she's an alien and come up with a funny line. You should try it," LaJune suggested.

"Funny like what?"

"Like this morning, she started in on Parren not being around for my pregnancy, ignoring the fact that the man is in the Navy and had to go back to his ship. While she complained, I thought, 'Do they ever shut up on your planet?' "

Serpentine laughed out loud with her sister, then they got out of the car and walked up to the house. Sometimes Serpentine compared Nolita with the Road Runner because her mother was small, sharp, and fast. She had also seen most of her mother's enemies meet with fates similar to Wile E. Coyote's.

Serpentine actually admired the confidence and determination that Nolita wielded with scary proficiency. Nolita would neither confirm nor deny it, but the family myth suggested that Serpentine's own birth was part of a well-thought-out and executed plan. As the legend went, Nolita got pregnant on purpose to catch Kendrick, Serpentine's father.

The story began on a cold January morning in 1958 when Nolita first opened swollen eyes and knew there was a child forming inside her. For months, she had slept with Kendrick every Saturday night, and prayed in church every Sunday morning.

When she hopped out of her twin bed that particular morning and ran through the frigid air into the tiny bathroom, there was no doubt in her mind that she had accomplished her goal. She dropped her terry cloth gown on the floor and stepped into the shower. As the hot flow of water ran down her body she relived the ecstasy of Kendrick's heated, satin lips the night before.

Kendrick was one of the finest boys at Western College, a mature senior with his own car. He worked part-time every evening at Shops Bakery, so he always had money in his pocket. Because Nolita was still in high school, many women on Western's campus didn't think she could handle Kendrick. They gossiped and teased, complained and prophesied about her inability to make a college man happy. When she and Kendrick first started dating,

Nolita was infuriated by the rumors. Yes, she was young, and no, she wasn't the prettiest girl in the world, but she was a long way from ugly. She had a dynamite figure and sultry eyes that she'd started accenting with mascara as early as fourteen. When she and Kendrick celebrated their first year together, the whispers finally stopped.

The Paseo YMCA sponsored dances almost every Friday night.

It was called the "black YMCA" because a Jewish philanthropist who wanted to do something to help black people offered twenty-five thousand dollars if the city would raise another seventy-five thousand for the building. Kansas City took the challenge, black folks raised thirty thousand dollars and white folks collected the other forty-five.

Nolita met Kendrick at one of those Friday night parties. She decided after just one dance that he was the man she was going to marry. She worked on getting his attention for weeks; showing up in places where she knew he'd be, making sure she was noticeable. She studied him, paying careful attention to his color and style. Kendrick often wore tight Levi's jeans and a white dress shirt, so Nolita countered with similar, hip-hugging Levi's and a white cardigan sweater.

"You look nice tonight," Kendrick told her one Friday, leaning against a tall wooden post.

"Thanks," she said, dropping her eyes to the floor to falsely suggest shyness. Nolita waited, lifting her head only after he spoke again.

"I've seen you a lot lately, but I haven't been able to find out much about you. You're a mystery to most of the people I know," Kendrick said.

"That means you don't know the right people," Nolita replied.

"If I asked you out, would you say yes?" he asked, rubbing his gold-plated belt buckle.

"Are you asking me out?"

"Yeah, I think I am," he added, then looked around as if he were afraid that someone might have heard him.

Nolita suddenly turned cold. "When you know for sure, ask again," she told him and walked away.

Kendrick followed her around for several weeks after that. She sometimes threw him a smile or honored him with a brief conversation to keep his hopes up, but it was three months later before they finally went on their first date.

When Kendrick officially became her boyfriend, Nolita knew she still had a lot of work to do. She confided in her sister, Regina, who was five years older and the only sexually active woman she knew.

"You can't allow just any fool to get some of your good stuff," Regina warned. "You better believe Sam earns everything he enjoys."

"I love him, Regina, and he's good to me," Nolita pleaded. "I just don't want to lose him to one of those college girls who doesn't mind putting out."

Regina sucked her teeth and rolled her eyes up into her head. "You don't need to be having sex with that Negro—girl, he's too old, and you're too inexperienced."

"I don't want to have sex, but I got to do something," Nolita explained.

Regina shook her head as patented words of wisdom flew out of her mouth. "Well, I can tell you how to keep him without really giving anything up. But you've got to promise me you're not gonna go all the way. He's gonna want to, but you have to say no. Don't come up with no babies on me, little girl."

Nolita nodded her head and promised, so Regina continued, threading the needle on her sewing machine.

"Men are really sensitive, so once you know the right spots to hit, you can easily bring him to a climax using your hand without risking a baby. I wouldn't put nothing in my mouth until after you got that wedding band on your finger."

Nolita frowned. "That sounds so nasty." She made a gagging noise.

"Sex is nasty, but that's why it's good. Now, are you ready for this or not?" Regina asked. She turned back to her sewing machine and pressed on the pedal.

Nolita hesitated. "I guess so," she replied.

Regina guided the needle over the seam of a pair of black-and-white pants. "It don't sound like you ready to me, little girl. Maybe you should just let this man go on about his business."

"No, I'm ready, Regina. Tell me, please," Nolita pleaded.

The conversation lasted late into the night, then Nolita implemented her plan. In the back row at the theater, she helped Kendrick explode. In his cousin's basement, she made the darkness seem much brighter. And Kendrick's favorite place was in his car as they drove across the bridge between Kansas City, Missouri, and Kansas City, Kansas. After several efforts, Nolita got the timing down, so that just as they drove onto the bridge Kendrick would raise his right foot from the gas pedal and allow his body to grow tense with pleasure. They would coast along for a minute or so with Kendrick screaming her praises.

The day Nolita told Kendrick about Serpentine's impending arrival, most of the snow from the weekend had melted, and the sun was taking care of anything that was left. She met Kendrick at the college for lunch. They had just finished eating when she guided him out onto the adjacent softball field to talk.

"Kendrick, what are *we* going to do when you graduate in May?" she asked as they walked over toward the bleachers.

"What do you mean? We'll still be together," Kendrick replied, then sat down on the bottom row. "I'm going to get a good job, save some money, and we'll get married in a couple of years."

Nolita paced slowly in front of him. "But we won't really be together and I'm afraid things will change."

"Change is sometimes good, baby, if you open yourself up to it. Come here, so I can tell you the changes I see happening for us." Kendrick grabbed her hand and pulled her down onto his lap. "I'm going to finish college, and get a full-time job teaching. We'll get married and have several little Kendricks running around."

"What if I don't want to wait a year or two to get married?" Nolita asked, sliding off his lap.

Kendrick's smile quickly turned into a look of frustration. "You know we can't afford to do it sooner than that, Nolita. We've already had this discussion."

Nolita took a deep breath and just let the information float out over her tongue. "I have a little Kendrick growing inside me right now."

Kendrick coiled back, taking Nolita by surprise. His eyes held a look of disbelief until he allowed the words to register thoroughly.

Nolita wasn't sure what to say next. She waited and embraced the fear that viciously ripped through her small body.

"You're pregnant?" he finally asked, hopping up from the bleachers in a daze.

"You're suppose to be as happy as I am, Kendrick. This is what we wanted. This means you and me forever."

"But now is not the time, Nolita. A baby costs money, and you haven't even finished high school yet."

"I can finish school later. The most important thing is this little person that we've made," Nolita said, then suddenly changed her tone. "I thought you would understand that. But hey, the last thing I want to do is force you into anything, Mr. Williamson!"

Nolita turned and walked away, praying silently for Kendrick to call her back or follow her. Moments later, when she twisted around, she saw him disappear behind the large wooden doors of the chemistry building. She stopped and watched the doors slam shut, then walked across the field toward the outside gate, lost in thought. As the tears flowed, she stepped off the curb right in front of a rusted, red Chevy Impala. The driver slammed on his brakes and cut to his left in an attempt to miss her, but he failed.

Nolita woke up in the emergency room at General Hospital. She had a broken leg, along with minor cuts and bruises. Just as the nurse finished telling Nolita how she had met Cab Calloway in 1945, when he was hit on the head by a policeman at the Pla-Mor Ballroom and rushed to emergency for eight stitches, her mother came in.

She sat down on the edge of the bed bewildered, staring at Nolita. "Why didn't you come to me?" she asked.

Nolita lowered her eyes, and used a cracked voice. "I'm sorry, Mom, but I didn't know how to tell you, especially when Kendrick didn't want to marry me."

"Do you know how much I love you?" her mother asked, leaning over Nolita and kissing her cheek.

Nolita shook her head. She was surprised at how calm her mother remained.

"If I love you and this baby is a part of you, I have to love the baby. You should know that."

"Why didn't Kendrick feel that way, Mom? It's his baby, too!"

Her mother sighed. "Sometimes men get scared, Nolita, especially black men. No matter how macho they act, they don't process things the way we do. It's a day-to-day struggle for them. So when the big picture hits them upside the head, they sometimes panic. Give Kendrick some time and he might surprise you."

When Nolita reached up to hug her mother she noticed that the pain medication was wearing off. For the first time, she could feel the dull ache of her broken leg bone, along with the butterfly movements of Serpentine inside her stomach. She closed her eyes and concentrated on the distinct sensations. She winced as she thought about how poorly she had judged the reactions of the two people closest to her.

One week later, when Nolita got home, a bouquet of red and yellow roses and a beige teddy bear were waiting from Kendrick. Within a month, they were talking on the phone. And when it was time, he stayed at the hospital through the sixteen-hour labor and delivery of their baby girl, Serpentine. Once he graduated, Kendrick took a job teaching math at Booker T. Washington Elementary School, and he and Nolita were married soon after.

Serpentine smiled, thinking about her father's trained response to the tale. A big grin would spread across his face and his chest would expand as he bragged that he knew what was going on all along. He'd say, "I thought any woman who would work that hard to get me should be rewarded."

Standing at the front door, Serpentine hesitated. She knew that people, even her family, would treat her differently than before. As she reached for the knob, the door flew open.

"Teenie, baby," Nolita said, rushing over and throwing her arms around Serpentine's neck.

"Hey, Mama." Serpentine returned the hug half-heartedly.

"There's my girl," Kendrick said, hustling in from the kitchen.

He reached over and slung his arms around both Nolita and Serpentine.

LaJune waddled over to the huddle. "Wait a minute, don't leave me out," she protested, turning her protruding stomach sideways.

Serpentine was the first to pull away. She snatched up her bag and carried it into the bedroom, where she kicked off her shoes and sat for a moment on the edge of her bed. She truthfully didn't know what was wrong. She appreciated their love and concern, but she wanted to be alone. She needed time to adjust.

"So, Teenie, how are you?" Nolita asked, stepping into the doorway, then continued without waiting for a reply. "You can stay in here and rest for a while, if you like. I'm staying all week to take good care of you."

"I'm fine, Mama. I can take care of myself. And please stop calling me Teenie," Serpentine growled. "I've told you a thousand times, I hate that name. I'm a lot of things, but I'm not teeny and it sounds stupid."

Nolita bristled, then immediately backed down. "It's just a nickname, baby, you know that," she said calmly. "I've been calling you Teenie for forty years, and I'm sorry, but it's going to take some time to stop."

Serpentine stared at Nolita. Her mother rarely retreated during a battle and Serpentine wanted to make note of the small victory.

"Hey, are you guys hungry?" Kendrick interrupted. He stepped into the door waving a chicken leg in his right hand. "Mom has some good stuff in here, Serpentine: fried chicken, macaroni and cheese, creamed corn, and salad."

"I think Serpentine wants to rest, honey," Nolita volunteered. "She can eat later."

"I can talk for myself, Mama. Please, don't treat me like something's wrong. I'm fine. It happened, it's over, and let's please move on!"

A buzzer sounded from the kitchen and Nolita hurried away to pull the rolls out of the oven.

"Sugar, you do whatever you need to do," Kendrick said. "I'm going back in the kitchen and fix me a plate."

Serpentine knew Nolita was basically a good person, but she had a hard time accepting human frailties. The fact that she had made all of Serpentine's favorite fattening foods brought forth a smothering fear. When she supported Serpentine's efforts to lose weight over the years, it was because she cared. But now Serpentine realized that her mother's support had also given her the wrong message. Nolita had always confirmed that Serpentine's weight was a problem, rather than helping her to recognize her beauty. Her mother's efforts, although designed to help, actually did just the opposite. She reinforced the burning shame and doubt that Serpentine harbored when it came to her Rubenesque frame.

Serpentine massaged the back of her neck. It was too difficult to interact with everybody right now, so she slipped her shoes back on, rushed through the living room, and out the front door. "I'll be back," she tossed out just before the door slammed.

Serpentine found herself pulled in the direction of laughing children. Two blocks down, she arrived at a playground where kids were running and jumping and sliding and bouncing, taking every possible advantage of life. She walked over to an empty sandbox and sat down. Taking her shoes off, she enjoyed the feeling of cold, hard sand against the bottoms of her feet. She stood up and created a set of perfect footprints in the sand the way she used to do as a child. Then prayed for the strength to put her life back together.

Relationships

A relationship that does nothing, gives nothing, costs nothing, and suffers nothing is actually worth nothing.

This includes all relationships. The loving relationship with your mother. The devoted relationship with your father. The give-and-take relationship with your boyfriend. The competitive relationship with your sister. The protective relationship with your brother. The caring relationship with your aunt. The warmhearted relationship with your uncle. The faithful relationships with friends; and even the strained relationship with enemies.

Mount Glory Baptist Church rocked on Sunday mornings, and this Sunday, Serpentine woke up missing that Holy Spirit. As she dressed, she found herself nervous about seeing Aunt Regina. Regina hadn't called or come by the week since she'd been home. Serpentine had let Regina down too and she worried that their relationship might never be the same.

Serpentine talked to her aunt about a lot of issues in her life because they shared a unique spiritual connection. She found it easy to talk to Regina about everything except the thoughts of suicide. When they'd first come, five years ago, they were sporadic. Something would happen; a frightening pain or fear would emerge, and a powerful need to escape took over. Eventually, the thoughts started coming monthly, then weekly and sometimes daily, constantly tormenting her soul.

Serpentine often wished, on those days, that she had been born with a stronger spirit like her aunt's. It seemed like nothing bad could ever touch Regina's soul. As Serpentine slipped on her panty hose, she relaxed a little, knowing that somehow Regina would understand what happened. She had to understand.

Serpentine pulled up in front of the contemporary chapel an hour later. Smiling, she noted the variety of folks hustling inside. Women wearing large floppy hats, mid-length dresses, and high-heeled shoes. Men sporting jackets, suits, sweaters, and ties. In the ten years since the Reverend Doctor Jeremiah Middleton had come to Mount Glory, the congregation had grown from one hundred to nine hundred members.

The Reverend Doctor believed in community ministry, so, building on the strengths of his members, he'd established a number of programs. There was a singles program, after-school care, income tax preparation for families, a political education service, assistance for the elderly, a program to feed the hungry, a popular radio show on WGOD Monday through Friday mornings, and the jewel in his crown, the award-winning gospel choir, Glory.

Serpentine could envision her aunt, as choir director, standing in front of Glory, arms raised high and mouth open wide. Glory's membership hovered around one hundred and fifty souls, and Regina Bentley knew how to bring out the best in each one of them. After many years of success, you couldn't pay the Reverend Doctor, deacons, stewards, or even choir members to question her decisions when it came to Glory.

The name Glory was chosen because they were singing for the glory of God, and the glory of God was what listeners experienced whenever they sang. Glory had won many local and state awards, including first place in last year's Chicago Gospel Music Fest and the Baptist Musical Achievement award two years in a row. The choir was in the middle of negotiating a contract for their first CD at a local recording studio.

Serpentine had been a member of Glory for many years. But working ten and twelve hours a day at the television station made it difficult for her to attend the biweekly practices. She had promised the Lord a number of times that she would do better, but somehow always fell short. Even church service on Sundays was a hit and miss proposition.

"Hey stranger," her cousin Tevan yelled as Serpentine walked in the door of the chapel.

"Hey yourself," Serpentine replied, moving toward him, expecting the warm hug they had always shared.

Tevan put his arms around her lightly and stepped back. "You don't return phone calls anymore?" he asked.

Serpentine caught the obvious strain in his voice.

"I did call back, but I didn't leave a message," she explained as she grabbed copies of the three songs they would sing for service that morning.

"Where's Aunt Regina?" she asked as she slipped on her orange- and green-striped choir robe.

"She's probably talking to the Reverend about the record contract. She'll be here soon," he answered. "How are you?"

Serpentine took her place in the choir line without answering. The distance she felt between her and Tevan now added to her pain, but she didn't know what to do about it. He was her father's brother's only son and even though he grew up in Detroit, they were very close. Tevan had followed her to the University of Iowa on a football scholarship, then moved to Chicago to work as an athletic counselor at Chicago State after his graduation. She had always appreciated the way he looked out for her, but there was nothing he could have done to stop what happened that night, and she knew he'd never understand that.

"I asked, how are you, Ms. Williamson?" Tevan asked again in a more serious tone.

Serpentine leaned against the wall. "I'm okay. You don't have to worry about me," she finally responded.

Tevan stepped in line behind her. "I have Chicago Bulls tickets for next week. The six-time champion Chicago Bulls. How about going with me?" he asked cautiously.

Serpentine smiled. "Thanks. But I'm not ready to jump back into things just yet. Why don't you invite one of your honeys?"

Tevan shifted his husky body sideways and breathed an exaggerated sigh. "Serpentine, you don't take a honey to a Bulls game, you take family or a friend."

Serpentine clicked her teeth and shook her head. "No, thank you."

"Well, maybe that fine friend of yours, Marleen, could come. You think she's ready to treat a brother right yet?" Tevan asked with raised eyebrows.

"Boy, please," Serpentine replied, finding it hard to keep a straight face. "You and Marleen together would be like hitting rock bottom, then digging even further down."

"How can you say that? She's the woman I'm going to marry," Tevan teased.

"Yeah, right," Serpentine grunted.

"The first day we met, I knew we were meant for each other," he insisted.

Serpentine laughed. She remembered that day, but with a slightly different spin.

She had entered the Hillcrest cafeteria, took a tray off the rack, and slid it down the rail. She placed several napkins and silverware on her tray, then pulled a small bowl of chunk-cut watermelon, a whole wheat roll, and a tossed salad with a packet of French salad dressing from the counter. She filled a glass with lemonade and took a plate with something that looked like a chicken potpie on it. Marleen was already sitting at a large table by the window, so she joined her.

"You going to the Greek mixer this Saturday?" Marleen asked as Serpentine sat down.

"I'm not sure," Serpentine answered, pulling Toni Morrison's *Sula* out of her coat pocket and laying it open on the table. "I've got a lot of reading to do."

Marleen looked over at Serpentine's book. "You don't have to read during your dinner to make good grades," she said sarcastically.

Serpentine was just about to reply when Tevan's deep voice echoed behind her head.

"Hey, Serpentine?" he bellowed, then dropped down onto the empty chair beside her.

"Hi, cuz," she said, smiling.

"So you're Serpentine's cousin," Marleen mused, nibbling on a french fry. "I've heard a lot about you."

"Serpentine didn't tell me enough about you, but now that we've met, I think I could be the answer to your dreams," Tevan replied.

Serpentine laughed as Marleen tossed her a "What the hell?" look, complete with furrowed brow.

"Where you from?" Tevan continued, then took a big bite from one of two hamburgers on his tray.

"My family lives up the road in Des Moines," Marleen answered, visibly admiring the mahogany skin that covered mounds of muscles. "Where are you from?"

"Detroit, the Motown City," he said, then sang, "Oooooooh,

Baby Baby," in a brief rendition of the Smokey Robinson and the Miracles tune.

"I thought Detroit was the Motor City," Marleen corrected him.

"Yep, that's us too. We got cars for days. Cadillacs, Pontiacs, Chevys, Fords, Buicks, Chryslers, Oldsmobiles, any brand you want. My dad knows everybody. He can get you a great price!"

Serpentine took a bite of her chicken potpie and tried not to laugh at her cousin's antics.

"So what position do you play?" Marleen asked, glancing at the sleeve of the black and gold Iowa jacket hanging on the back of his chair.

"Defense, and I'm a bad mother, if I do say so myself," he replied, allowing his eyes to drop down and survey Marleen's ample chest.

Marleen grinned in a flirty way. "You planning to go pro?"

"Of course, everybody plans to go pro. But I'm also setting up a solid foundation for myself. I ain't the typical stupid jock, if that's what you're hinting at."

"Did I say you were a stupid jock?" Marleen asked.

"Girl, you just don't know how happy you could be if you gave me a chance," Tevan teased.

"Sorry, sugar, you're too young," Marleen snapped.

"I guarantee I could make you forget my age," he countered.

Marleen turned to Serpentine. "If I throw a stick, is he trained to fetch it?" she joked.

Serpentine was jarred out of the memory as the choir line bolted forward.

"You know, you could hook a brother up with Marleen, if you wanted to," Tevan whispered.

"Get a grip," she mumbled as they reached the center of the third riser and stopped.

Serpentine looked around for Aunt Regina, realizing she had never come into the room. The pianist's initial chords set the choir in motion and they rocked back and forth with the beat. It was then that Regina stepped into the sanctuary. Her choir robe crisply flowing from her shoulders to the floor. Regina moved as if she were floating, and the congregation stood up to acknowledge her presence, clapping their hands and stomping their feet with all the energy they could muster.

Regina stood in front of the group, and Serpentine noticed an instinctive glance in her direction. When their eyes met, Regina smiled. Serpentine smiled back and thought about what Reverend Middleton always said: "Regina was the keyhole through which many lost souls saw God."

Regina raised her hands to ready the group as Sister Chevon slid over to the center of the first riser, took the microphone, and rocked her shapely hips from side to side.

"In the spirit, glorious, glorious spirit," she sang.

"You checking out those hips?" Serpentine whispered to Tevan, trying to get back into their usual banter. "That's who you need to be getting with."

Tevan bumped her gently with his shoulder and stifled his laughter as the choir joined in.

"In the spirit, glorious, glorious spirit," the choir sang. "In the spirit, glorious, glorious spirit."

Chevon began the solo verse, reading the words from her photocopied sheet.

Regina jerked her hands faster to communicate the need for more speed. Then she glanced over at Serpentine and winked.

"In the spirit, glorious, glorious spirit," Glory sang. "In the spirit, glorious, glorious spirit."

Regina raised her right hand to indicate a repeat of the last chorus and lowered both arms for the finish. When the song ended, the congregation clapped and praised God.

Serpentine wasn't focused on the service like she should have been. Her mind kept drifting back to the sound of sirens, Dr. Greeley's face, and her spider dream.

After the service, Glory marched out of the sanctuary and down into the large multipurpose room in back. They quickly stripped the choir robes off and prepared to meet family and friends out front.

"So you're sure you won't set that thing up between me and

Marleen?" Tevan asked as he slipped off his robe and hung it on a waiting hanger.

Serpentine snapped back: "I can see the wheel turning, but the hamster must be dead!" she teased.

"Ha, ha, ha," Tevan said as Sister Chevon walked up behind them.

"Hello, Tevan," the maple-honey widow cooed, holding out a brown paper sack. "I baked this for you."

Serpentine winked at Tevan then hung her robe on the silver rack.

Tevan reached for the bag with thick fingers connected by ashy knuckles. "Thanks, Chevon," he said. "You know I love your peach cobblers."

Sister Chevon ran her hand down her right hip. "Well, I aim to please," she said. "I'll look forward to your call."

Serpentine watched as Sister Chevon swiveled her hips out the door. "Boy, the good church women are still hot after you, aren't they?"

"She's nice, but she's not the one," Tevan replied.

Serpentine gave him a crooked eye. "So why did you accept her pie?"

"A man gotta eat," he answered, patting his stomach.

"Yeah, right." Serpentine grabbed her purse, pulling it over her shoulder. "You'll never lose those pounds you keep complaining about if you continue to accept peach cobblers from Ms. Not the One," she warned.

Tevan sucked in his gut. "Well, you know a lot of women see a big, strong, healthy brother like myself as a cuddly teddy bear who needs somebody to take care of him."

"And why don't brothers look at sisters the same way," Serpentine countered.

"Some brothers are ignorant, and you don't want to be bothered with them anyway," Tevan assured her.

"Those seem to be the only brothers out there, as far as I can tell."

"I need an answer from you about the tickets by Friday and no is not acceptable," Tevan persisted under his breath just as Reverend Middleton entered the room and moved through the crowd exchanging courtesies.

"Serpentine, it's great to see you," the Reverend said as he stopped in front of her and grabbed her hand.

"Hi, Reverend, it's good to be back," Serpentine responded.

"If you need anything, please let me know," he added, holding on tightly as if he didn't want to let go.

"I will, thank you," Serpentine answered, pulling her captive fingers free. She smiled, wanting him to go away. Others were now looking in their direction and the last thing she needed was a pity party.

At that moment, Regina entered the room and slapped her chubby hands together to get everyone's attention.

"We're scheduled to perform a spiritual concert at Big Muddy River Correctional Facility in Ina, Illinois, this Saturday, two o'clock. How many of you are planning to come?" Regina asked, then looked around the room at the hands that were raised. She stopped at Tevan and Serpentine and stared until Tevan grabbed Serpentine's right hand with his left to lift both arms upward.

"Good," Regina said, nodding. "Be here at Mount Glory at noon on Saturday to get on the bus. We'll add three songs to our basic repertoire, 'God Specializes,' 'Oh, Happy Day,' and 'He's Able.' Any questions?"

"Why'd you do that?" Serpentine hissed at Tevan as the group started to scatter.

"The spirit hit me," Tevan replied with a smirk.

"You know Aunt Regina is serious about this prison ministry thing. If I cancel I'll never hear the end of it." Serpentine picked up her coat off a folding chair.

"Then don't cancel," Tevan said. "You need to spend more time with your family, and I can't think of a better way than singing this Saturday with me and Aunt Regina."

By now, Regina had made her way through the crowd and over to Serpentine. She flung her arms around her niece's neck, repeating, "Thank God, thank God, thank God for his mercy."

Bad Habits

Do you know how long it takes to break a habit? Try something simple, like moving a trash can to the opposite side of the room. It's interesting how the mind operates concerning change. The first few days you have to make a specific effort to recognize the change, because your mind will want to continue to throw the trash in the same spot.

Over the next few days your mind tries to adjust. You'll reach to throw the piece of paper in the wrong place, but stop yourself in midstream, then make the proper change. Finally, the mind registers the change and a new habit is created. Your mind will automatically have you turn in the right direction to throw the trash away.

It takes me approximately twenty-two days to change a habit. I know because it was on the twenty-second day that I finally threw a wad of paper into the trash can in its new spot on the other side of the room with no hesitation or doubt.

Now, what other habits do I need to change?

Serpentine was getting on with her life, and that meant going back to work. This was the final hurdle and she wondered if she could handle it. As she parked in the lot, Serpentine waved at the security guard.

"Hey, Serpentine. Good to see you back," he shouted.

"Good to be back," she replied.

The guard opened her door for her. "Do you know why we have wakes before funerals?" he asked.

Serpentine shook her head and chuckled. She didn't remember his name but he always had something interesting to tell her.

"In the early days people drank whiskey from lead cups and the combination would sometimes knock 'em out for days. So whenever a body was found, the family couldn't bury it right away. They'd take it home and folks would gather around to see if the person was gonna wake up. That's where the custom of holding a wake comes from."

Serpentine stepped out of the car, smiling. "Where do you get this stuff?" she asked in a journalistic tone.

"I read everything," he bragged, shutting her car door, then rushing over to another arriving vehicle.

To her surprise, Serpentine felt at home as soon as she stepped inside the massive building that held six satellite dishes on the roof. She walked down the front hallway admiring the state-of-the-art equipment in the editing studios to her right and absorbing the immediate comfort from friendly faces offering smiles of welcome on her left.

Serpentine checked her gold Timex, grabbed a pad, and gingerly walked over to Terry's office for the regular morning story meeting. She knocked on the door and waited to hear "come in."

Instead, the door flew open and a short, stocky man wearing a barely noticeable toupée stood in front of her.

"Yes?" he huffed with a disgusted look on his face until he saw Serpentine. "Hey, Serpentine! Good to see you!"

He patted her on the shoulder and motioned for her to come in and sit down. She followed his directions.

Terry positioned the left cheek of his behind on the edge of the desk and balanced himself with his right leg. "How ya feeling? You sure you don't need another week or two?" he asked, but didn't stop for her to respond. "Not that we don't have plenty of work for you to do."

"I've actually missed this place," she replied nervously.

"Well, we missed you too," he said just as someone knocked on the door and it opened. The rest of the team filed inside exchanging greetings and words of goodwill until the meeting got under way.

"Before we get started I want to let you guys know that the rumors about bringing in consultants is just that, rumors. I've already spoken with Marshall, upstairs, and gotten things straight. There will be no consultants telling me what to do," Terry said with pride.

"I thought Mr. Marshall had already hired the company." Trina Elman, one of the newest reporters, said.

Serpentine eyed Trina carefully. She was a hustler with no qualms about knocking you down if you got in her way.

"Well, he'll have to unhire them," Terry spit out. "We will continue to cover the news like newspeople, not like bureaucratic commercial puppets. Now, what's going on with Benton?"

"He's out at the hostage site on the north side of town," Trina answered.

Terry turned to Serpentine to offer details. "A man is holding his wife and three kids at gunpoint. The police SWAT teams are covering the house, and Benton is feeding us live reports."

"What else do we have?" asked Arthur Richards, the senior reporter on staff.

"I'd like to suggest a story about tourist robberies in Chicago. The numbers are up again, by almost twenty percent," Trina responded.

"Make sure you get a statement from the tourist bureau this time so they can feel like they're appreciated," Terry warned.

"The first segment of my phone-sex special report can be ready if we need it," Arthur told them. "I've edited interviews from three of the phone workers and a local company owner. Check it out," he said, pulling the videotape out of his briefcase. He popped it into the VCR next to Terry's desk.

The group watched a two-minute piece on phone-sex filled with suggestive shots; close ups of deep-red lips, bulging cleavage, and a woman rubbing her hand across her thigh while speaking in a seductive tone.

"That's horrible," Trina immediately complained. "Those shots are so stereotypical and exploitative. You should be ashamed, Arthur."

Serpentine immediately felt comfortable, seeing that very little had changed. Trina and Arthur were always at each other's throats about one thing or another.

"What's wrong with it? I think it's a powerful piece," Arthur protested.

Trina bristled in her seat. "You *would* believe that, because you're thinking with your little head instead of your big one." She pointed her finger between his eyes.

"I don't have to listen to her ridicule me like this," Arthur protested.

Terry finally stepped in. "Both of you need to just calm down," he told them forcefully.

Serpentine noticed that Terry swayed for a moment as if off balance, but he quickly regrouped.

"It's tabloid journalism," Trina mumbled. "And I won't work in a place that accepts it!"

Arthur stood up and bounced around like a kid having a temper tantrum. "It is *not* tabloid! I used those shots to emphasize the subject of the piece: sex. I've been doing this much longer than you, and I know what I'm doing!"

"It's sick, and I'm going to make sure that anyone who calls in to complain gets your home phone number!" Trina threatened.

"Look, we'll deal with this later. You two are going to drive me nuts," Terry said, waving everybody out of his office. He glanced at Serpentine almost apologetically and she stopped. He looked so much older than he was.

"Is everything all right?" she asked, ignoring the slip.

"Yeah, I'm going to start you out with something slow. A local computer company is marketing home IQ tests. There's some controversy about the impact; see what you can do with it," he said, handing her the background materials.

"You sure you're okay?" Serpentine asked as she took the papers from his trembling hand.

"Just caught some kind of bug, I think. I'll be fine."

Serpentine felt a rush as she left Terry's office. Thinking about how to organize a story had always been the most exciting part of the job. Of course, the issue of cultural bias was a juicy one. But she would also need to explore reliability and fairness issues. Serpentine stopped at her desk and grinned. It was nothing special, just one of ten desks set back to back in the center of the huge newsroom, but she had truly missed it.

She flopped down in her brown swivel chair, closed her eyes, and took in the wonderful sounds of conflicting TV monitors, police scanners, and ringing telephones. Then she opened her eyes and watched the organized chaos of people excitedly rushing back and forth past computers, desks, chairs, papers, tapes, and bulletin boards with deadlines to meet.

Serpentine was one of the youngest assistant producers ever hired at WXYZ for the six and ten o'clock newscasts. After five years, she decided to test her skills as an outside reporter. That was four years ago and she had excelled because she was a thorough researcher.

"Hey girl!" Marleen screamed when she saw Serpentine sitting at her desk. She rushed over and they hugged.

"Hi, Marleen," Serpentine replied, standing up. "I was going to come find you in a few minutes."

Marleen bounced up and down as she spoke. "I am so glad you're back. This place hasn't been the same without you."

"Thanks," Serpentine said with a smile meant for her best friend.

"Nobody knows what happened, except Terry," Marleen whispered. "Everybody else thinks you had your appendix out back in Kansas City."

"Appendix? You couldn't think of a better story than that?" Serpentine teased.

Marleen winked. "Just go with the flow, girl, and I'll see you at lunch," she said, strutting away.

Serpentine sat back down at her desk and beamed. Seeing Marleen almost made her believe that everything would be okay again. Serpentine had to admit she was grateful that Marleen was a constant in her life. Serpentine knew that Marleen would always be the same wonderful soul who'd befriended her twenty years go.

They'd met in the middle of their freshman year at the University of Iowa. Marleen was tall and shapely thin. Serpentine had lost almost twenty pounds in the excitement of being away from home, so her curvy medium build could stand its ground.

They met at a Chi Cutie rush. Both girls had been asked to join the black Greek auxiliary group, and they both attended the meeting out of curiosity. The Chis were known as the pretty boys on campus, and Serpentine had to admit that her invitation came from one of the finest men she'd ever seen in her life: Patrick Anderson.

She remembered strolling into the Burge dorm lounge a few minutes before the meeting was supposed to start. About fifteen girls were sitting in a circle on orange vinyl chairs. Most of them ignored Serpentine after taking a quick initial look, but when her eyes met Marleen's they smiled at each other without knowing why.

John Lambert, a slender, cream-colored brother, came into the room. He was followed by Patrick, who was about the same hue, but a couple of inches shorter and ten pounds heavier.

"I'm John, president of Chi Omega. I want to welcome you to the first meeting of the Chi Cuties. All of you are here because one or more of the brothers felt that you would be an asset to our organization. We only accept the best, and we'd like you to consider joining us."

A yellow hand with freshly manicured nails shot up in the back, and John pointed to it. "What is the pledge period like? I've heard all kinds of crazy stuff."

"Good question. We want you to understand completely what our organization is about. We know there are many rumors out there, but the truth is we don't have a pledge period. We have a probationary period. That means that we will evaluate your behavior and personality for six weeks. If your evaluation is satisfactory you will remain a Cutie; if not, we will thank you for your service and send you on your way."

"So what kinds of things do you look for?" a pair of strawberry-red lips parted to ask.

"I'll let Patrick explain that." John stepped back, giving Patrick the floor.

"As Chi Cuties, you should respect the brothers at all times. That means you will greet us by our appointed names whenever you see us, whether in public or private. For example," Patrick said, twisting his pelvis seductively as the words glided from his mouth, "I'm 'Big Brother Oh So Fine, Always Got You on My Mind.' "

Serpentine and Marleen looked at each other and smirked.

"We also expect the Cuties to be of service to the organization. We sometimes need help with things like homework, housework, and laundry, and of course, our super-bad parties, which are hailed as the best on campus."

"You expect us to do your laundry and shit?" Marleen asked in an agitated tone without waiting to be recognized.

"We sometimes need help around the Chi house, including laundry, yes. But it's not a requirement, it's a request."

"So we can say no to doing your dirty dishes and funky laundry and still be Cuties?" Serpentine added in a raised voice.

"We would hope that if a brother asks you to do something for the organization you wouldn't say no, because if he asks for your help, he needs it. For example, for our party next weekend, we will need the Cuties to help us get organized. We would need you ladies to set up decorations, prepare food, and take charge of the cleanup afterwards."

Marleen bristled in her chair. "And while the Cuties are doin' all that, what the hell are y'all gonna be doin'?" she asked with a grimace.

"We'll be taking care of fraternity business."

Serpentine cocked her head and jumped in again. "Like what?"

John shot her an awkward look. "The brothers have a lot of projects going on. We take care of the financial business of the house and run our public service programs for the elderly and minority youths in the community, things like that."

Marleen stood up and cocked her head sideways. "Well, I've heard enough. Thanks but no thanks, Patrick. You're fine, but not that fine," she said and left the room.

Voices murmured with surprise and disagreement.

Serpentine wanted to leave, too, and this seemed like the best time, so she hopped up behind Marleen. "I'm sorry, but I don't have a lot of time to spare," she said, slipping into the hallway.

Serpentine had to laugh at herself as she shoved the heavy steel doors open. What was she thinking? She truly didn't fit in with *that* crowd.

She spotted Marleen sitting at the bus stop smoking a cigarette, and realized that she liked her bold, straightforward style. It was refreshing.

She walked over and stood next to her. "I know this is going to sound weird, but I feel like we might be kindred spirits or something," she told her.

"I don't believe in that spiritual mumbo-jumbo," Marleen quickly replied with a half-grin, then took a long suck from her filtered Kool cigarette.

"Well, it's the effort that counts, my father always says," Serpentine snapped back, ready to walk away.

Marleen blew the smoke out of her nose. "If the effort counts, why are you giving up so easily?" she asked.

Serpentine faced her squarely. "I make it a practice to only hit a brick wall one time with my head, then I recognize the pain and go around."

Marleen let go of a deep, throaty laugh. "That's cool," she said. "Maybe we can hang out sometime, once the knot on your head goes away."

They both ended up in the journalism program at Iowa; both graduated at the same time. When Serpentine moved to Chicago, Marleen accepted a public relations position in Boston. She hated it, complaining that the people weren't friendly, the city was racist, and the men were flaky. Right after Serpentine landed the reporter spot at WXYZ, she talked Terry into bringing Marleen in to take her place as the assistant producer.

At five-thirty, Serpentine made her way to the studio area to watch the anchors prepare for the six o'clock report. That was her ultimate goal, to sit in one of those chairs at the anchor desk every evening to deliver the news to the people of Chicago.

A glass-enclosed control room looked down over the spacious studio. Racks of spot, key, and fill lights hovered above the blue-and-maroon anchor desks to illuminate the made-up faces and drive out the dark shadows across the back wall. Serpentine watched the three remote-controlled cameras move as if by magic. With the touch of a switch from the control room, one person maneuvered all of them. Serpentine took a moment to feel sad about the three cameramen who had lost their jobs because of this new technology.

Along with that sadness came an apprehension about the job itself. The deadlines, work schedule, and bad habits had helped to push her to the edge before. The lifestyle meant living on fast food, often eating in the car on the run; drive-up windows were invaluable. Even at home, she often ate pizza, because they delivered and she was usually too tired to cook.

The really bad days were those when she got so busy at the station that she went most of the day without eating. Later, at home, when she started eating, she couldn't stop. She would rummage through the leftovers, then down a bowl of cereal, and follow it with something sweet. Serpentine took a moment and counted to ten in her head, reminding herself not to think negatively.

Lackadickaphobia

LaJune once told me that she had lackadickaphobia. Parren was out to sea and she hadn't had sex in a couple of months. She said she saw dicks everywhere, big, small, long, short, fat, slim, crooked, and straight. She imagined them in the shape of tusks on her favorite elephant at home. The arch of the waterspout at a public fountain. The tip of the hose on the fire extinguisher at work. Even the arrow at the recreation center where she walked twice a week that tells runners and walkers which way to go was suspect.

At the time I laughed and told her she was crazy. But I'm going to apologize next time I see her, because tonight I finally understand. There are suggestive images everywhere. I watch the hands on the clock as they move in a gentle, circular motion. My toothbrush works its way in, out, and around my mouth with a stimulating power. Oh, and the showerhead was simply magnificent. When that sultry water came pulsing out across my tense body, the old knees went limp.

Even though Serpentine dreaded her Monday and Wednesday therapy sessions, she knew they were helping. Today as she waited for Dr. Greeley to get off the phone she studied a huge abstract painting that covered most of his back wall. She carefully examined the bright blue looping swirls and burnt-orange swatches. She truly didn't understand abstract art because it looked like something any monkey could have done with the right paint and brushes.

"Are you ready to begin, Serpentine?" Dr. Greeley asked as he hung up the receiver.

Serpentine slipped off her shoes and pulled her legs up under her on the well-worn couch. "Sure," she responded in a practiced, nonchalant tone.

Without warning Dr. Greeley handed her a piece of paper. "What does this mean?" he asked.

Serpentine trembled as she read the phrase out loud: "Don't be afraid of tomorrow; God is already there."

Tension immediately engulfed the room.

"Can you tell me why you left this note?" he continued.

She had talked about a lot of things with Dr. Greeley, but the real issue was still off limits. Serpentine swallowed. "It means what it says," she told him irritably.

"Serpentine, what were you trying to tell your loved ones with this note?" Dr. Greeley pushed.

Serpentine stood up and moved to the large wingback chair. "I don't know. I guess I wanted them to know that God understood. I didn't want them to worry," she finally answered.

Dr. Greeley sensed her distress.

"Maybe we should come back to this at another time."

Serpentine crossed her arms and looked down at the floor.

Dr. Greeley went on. "A person's self-esteem, value, and worth are often tied to issues of love and sex. Do you think that was part of what happened to you?"

Serpentine hesitated. "There was a man involved, but a lot more was going on in my head at that time. I didn't attempt suicide because of a man, if that's what you're asking."

"It doesn't have to be a question specifically about the suicide. Do you know to what extent your self-esteem and value are tied to love and sex?" he asked.

Serpentine shrugged. "I did have one lover who could have driven me to suicide because the sex was so bad." She chuckled.

Dr. Greeley rubbed his hand against his smooth beige chin and grinned. "Tell me about him. What happened?"

Serpentine's smile went away. "He was a nice guy," she said, fidgeting with her class ring.

"Did you love him?" The doctor kept probing.

"No, it definitely wasn't love," she answered. "It was more like lust, or maybe just plain old lackadickaphobia."

"What kind of phobia?"

"Lackadickaphobia, the fear of not getting any for a long time."

Dr. Greeley wrote the term down in his notebook and shook his head. "Okay, so how did you two meet?"

Serpentine cleared her throat. "I met Neal at the TV station. He was into investing and stuff like that," she said. "He was older and very mature. Nobody had been interested in me in a long time." She paused for a moment. "Right after I moved to Chicago, I threw myself into my work and gained a bunch of weight, so I didn't have time to worry about a man in my life."

"So, how did Neal get in?" Dr. Greeley asked, abruptly.

"Neal was always preaching about how you gotta pay yourself first and complaining that black people throw their money away on too many material things, not thinking about the future."

Serpentine searched her mind for the right words to weave the story together. "I liked to listen to him talk. That was the main thing that drew me to Neal. He was a black man with his own successful business. A positive example of what education can do for a serious brother who's after his piece of the pie."

Serpentine cleared her throat. She remembered watching Neal's hands rise and fall that day at WXYZ as he talked to a salesman in the reception area. She had seen Neal several times, but they had only exchanged a few casual hellos.

"It's so sad," Neal told the guy sitting next to him. "We live in the richest country in the world and we don't understand what makes us rich. We don't take advantage of all the opportunity that's out there."

As Neal spoke he rocked back and forth causing a long silver chain he always wore against his chest to swing.

"I ain't talking about giving lots of money. You're in your twenties, right? Well, if you start paying yourself right now, just ten dollars a month and make ten or twelve percent interest on it, by the time you turn sixty-five, you would have more than a hundred thousand dollars to draw from," he continued.

"I'm gonna just have to pray on Social Security," the man finally replied and Serpentine watched Neal's head drop.

"This would be in addition to your Social Security," he explained.

"Look, I'll think about it, man," the guy finally told him in desperation before he hurried away.

"Still trying to get folks to pay attention to their future, I see," Serpentine teased, moving toward Neal.

"I'm always looking out for my brothers," Neal replied, gently squeezing her outstretched hand.

"And what about your sisters?" she asked.

Neal played along. "I look out for sisters, too, when they let me," he responded.

Serpentine stopped as the moment grew deep. She thought he was flirting with her, then he winked and confirmed it.

"Maybe you should come to my office and discuss the possibilities," he added.

"Maybe I should," Serpentine replied and offered a big smile.

"You'd be surprised what the right investment can do for a person. Here's my card. My home number is on the back, in case you need it." Then almost as if it was a challenge, he added: "Call me when you're ready."

Serpentine gently pulled the card from his hand. "I will, I promise."

It was several days before she called. Serpentine was sitting at her desk editing a story on the murder of three fast-food workers when she noticed the card poking out from under the phone. Without thinking about it, she picked up the receiver and dialed.

"Neal Rayhill," the voice on the other side boomed.

"Hi, Neal, it's Serpentine," she said.

"Hi, Serpentine, you got some good news for me?" he asked.

"I think so," she said, trying to ignore the irritating static on the phone line.

"I'm ready to set up an appointment, but it has to be early morning or late night because of my hours at the station."

"How about tonight?" Neal asked.

Serpentine took a moment to respond. "I don't get off until eight," she said.

"Eight-thirty is fine with me," he replied.

"Are you sure?" Serpentine asked.

"Very sure," he told her. "You know where my office is?"

Serpentine glanced at the address on the card, adding: "I think I can find it."

"Okay, I'll see you tonight, then," Neal said cheerfully, and hung up.

Serpentine did find the office easily. It was in the Chatham section of the city, in a five-story brick office building on 79th Street.

Serpentine knocked on the door and waited.

"Serpentine," Neal called as he opened the door and shook her hand.

"Hi, Neal," she replied, taking note of a slight sensation from his touch.

"Come in, sit down," he continued, walking her through his three rooms on the fifth floor; a modestly furnished reception area, a combination break/supply room, and his large private office.

Serpentine sat in one of the tan pleather chairs while Neal leaned back against his scarred oak desk.

He opened the discussion in a very businesslike manner. "I've put together a package of information for you. It should explain everything. Did you think of any initial questions?"

"I really don't know if I need to worry about this right now. I have a long way to go before retirement, and the station does some investing for me," Serpentine replied. She liked the way his light brown eyes twinkled and his graying temples flexed when he spoke.

Neal nodded. She could feel his eyes focus on the movement of her lips as she spoke. She also noticed how his focus shifted to her left thigh when the tight, blue-weave skirt she was wearing worked its way upward after she crossed her legs.

"One of the worst things you can do is underestimate the amount of time needed to prepare financially for your retirement," Neal explained. He snatched a brown folder off his desk. "I'm not trying to sell you today. I want you to take these materials home and read them carefully. There is information here on emergency funds, life insurance, IRAs, municipal bonds, and professional management. Once you've read everything, we can meet again."

Serpentine took the folder and set it in her lap. She felt awkward, but there was something intriguing about the man. He seemed so settled and so confident, she found herself wondering why he wasn't married.

Neal grinned, spread his long legs apart, and leaned over to whisper in her ear, "Do you have a boyfriend, Serpentine?"

She smiled at him curiously. "No, I don't," she answered in a flirtatious tone.

Neal studied the blue carpet, as if trying to muster up enough nerve to continue. "Let me ask this another way," he eventually said. "I'd like to take you out sometime, Serpentine. What do you think about that?"

Serpentine sat very still and considered the question. "I don't know, Neal," she said.

He smiled and sat down in the chair beside her. "You're a gorgeous girl, and I think we would be real good together," he murmured seductively. "I imagine those hips could take a man on up into heaven."

Serpentine blushed. She hadn't been with a man in over two years. She took a deep breath and sucked in her stomach, brooding about her main excuse: the weight she'd gained. She had told herself she wouldn't look for anybody until she got down to a more desirable size. But here, sitting next to her, was a good man, a mature man, who liked her just the way she was.

"How about having a drink with me?" Neal asked. He got up and walked over to a small bar along the wall.

"A white wine would be nice," she replied.

"Coming up."

Neal pulled glasses out of a nearby cabinet and poured the drinks so confidently that she knew this wasn't the first time he'd entertained in his office. She had to chuckle when she thought about Neal trying to be a player. He had potential, but his talent was raw.

When he handed her the glass, Serpentine noticed how broad his shoulders were. "You seem well prepared" she said, temptingly.

Neal lifted her left hand off her thigh and kissed the back of it softly. "I was a Boy Scout," he replied.

They had several drinks, talked, flirted, and even danced to music from the radio late into the night. Serpentine enjoyed his company and thought, maybe, it was a relationship she wanted to pursue. She was excited about the possibilities, especially when he kissed her hungrily. It was obvious that he needed her as much as she needed him. They kissed again, then he led her over to the couch.

"We'll be more comfortable here," he said.

Serpentine smiled. "It's getting late. I'd better go," she told him, but followed the comment with another steamy kiss.

"Don't go, please," Neal begged.

As their lips melded again, Serpentine focused on how good it felt. She didn't really want to go. She enjoyed being there with Neal, and if she were honest, she'd have come right out and told him she wanted to make love.

She didn't have to tell him. They kissed and petted on the couch for a while longer, until Neal took it to the next level, himself. She massaged the arch of his back when he held her tightly and let him know through her submission that she wanted the same thing he did. But the experience took a turn when Neal began pulling and pawing at her in a clumsy, forceful manner.

"Wait a minute, baby," Serpentine said softly. She wanted to slow him down, but his train of thought had no caboose. He shoved his moist lips onto hers and grabbed the hem of her skirt, yanking it upward. "Neal, just give me a minute, please?" she asked again, raising her voice above his sensual moans.

With what seemed like one quick motion, Neal's hand was under her skirt and her panties were down around her ankles. Serpentine bolted up and tried to push him off her. She registered confusion at that moment. She wanted him, probably as badly as he wanted her, but she didn't like this frantic, awkward approach.

"Wait, Neal, please!" she said in a more forceful tone. He needed to, at least, get a rubber.

Neal pressed his heated body up against hers, pushing her back down onto the couch. "Ummm, baby, you can't stop me now. I'm ready to give it all to you," he groaned through lips that left a saliva trail across her neck and shoulder.

Serpentine attempted to free herself, but his body wouldn't budge. Her right arm was pinned between the couch and his shoulder. Her left arm was pinned under his chest. Serpentine remembered hating the feeling of his rough fingers poking between her legs. The too-long fingernails scratched and pulled at her private parts. When he separated her thighs with his knee, tears rolled down her face. She had wanted Neal, maybe even needed him, but not like this.

Suddenly, he pushed hard up inside her and a cycle of pounding and grunting began. Her tears become more intense with each sweaty thrust. Then, almost as quickly as it had started, it was over. Neal yelled loudly with relief and lay limp on top of her.

"Oh baby, that was great!" he eventually said, sticking his tongue in her ear. "You are definitely one hot mama who I could fall in love with if I'm not careful."

She listened to his heavy breathing for a moment before speaking. "Neal, please get up off me," she finally said in a subdued voice.

Neal lifted himself up and noticed the tears, now back in his right mind. "What you crying for, girl? Was I that good?" he asked with a stupid grin spreading across his face.

Serpentine stood up, pulled her skirt down, and picked up her panties from the floor. "I—I've got to go," she told him. The smell of sweat and sex mixed with Jim Beam was starting to make her sick.

"Hey, sugar, is something wrong? I was hoping we could go get something to eat and maybe go to my place for a second round," Neal said, in a silky tone.

Serpentine stood in the center of the floor and stared at him. "What the hell is wrong with you? I asked you to wait, Neal, and you ignored me!"

"I didn't think you were serious, girl. I thought you was into it, too," he explained defensively. "I thought you wanted it as much as I did. I know I heard you moan a few times when I was hittin' it real good."

Serpentine wanted to walk over and smack the shit out of him, but she couldn't get her legs to move in that direction. She shook her head and wondered how she could ever have found him attractive. The gap between his two front teeth suddenly looked wider, and his ears stuck out in a comical kind of way.

"You're an asshole, Neal," she spat out, grabbed her purse, and stormed out the door.

"**I** thought about calling the police or my aunt to tell them what happened," Serpentine told Dr. Greeley. "They would have probably called it rape. But I wanted to feel Neal inside me, so I don't think it was rape. I think he was just a lousy screw."

"Can you forgive him?"

Serpentine shrugged. "I don't know. Neal didn't make love to me, which was what I wanted. He fucked me, and there's a huge difference."

"Have you forgiven yourself?"

Serpentine took a minute to think seriously about the question. "I just buried the experience in a shallow grave."

Sunset Clouds

This was the third evening in a row that I sat outside in my back-yard and watched fuchsia-colored sunset clouds laughing, dancing, and sweeping across a dusky sky. Some were full, dense, dark, and hulking; others were barren, sparse, light, and rambling. One cloud seemed to be carrying the shadowy full moon on its back.

Around seven o'clock, I welcomed a warm breeze that pushed its way across the backyard and gently caressed my arms, legs, and face like a long-lost lover.

ⓞ ⓞ ⓞ

Saturday morning Serpentine practiced making excuses to get out of going to the prison, but at fifteen minutes before noon she was obediently sitting in her car in Mount Glory's parking lot, watching the church bus pull up.

She fast-forwarded to her favorite song, "I'll Take You There," singing along with Bebe and Cece Winans, until a knock on the passenger window startled her. Serpentine glanced over, saw her aunt's face, and unlocked the door.

Regina slid inside. "I'm so glad you came," she said. "I was expecting the phone to ring with an excuse this morning."

"I tried to come up with something, but I knew you'd be expecting it," Serpentine admitted.

Regina leaned across the front seat of the car and kissed her niece on the forehead. "That's why you're wonderful and we all love you very much," she cooed.

" 'We' who?"

"Me, God, everybody!"

"How does God feel about the fact that I don't really want to be here today?" Serpentine asked.

"That's okay. It only matters to Him that you *are* here. God loves that beautiful voice of yours and you need to share it with the world."

"Aunt Regina, let's not have this conversation again, please?"

"I'm sorry, but I've got to keep trying. You should be a soloist with Glory, not hiding in the background."

"It's just not something I feel comfortable with, okay?"

"Okay, but it's just such a waste," Regina complained.

At twelve o'clock, the bus driver opened the doors, and everybody boarded. Serpentine slept on Tevan's shoulder most of the way. She had worked late into the night, editing her story on the deadly practice of teenagers sniffing chemical household products, to free up the afternoon.

At the prison, the choir was greeted by the warden and taken straight to the chapel. As they prepared for their concert, Serpentine watched her aunt Regina with admiration. She was a kind soul, always trying to help somebody.

She'd committed Glory to perform at a different Illinois prison one Saturday a month for the entire year. She was leading Reverend Middleton's ministry to reach those who might be released back into society one day.

The prisoners filed in at exactly three o'clock and took their seats as the choir members organized themselves in formation at the front of the chapel. Serpentine felt sad when she looked out at the audience and saw that the majority were black men her age and younger. She had read the statistics in magazine articles and seen them on television reports, but to witness the reality first-hand was unnerving.

As the choir began to sing "God Specializes," Serpentine found herself scanning the condemned faces. She couldn't shake the feeling that most didn't even look like criminals. She could picture the guy at the end of the fourth row bobbing his head at that popular club "Dazzled" on a Friday night. The older, balding man who stood in the back of the room clapping could easily have been a member of Mount Glory Baptist. Her eyes stopped suddenly at a familiar face in the second row. She couldn't believe it, but there sat Creighton Johnson.

Serpentine struggled for air. She swallowed and tried not to stare at his milk-chocolate face. They'd grown up in Kansas City together. He'd gone from nice guy, to hoodlum, to star high school basketball player, and apparently back to hoodlum again. Serpentine clapped her hands and moved back and forth with the choir, still in shock. There almost directly in front of her sat Creighton Johnson, the first man she ever loved.

Her mind leaped back to the day when he asked to walk her home after math class. She didn't think too much about it because they had been friends for a while. Serpentine and Creighton originally became friends at Franklin Junior High when their mothers studied together to earn their GED's. While their mothers attended math, science, and English classes three nights a week, Creighton stayed at Serpentine's house doing homework and watching television with her and Kendrick.

Creighton's well-muscled shoulders were designed to shoot basketballs into a small hoop fifteen and twenty feet away. He had become Lincoln Senior High School's best shooting guard, nicknamed "the Ringer" because of his skilled technique in both defense and offense.

After the last bell rang that day, Serpentine went to her locker. Just as she shut the door, Creighton slipped up behind her.

"Hey you," he whispered from the left side, then stepped to her right.

Serpentine jumped. "Hi, Creighton," she said. "You ready?"

"Lead the way," he replied with a mouth-watering smile.

They headed out the east door of Lincoln, making their way through the eight hundred other students also headed home. They passed the school's mascot, a stone replica of a golden tiger that sat guarding the front entryway, then strolled east down Twenty-second Street toward Prospect.

"You're really good in math, aren't you?" Creighton asked, breaking the awkward silence that hung between them.

Serpentine had mainly gotten A's in class, so she nodded. "My dad teaches math at Washington Elementary."

"I like math, but some of it doesn't make sense to me," Creighton continued.

"You got an A on your last test," Serpentine reminded him.

Creighton smiled. He seemed surprised that she'd noticed. "I do okay in some areas. I understood percentages, but fractions killed me."

As they stood and waited for a noisy city bus to pass, they glanced at each other, locking eyes for a brief moment. Serpentine's heart pounded so vigorously that she was afraid it would push right through her chest. She took deep, slow breaths to calm herself until the light turned green, then Creighton gently grabbed her hand, pulling her across the street, and she lost control all over again.

"I wanted to talk to you before, but when I'm in basketball season I don't think about nothing but the next game. Now the season's over."

Serpentine watched his lips slide across the gap between his two front teeth. How could Creighton Johnson be interested in her? As they turned down Prospect, she gathered up her nerve and threw the question out there.

"Why me?" she asked, hoping she wouldn't hate his response.

Creighton didn't answer right away, which made her nervous. He looked up at the sky and then off into the distance, taking the time to think about her question. "I like you," he finally replied, plain and simple. "I was hoping we could get to know each other better."

Serpentine was happy with his response, yet she found herself needing more assurance from the pretty, brown eyes that hovered above the thick brown nose which was spread above soft, brown lips. Serpentine continued with the direct approach because she didn't have time to appear in an episode of Creighton's Heartbreak Theater.

"What about Melissa?" she asked. "I thought you two were going together."

Creighton frowned. "Melissa and I broke up just before basketball season started," he replied.

Serpentine eyed him carefully. She hadn't heard about a breakup, and news like that would have spread like floodwaters. "Melissa's really pretty," she added, picturing the small, almond-skinned beauty, afraid that she couldn't compete and not sure she wanted to try.

Creighton grabbed Serpentine's arm and yanked her to a halt. He looked into her frightened eyes. "You're just as pretty as Melissa," he said. "But you don't know that, do you?"

Serpentine trembled. He thought she was pretty. She wanted to sing and shout and dance with the news, but instead she zeroed in on the doubt that clung to her self-image. "I'm not sure I want to get into anything right now. I need to focus on my grades," Serpentine finally answered while staring at the sidewalk.

"I don't consider myself just 'anything,' " Creighton teased.

Serpentine glanced up at him. "I didn't mean it like that."

"But that's what you said."

Serpentine shifted her science book from her right hand to her left.

"Here, let me help you with that." Creighton reached for the book.

"No, that's okay, I can handle it," she told him as uncertainty crept from her heart back into her mind.

"You gonna give a brother a hard time like this every day?" he asked.

"Maybe," she answered.

They went together all through high school. It seemed as if Creighton had dinner with Serpentine and her family more often than he ate at home. She was in the front row at every game and they often joined other couples afterward to celebrate the team's victories.

Unfortunately, Creighton's interest didn't help Serpentine feel more comfortable with her size; it only made her more determined to lose the so-called extra pounds.

Serpentine wanted Creighton to be the first man she made love to, and her body had to be right.

As Serpentine sang with Glory, she looked up at the ceiling or over at the pianist or down toward Regina, trying not to stare at Creighton. But she found herself, every now and then, peeking in his direction.

In the middle of "He's Able" his well-defined, brown arm pointed at her, and Serpentine's knees buckled when he threw her a kiss.

She didn't really want to talk to Creighton. She didn't know what to say, but she did take note that it wasn't hate she was feeling, but sorrow. Creighton had had so much potential and he had overcome so many obstacles, only to end up in prison anyway.

When the last song came to an end, Creighton appeared beside her without warning.

"Hey, Serpentine, how are you?" he asked, obviously charged by her presence.

"Creighton," Serpentine responded awkwardly. "What are you doing here? I mean . . ."

Creighton didn't miss a beat. "Don't even try it—everybody knew this was where I was going to end up, including me. But you're looking great. I've always loved that bodacious behind of yours."

Serpentine blushed.

Creighton continued, "I like to watch you on WXYZ. You're good. I knew you'd do something positive with your life."

"Thanks," Serpentine replied, looking around for Regina to rescue her.

Creighton ignored her distraction. "You disappeared for a while. What happened?"

"I took a break, that's all," she explained, staring at her feet, the wall, the fluorescent lights, anything except Creighton.

"I'm a fool," he finally said. "You should know that better than anybody. I got involved with some dudes who decided to hold up a liquor store, and we got caught. I've been in here for five years. Got one more to go."

"That's great," she said, then stopped. "I mean, it's great that you're getting out in a year."

Serpentine waved at Tevan against the opposite wall, talking to several inmates. He nodded, but didn't move.

"I know what you meant," he assured her. "Actually, I've used my time in here wisely. I finished my bachelor's degree in general studies. And I've earned nine hours toward a master's degree in business, all free!" he bragged, sticking out his chest.

"That's good; that means when you get out, you'll have some options."

"When the parole board sets me free next year, I ain't coming back like most of these fools."

"Okay, folks, time to roll," Regina called, and the large mass headed toward the entrance.

Creighton raised his voice over the noise. "I'll look you up when I get out. Maybe we can get together."

"It was good to see you, Creighton," Serpentine replied briskly as she moved with the crowd.

"I think about you all the time, Serpentine. I made a mistake, but I want you to know that I've always loved you," Creighton told her as the doors swung open.

Serpentine managed to muster up a fake smile. How dare he say some shit like that to her after what he did? Homecoming weekend of her freshman year, Creighton snatched out her heart and left her for dead.

Serpentine couldn't concentrate on anything that week except Creighton's visit. She tried to wish the days away, but the clock wouldn't move any faster. At three o'clock Friday afternoon, when she finally heard his knock on her door, she jolted forward with excitement.

She opened the door and beamed at the six-foot-two dream who stood in the hallway with his arms spread apart. She lunged toward him without even thinking. She kissed him passionately, savoring the soft memories of his lips.

"How's my girl?" Creighton asked, picking up his duffel bag, following her inside.

Serpentine practically melted at the sound of that strong, sexy voice she had enjoyed only over the phone for months.

"I missed you so much," Serpentine told him as she joined her hand with his. "Now that you're here, I'm perfect," she added, and leaned into his lips again.

Creighton slid his bag onto the floor. "I missed you, too," he whispered, pulling her to his chest. Serpentine buried her nose deep in his left shoulder.

His black leather bomber jacket had a familiar smell that made her weak when he wrapped his long, powerful arms around her waist.

Potent fingers massaged her behind, bringing back other sensations, and before Serpentine could think straight, they were on each other like two actors in a torrid love scene. She realized that she had truly missed Creighton. She closed her eyes and let him take control.

As the light from the sun dissipated, and they lay in each other's tangled arms, the phone rang, but Serpentine didn't answer it. Didn't her friends know better than to call? She wanted some time alone with Creighton before she took him around to show him off. When the phone rang a second time, Serpentine picked it up, annoyed.

"Hello," she said in an irritated tone.

"Hey girl, did he make it?" Marleen asked, giggling.

"Yes, my baby is right here," Serpentine cooed.

"I take it you guys aren't coming out tonight," Marleen teased.

"Bingo! You're a winner! Now do you want to keep your prize or trade it for what's behind door number two?"

Marleen laughed. "Trade it."

"Buzzzz. Sorry, you lose. You get a dial tone." Serpentine told her, then hung up.

That night there was more of the passionate lovemaking, rekindling the desires she had desperately missed. For the first time, Serpentine questioned her decision to attend a college three hundred miles away from home or, more accurately, three hundred miles away from Creighton.

As he lay sleeping, she watched his hairy chest slowly rise and fall. She remembered the first night she'd made love with this man she adored. She had joined the hundreds of other high school virgins who became women after their senior proms, on that sacred night of passage.

They were both nervous and excited, acting more like immature newlyweds than young, experimenting teens. Creighton lifted her voluptuous frame and carried her into their room at the Red Roof Inn. They couldn't seem to get their clothes off gracefully, the way couples in the movies did. Creighton accidentally ripped a button off her pink satin formal as he fumbled with the neckline. Serpentine tried to help him with his pants but got in the way and they both tumbled onto the floor. Creighton came too quickly and Serpentine didn't reach a climax, but none of it mattered, because they were in love.

Over the summer, things got better. Each time they made love Serpentine discovered something new, and she was amazed that her weight didn't matter. They grew more and more comfortable together, trying new things and exploring ways to improve the old. She and Creighton had become experts at loving each other, and Serpentine couldn't imagine herself with any other man.

It was morning when the sound of Creighton pulling his duffel bag out of the closet woke Serpentine. She raised herself up on one elbow and rubbed the sleep from her eyes.

"You dressed already?" she asked through a smile, then shifted to the center of the bed.

Creighton didn't answer.

"Where you going?" Serpentine asked when she noticed his bag in the center of the floor.

Creighton walked over to the bed and sat on the edge. He rubbed her hand and dropped his head before he spoke. "I need to talk to you, Serpentine," he said.

Serpentine's smile disappeared. A conversation that started like that would probably not finish very well. She braced herself for his next words.

"The last thing I wanted to do was hurt you, baby, but I just can't say this any other way. I don't love you anymore."

Serpentine held her breath and tried to pull the long, imaginary knife from her heart. She tugged and strained, but it was buried deep and determined to stay. She prayed for some kind of joke to follow.

"I was hoping that I would feel differently with this trip; that's why I came. What I feel instead is terrible, so I think I should go."

"What are you talking about, Creighton?" Serpentine howled. "What the hell happened between last night and this morning?"

"I've started seeing somebody else at home. That's what I'm trying to tell you. It was her I was thinking about every time we made love, and that's not fair to you."

A frightening pain grabbed the spot in Serpentine's heart where the imaginary knife was rooted.

They sat in silence for a minute, then Creighton got up, grabbed his bag, and opened the door.

"I hope someday you can forgive me, but I know this is best," he said.

Serpentine's eyes followed each step out of the door. Her chest was pounding tightly. She wanted to beg him to stay. Maybe if she made a scene; lay on the floor, kicked and screamed and cried, maybe he would realize that their love was the ultimate love. It just couldn't get any better, not with anybody else.

Serpentine felt paralyzed. She sat in her bed watching shadows bounce against the wall. She wanted to get up, but couldn't. She wanted to scream, but couldn't. She wanted to cry, but couldn't. She simply lay there, still and silent. It was the phone ringing that moved her, almost four hours later. She lifted the receiver and mumbled hello.

"Get the hell out the bed, girl!" Marleen yelled into the phone. "You gonna bring that man around so somebody can meet him, or what?"

Serpentine's face suddenly contorted; she dropped the phone on the floor and staggered into the bathroom, sobbing.

Tevan's hand touching her left shoulder brought Serpentine back into the room. Her eyes found Creighton in the line of prisoners who were turning left to go back to their cells. She fell into step with the members of Glory who were turning right and heading for the exit.

Ignorance

Most people are ignorant and they don't even know it. I spent my high school days as ignorant as a virgin who uses a condom on her new vibrator. When I look at my photo album from high school now, I wish I could go back. I looked good and I didn't even realize it, because society said if I wasn't a size six or eight I was fat. I was heavy, I don't deny that, but I was stacked. I didn't look anything like that Twiggy model who was popular at the time. Most black women couldn't look like her if they wanted to.

I grew about three inches the summer between junior high and high school; the pounds didn't come off, but they shifted around and positioned themselves in all the right places. I was a stone fox, but unfortunately, I had bought into the hype. When I looked in the mirror I still saw fat.

It's a shame I couldn't truly enjoy my high school days because of ignorance, society's and mine.

Serpentine was a few minutes late when she rushed into Dr. Greeley's office. He looked up from his paperwork and smiled.

"I really need to vent today," she told him, then flopped down on the couch that was becoming a good friend.

Dr. Greeley moved over to the black chair and crossed his long pencil legs. "What would you like to vent about?" he asked.

Serpentine looked up at the ceiling. "I went with my choir to sing at a prison this weekend and saw an old boyfriend there."

Dr. Greeley cleared his throat. "Tell me about it," he said.

Serpentine took a deep breath and released all of the anger she felt inside. "It all comes down to racism!" she shouted. "Granted, I wished for something bad to happen to Creighton on many occasions after we broke up, but he's in jail because this is a racist society. It messes brothers up. Truth be told, it screws us all up in one way or another!"

Dr. Greeley's ears turned red as he sat quietly and listened to Serpentine's tirade. She closed her eyes and began by telling him about a desegregation project that she and Creighton took part in when they were thirteen years old.

She was glad at first when the Kansas City school board selected her for the special desegregation project. Fifty students from the predominantly black Central Junior High School were to be bused over to the predominantly white Franklin Junior High School for a one-year experimental program.

Her happiness was destroyed, however, on the very first day of school: Their bus pulled up to the curb and was bombarded with rocks and sticks. The school had hired two security guards to handle such problems, but they took their time getting the situation under control. The frightened, cocoa-colored human beings spent an extra thirty minutes on the bus waiting for assistance.

When they finally hurried into the large brick building, they were given a pep talk by the principal about the need for patience and determination if the project was going to work. He then proceeded to split them up and send them to their various homerooms.

It was rough going at Franklin, but the test group was making it until a group of hate mongers beat Creighton up just before Christmas break. Creighton's mahogany smile was infectious. He had big dreams to go with his even bigger talent in art. He chose to befriend a white student, Harold. They planned to show everybody that Dr. Martin Luther King, Jr.'s dream really was possible. They went to basketball games and science fairs together. They ate lunch and studied in the library together.

First came the threats. Serpentine found one note when she borrowed Creighton's science book. It said: "This is your last warning. If you know what's good for you you'll stay in your place, stupid nigger!"

When she asked him about it, Creighton claimed he wasn't scared. "So what?" he told her in an agitated voice.

"This note is serious, Creighton," Serpentine warned him. "You can't just ignore it."

"They're just stupid people trying to scare somebody," Creighton replied. "I'm sick of all this hatred. I'm not scared of these assholes. I can take care of myself."

After a Friday night basketball game, Creighton and Harold didn't notice that the halls had cleared except for three white boys who rounded the corner and came up behind them.

"Oh, there they are. The Bobbsey Twins," the tall, skinny white boy shouted in their direction.

"Get lost, asshole," Creighton shot back.

"I know you don't have the nerve to get smart with us," the football-player-sized guy added.

"I see we're going to have to show your nigger-loving ass what time it is." The short, pale boy spoke directly to Harold.

"L-look, we don't want any trouble. J-just leave us alone," Harold stuttered.

It was the spit that landed on Creighton's neck that caused him to snap. He lunged forward, grabbing a handful of stringy blond hair. The tall guy jerked away and the football player tackled Creighton as if they were opponents on the field. The short, pale boy lowered his head, ramming it into Harold's side, then sank his teeth into Harold's right arm. Harold screamed and pulled away, then ran down the deserted hallway to find help.

The trio pushed Creighton hard into the wall, chipping his front tooth. He shook his head, attempting to shake the dizziness, but suddenly the attackers were dragging him across the cement floor. They pulled him into the men's bathroom and shoved his face against a stall door. Creighton fell inside, pulling his attackers down with him.

Creighton tried to stand up, but he was stopped by hands that gripped his head and shoved it into the toilet bowl until he passed out. He was found unconscious minutes later. The doctor told his mother that he would need a hearing aide to compensate for the extensive damage to his right ear.

Several black parents pulled their kids from Franklin when they heard about the incident. Nolita and Kendrick wanted Serpentine to stick it out, but they told her she could make the final decision. Serpentine surprised everyone, including herself, and stayed.

Serpentine swallowed as she went on to explain to Dr. Greeley how the pilot desegregation project continued to fail miserably.

"Only twenty-one of the original fifty students returned for the spring term. Because the number of black students returning that January had dropped substantially, the school board made a financial decision to discontinue the chartered bus service that carried us safely to and from the school. We were expected to ride the city bus with the white students."

Dr. Greeley took a few notes as she spoke.

"I dreaded the tense, tiresome city bus ride. Each day I prayed that we could get to or from school without a fight, but my prayers were rarely answered. I couldn't blame God because when I looked at the news each night and saw the riots and marches going on all over the country, I knew He was busy."

It had been illegal to force blacks to the back of the bus since the Supreme Court decision on busing in 1956, but Serpentine and the other black students still considered the back of the bus their domain, because it was safer.

One dismal, wet Wednesday in March, Serpentine got on the bus and sat next to Creighton. After the beating, he had returned with a very different attitude. He quickly gained a reputation as a bad dude, not to be messed with. He would fight about almost anything.

When his mother told Nolita that Creighton's father was killed trying to get a college education somewhere in Alabama, it helped Serpentine to understand his actions. Up until that point, she had wondered why he came back to school at all. It was obvious that he didn't care anymore. He didn't apply himself to any of his courses and the only thing that saved him was a photographic memory that made up for his lack of effort.

"You see *Shaft* this weekend?" Creighton asked with a raised voice as Serpentine sat down.

A strand of long blond hair bounced on his lap. He brushed it away, and tapped the white girl sitting in front of him on the shoulder. "Excuse me, could you keep your hair off me?" he asked in an exasperated tone.

She turned around. "Sorry," she snapped, sweeping the long locks back over her shoulder with her left hand.

"I didn't see it, but I heard it was good. You see it?" Serpentine asked.

"Shaft was a bad mother shut your mouth!" Creighton sang. "He was a real black man in control of his life. He had his woman's respect, he had the respect of the bad guys, and even the white cops didn't mess with him. He was bad!"

The head in front of him continued to turn back and forth immersed in conversation and soon the hair made its way over the seat again.

Creighton tapped her on her shoulder a second time. "I'm not going to ask you to move your hair again," he said in a threatening tone.

"I heard the record by Isaac Hayes, and it's real good." Serpentine spoke quickly, noting the change in Creighton's tone of voice and trying to distract him.

Creighton grinned from ear to ear. "I got it at home, played it all weekend!" he said.

When the extensive mane swept across his legs for the third time, Creighton pulled a cigarette lighter out of his pocket and held it under the tapered gold ends.

"Creighton, don't," Serpentine warned, reaching for the lighter. But it was too late. As the fire shot up toward her scalp, the girl leaped into the air, screaming.

Serpentine jumped up and dashed out of the way, while Creighton sat and calmly watched the action. Several of the girl's friends tackled her and patted the fire out with jackets, scarves, and hats.

The bus driver immediately pulled over and opened the door to clear the smoke.

"What's going on back here?" he asked.

"He set her hair on fire!" one of the girl's friends shouted.

"What is your problem, boy?" the driver scolded.

Creighton stood up and walked toward the driver without fear. "I warned her to keep that slimy shit off me," he said.

"Are you all right?" the driver asked the shaking girl. When she nodded he turned back to Creighton. "You just wait right here. I'm gonna call the police." He hurried back up front.

Creighton glared at the bus driver, then exited out the back door and strolled down the street as if he didn't have a care in the world.

When the bus driver returned he looked around and didn't see Creighton. "Where'd he go?"

Several of the black students shrugged.

He looked directly at Serpentine. "Anybody know where he lives?"

Serpentine shook her head.

"All of you get the hell off my bus!" the driver shouted. "I don't want to see any of you niggers back on this bus ever again."

As they filed out the back door, Serpentine stepped around a pudgy white leg.

"That's right, get off the bus, you fat, ugly, black bitch," she heard the owner of that leg shout.

When Serpentine turned to face the voice, a heavy-set white girl with a beet-red face and short, curly brown hair leered at her. Serpentine was stunned to see she had three chins and a pot gut of her own.

Dr. Greeley's phone rang just as Serpentine ended her story.

"We've made it through some horrible times in America," he told her, ignoring the phone.

"Very few of us have made it, Dr. Greeley," Serpentine persisted.

Dr. Greeley scribbled something on his pad. "Before you leave, Serpentine," he said, "can you tell me from that experience what sticks in your mind most vividly?"

Serpentine thought for a moment, then responded almost too quickly: "I still can't believe that bitch had the nerve to call *me* fat!"

Postcards from the Edge

I saw a postcard today that I had to buy and put up on my bulletin board. It was a caricature of a woman walking from the left side of the card to the right. She's obese when she begins, but with each step she gets slimmer and slimmer.

The note on the other side reads: "Smothered pork chops, macaroni and cheese, bread and butter, spaghetti and meatballs, mashed potatoes and gravy, ice cream and cake, chocolate chip cookies, I sure miss you guys!"

Thick sheets of rain made it difficult to see on Monday morning as Serpentine drove into work. She turned her windshield wipers up faster and leaned forward as if that might help. She sat in the station parking lot for ten minutes until the rain let up, then dashed into the building. As she passed the receptionist's desk, Vera, who had obviously not heard Nolita's saying "busy souls have no time to be busy bodies," stopped her.

"Did you hear yet?" Vera whispered.

"Hear what?" Serpentine replied, somewhat annoyed.

"Terry had a heart attack this weekend. He's dead."

Startled, Serpentine searched Vera's eyes in disbelief. She jogged down the hallway over to Terry's office and rushed inside.

Evan Wilson looked up over his glasses from behind Terry's desk. "Serpentine, I guess you've heard the news," he said. "It's so sad. I'm really gonna miss him."

Serpentine leaned back against the door to steady herself. "What happened?" she asked.

"Apparently he was doing what he loved best, jogging, and his heart just stopped. He was already dead when he got to the hospital."

"I can't believe it," Serpentine mumbled.

"Me neither . . . I'm going to take charge," Evan told her. "We have to keep the department running smoothly. Don't you agree?"

In the six weeks that followed, Serpentine couldn't believe the changes Evan had made. He wanted everyone to know his word was law, so he had Vice President Cameron Marshall issue a memo to the news division confirming that the changes were a necessary part of the station's "quest for excellence."

The consultants were on board, and a focus group project was under way. The contract called for the consultants to observe each reporter, anchor, and staff member in the newsroom for two weeks. They also organized the focus group sessions in the community.

Evan called everyone into a meeting to prepare them. "These consultants will be a great tool for boosting ratings and cutting out dead wood," he started his speech. "They've already made some wonderful suggestions like brightening up the colors for the anchor desk and a new personalized theme for our newscasts, 'If it's news we've got it.' "

Serpentine took the time to dress especially nice the morning she was scheduled to meet with one of the evaluators. She pulled out her navy blue linen suit with matching pumps and added a sixteen-inch serpentine gold chain that had been a Christmas present from her father.

The willowy white female with dyed-red hair and black roots followed her around all morning, asking questions about everything. She only wrote one criticism in her report: Serpentine's preference for what the consultant called an antiquated writing style. Serpentine made the mistake of telling her that if she had time, she liked to write out a story by hand, then type it into the computer. The reviewer reported that the process was slow and time consuming.

Serpentine didn't focus on anything positive in the report. Instead she cursed the woman under her breath: "May a thousand bumblebees infest her nostrils," she mumbled, then laughed, thinking about a thousand bumblebees crammed into those tiny openings.

The focus group sessions proved to be much more problematic. Each consisted of ten participants chosen from surveys that people had filled out in various parts of town. The sample was supposed to be a good cross section of the Chicago population. Group One was selected because they said they watched WXYZ news almost every evening. Group Two claimed they rarely or never watched the station.

At the end of the evaluation period, Evan summoned Serpentine and her colleagues into editing studio C to watch a hodge-podge of community viewers critique their ability.

Evan showed the twenty-seven-minute tape of the WXYZ viewers' opinions first.

"We love Thomas Benton," a mixed-race couple chimed. "He's very professional and articulate."

A young artist spoke next. "He seems stiff to me, like there's a stick up his butt."

"Trina and Thomas make a wonderful team. They help me to feel more secure and confident about our community," the wife from a Gold Coast family of four commented, with her husband nodding in agreement.

A woman from Little Greece made a suggestion: "Serpentine Williamson and Arthur Richards are really good reporters. I enjoy their stories, but I wish they would report less detail about violent acts. Mr. Richards's story on the cat killings in Skokie last week gave me nightmares."

"Can you tell us specifically what about the coverage bothered you?" one of the consultants asked.

The lady thought for a moment. "I don't know, I just didn't like it," she replied. "What those kids did was sick, and it's hard to watch things like that. I know that's part of the news, but I don't like it."

A businessman from the near north and northwest side cleared his throat. "For me, Ms. Williamson doesn't seem to be as sharp as she once was," he said. "When I first noticed her, several years ago, she had a spunk that was contagious, but lately she's been steadily putting on weight and most of her stories seem to be racially focused."

Serpentine sat up and paid attention when she heard her name. At first, these people were just batting issues back and forth; but now somebody had gotten personal.

"I don't know," the husband from a black South Side family retorted. "Her report on those computer IQ tests was excellent. And she also did that great story about the Supreme Court decision which allowed the Ku Klux Klan to erect a cross in a public park in Columbus, Ohio."

"It's hard to believe that something like that could happen during the Christmas season, of all times. When we're supposed to be honoring Jesus," the man's wife added.

A black college student jumped in. "Sorry Clarence Thomas used some legal bullshit about an Establishment Clause and sided with the majority."

"I know Mr. Thurgood Marshall's soul is restless in his grave with that man as his replacement," an Asian male parking-lot attendant added.

The second group was unfamiliar with the station, so they agreed to watch several past WXYZ newscasts, then give their opinion. Midway through the second tape, Serpentine's name came up again.

"I didn't really like that guy Thomas Benton," a hotel manager said. "He seems almost anal retentive. But the lady anchor was cool."

"Arthur Richards has nice eyes. You can tell he's giving you the truth," the wife of a Polish couple said. "Doesn't he look like Martha's boy?" she asked her husband.

A white college female shook her head. "The two anchors don't really work well for me. WGN's anchors seem to fit together better."

"I liked that story by Serpentine Williamson, but she's too thick," a South Side black male jumped in.

"What do you mean by 'thick'?" asked one of the consultants.

"She has a really pretty face, but she's too big," he answered.

A South Side black female, who was plump herself, spoke up. "I disagree. I think it's nice to see a healthy woman on television. Everybody is not thin and she's representing that segment of our society."

"Well, I do know some fellas who like 'em big; they're chubby-chasers. But I'm not into it myself," the man explained.

A consultant again needed clarification. "Can you define a 'chubby-chaser' for us?"

"A fat woman usually has low self-esteem and she's more likely to let a man slide because she don't have as many options."

Serpentine rolled her eyes up into her head. "Oh, Lord," she moaned, just before she stormed out of the room.

Evan rushed after her. "Serpentine, wait," he called.

She stopped and turned around.

"Look, I know this stuff is hard to listen to, but these consultants have been really successful at turning stations around," he told her.

"Those tapes don't mean anything, Evan, and you know it. One person says good and another says bad.

Evan sighed. "They're telling us a lot if we listen, Serpentine. Both groups mentioned that your weight gain is a problem."

Serpentine stared at Evan and their eyes locked as if it were a contest of strength.

"My weight does not affect the quality of my work, Evan, and you know it," she told him.

Evan blinked, looked down, then back up again. "Listen, Serpentine. You are a very good reporter, but your weight does matter. Television is not only about reporting skills, it's about the total package: skills, looks, voice tone, even personality. Viewers have to want to invite you into their living room on a daily basis."

"So what happens if I don't lose weight, Evan? Are you going to fire me?" Serpentine asked sarcastically.

"Of course not, you have a strong following here in the Chicago market. But, unfortunately, your future in television could be greatly impacted."

"Is that a threat?"

"Look, Serpentine, I'm not the enemy here. I'm trying to look out for you. I know you've been interested in moving to an anchor position and the weekend slot will be opening up soon. Mitsy is pregnant and she plans to stay home to raise her child. You'll never land that kind of position the way you look now."

"How the hell do you know what I can land?" she spat out.

"I know that outfit you have on today is a good example of what I'm talking about. With all that purple, you look like Barney around the hips."

Serpentine was shocked. She stopped arguing, turned, and walked away thinking about something her father always said. "You can't trust a dog to watch your food."

When it was all said and done, however, nobody could dispute the numbers: the ratings for WXYZ news shot up two points, which meant thousands of additional dollars in advertising revenue for the station. The consultants' final report looked very much like other final reports received by hundreds of stations across the country.

According to their vision, everybody was supposed to look the same, and sound the same, then they would rate the same. The goal was mediocrity, with everything aimed at the same old target whether it hit the bull's-eye or not.

Serpentine missed Terry so much. He would never have allowed this to happen. Every time management started one of their "we need to modernize campaigns," Terry would growl about how he had been around too long and he wasn't going to tolerate that crap. Vice President Marshall had tried to force those news consultants down Terry's throat for years, but somehow he always won out.

As she walked past the newly painted anchor desk she knew Terry would have hated it. The rich blue and maroon colors that had meant quality and professionalism for more than twenty years were gone. It was now a bright yellow and orange that seemed loud and childish, more in tune with Bugs Bunny fans.

THE BEGINNING

(Last Summer and Fall)

Fat Jokes

I remember many of the fat jokes I've heard over the years. I love to laugh, but it's hard to laugh at yourself.

—Your mama's so fat, Richard Simmons wouldn't deal her a meal.

—Two fat people are making love. "You get on top." "No, I'm tired. You get on top." "I got on top last time." "Well I'm not getting on top." "Forget it then, let's go get something to eat."

—Your mama's so fat, when she hauls ass, she has to make two trips.

—If you're thin, you're in. If you're fat, get back.

—How do you make love to a fat woman? Roll her in flour and find the wet spot.

—A fat lady stepped on a pay scale and put in a quarter. The scale read: "To be continued. Another quarter, please."

One of the first fat jokes that I remember, I heard when I was fourteen years old. A lot of people thought it was funny, and they laughed. But I didn't, I couldn't, because it was about me.

Today when Serpentine entered Dr. Greeley's inner sanctum she was ready to talk. Just as she got comfortable on the faded couch, Dr. Greeley rushed in and plopped down at his desk. "Give me a couple of minutes, Serpentine, please," he said.

Serpentine leaned back, and listened impatiently as he talked to his wife concerning a dinner party they were hosting that weekend. She crossed her legs and closed her eyes. It was difficult to know where to begin, but today was the day she would tell Dr. Greeley what he wanted to know most. She had replayed the mental tape over in her mind.

Dr. Greeley hung up the phone, twirled his chair around, and smiled. "Okay, are we ready to begin?"

Serpentine opened her eyes and nodded. She didn't know why she had chosen today to talk about her suicide attempt. When she got dressed this morning it wasn't on her mind. Driving to his office it didn't come up. Even in the elevator she didn't have a clue. But when Serpentine walked inside that room she immediately knew that it was time.

"I didn't decide to die in that one day," Serpentine told him. "That decision was the culmination of many years of personal turmoil."

Dr. Greeley quickly erased the look of surprise from his face and started writing.

"There has always been a constant drumbeat in my head that seemed to get louder and louder over the years. When comfortable situations would collapse, the beat would get stronger. When my needs would collide with reality, the beat would move faster. Probably, the main thrust of it started last summer at the Beechnut Club, one of the most popular black nightspots in Chicago."

Dr. Greeley put his pen down and leaned forward in the chair.

"According to LaJune, a night out was exactly what I needed. I had been depressed for a while. There was nothing specific that I could pinpoint, just an overwhelming dismal feeling that included the hectic nature of my job, the steady climbing of my weight, and the empty perception of being alone. The last man in my life had been a crazy blind date that Marleen set me up with—which automatically tells you how desperate I was. He had the audacity to call the next day and say I was nice, but my weight was a turnoff for him. Asshole!"

Parren was out to sea and LaJune always got a little crazy by the end of the first month, so Serpentine had agreed to go out, for a little while, for her sake. They had been at the club for about an hour and Serpentine was already bored shitless.

LaJune couldn't stay in her seat. She danced almost every song with anyone who asked. Serpentine watched as the men in the room gravitated toward the skinny, hot mamas with everything "hanging and swinging." She sighed and opened a recent issue of *N'digo* newspaper, which she had grabbed from the silver stand up front when they entered. She leaned over into the faint light and skimmed the front page.

She was annoyed, at first, when somebody stepped up to the table and blocked the minimal light. But when she looked up she immediately recognized Carlin. It had been more than twenty years, but even with a dark mustache and tapered beard, he looked the same.

Carlin waited, judging her response before he spoke. "Serpentine Williamson?" he asked.

"Carlin Dumont," Serpentine responded.

"How are you?"

"Okay, and you?"

Carlin bobbed his head with the beat. "Good, good. Why aren't you out dancing on this jam?"

Serpentine scowled. "I don't know," she finally answered, picking up her newspaper again.

"Well, I can tell you the problem, if you really want to know," Carlin continued, leaning against the table.

Serpentine set down the paper and smiled skeptically. "Sure, tell me," she said.

"It's this reading material on your table," Carlin explained with a playful charm, pointing to the various spread-out sections of the paper. "You scarin' the brothers away. A sister at a club readin' is hard to get with."

Serpentine couldn't stop the real smile that appeared. He was still Carlin Patrick Dumont, the silly eleven-year-old that used to make her laugh all the time. Serpentine looked into his face, remembering their past. She noticed the dimples in each smooth, golden cheek had grown deeper.

"I guess you could have a point," she admitted.

Carlin looked around the room. "Trust me. These brothers are thoroughly intimidated."

"And, of course, you're not?" she asked, anticipating his response.

"I am, but you know me. I believe in leaps of faith." He held out his hand. "You gonna dance with me, or what?"

Serpentine frowned. "I'm not sure."

"Don't be that way," he said, emitting his own unique brand of urban confidence. "If you give me a chance, I could make it up to you."

"With a dance?" Serpentine asked, cutting her eyes at him.

"What about dinner and my sincerest apology?" Carlin begged. "I'm starving."

"You think dinner will make a difference?" Serpentine asked.

"I think it would be better than staying here and reading in the dark."

Serpentine laughed out loud. Carlin could still make her laugh. She found LaJune and told her she was leaving. Then she and Carlin headed for a new Caribbean spot on the southwest side. The place was dark and romantic, with candles on each table that flickered passionately. Serpentine ordered the bacon-and-cheddar-cheese soup with a Caesar salad. Carlin had blackened catfish and baby carrots.

After they had given the waiter their orders, Serpentine took a sip of her margarita on the rocks, and looked for more traces of the bug-loving boy she'd befriended that summer.

Serpentine remembered sitting on her parents' front porch that day, reading *Brown Girl, Brownstones* by Paule Marshall for the second time. She laughed at the fact that she had struggled earlier with a diaper pin, to hold up the too-big hand-me-down cotton shorts she wore.

It was a normal, fiery-hot summer day in June, when the Ryder moving truck stopped two houses down the street. Serpentine stood up and inched her way over to the sidewalk to get a better look. Two adults and one child got out of the front cab of the truck. She immediately noticed that the nerdy boy looked about her age. She moved in a little closer, masking her excitement.

The gangly five-foot-eight boy noticed Serpentine right away and took several steps in her direction.

"Hi, I'm Carlin," he said.

"Hello, I'm Serpentine," she replied, but stayed planted within the comfortable boundary of her front yard.

"Wanna see something cool?" Carlin asked.

Before Serpentine could reply, he took a small white box out of his pants pocket.

"It's a spider skin," he explained, pulling the wrinkled substance out and handing it to her. "I collect them."

Serpentine stiffly held the thin layer of dry skin trying to act interested.

"Spiders shed several times a year. Look, this is a dead one," he added, dumping a huge, black, hairy spider out of the box into his palm. He pointed to the neck area. "That's where the poison sacs are."

Serpentine peered into his hand, but kept her distance. She asked the first question that came to her mind. "Have you ever been bit by a spider?"

Carlin stuck his chest out proudly. "Sure," he replied with a self-assured air. "It swells and hurts for a few days, but most of them don't carry enough poison to kill anybody. Maybe the tarantula or the black widow could kill a little kid."

Serpentine shivered and turned up her nose.

"Have you ever seen a spider eat?" Carlin continued, ignoring her disgust.

Serpentine shook her head no, so he grabbed her arm and pulled her toward the driveway.

"Just check this out. I'm gonna show you how to feed a spider. It's cool," he said, then dropped his head and searched the ground for movement. "The key is to hit the bug softly so that it doesn't die, because spiders prefer live food. Here's a black ant," he said, pointing his right foot toward a moving black dot.

Carlin tapped the figure-eight-shaped bug just hard enough to stun it into submission. Then he picked it up carefully, trying not to squeeze it too much. He walked across the yard to a big web and dropped the ant onto it. Once the ant hit the middle of that silk orb, there was nothing left to do but wait.

As he talked, Carlin never took his eyes off the large elastic web that stretched between two gold-flame spirea bushes like a huge fishing net. "I think I saw two spiders doing it once," he whispered. "Did you know that female spiders sometimes eat the male spiders after sex?"

Serpentine turned toward him and spoke: "That's gross! Why would she want to eat him?"

Carlin put his index finger up to his lips. "Shhhhhhh, watch the web and lower your voice," he warned.

Serpentine followed his instructions.

Carlin scratched just above his right ear, then patted his curly afro back into place. "A lot of spiders don't see well. They mainly use their sense of touch. Since the male is smaller than the female, she sometimes mistakes him for food caught in the web."

Just then the ant woke up and started to struggle against the sticky thread.

Carlin called for her complete silence. "Shhhhhhh," he hissed. "Watch."

The vibrations from the ant's frantic movement sent signals to the small, fuzzy, brown spider bringing it cautiously out of its perfectly shaped hole. They watched as the spider circled its victim, wrapping it tightly in thread, then dragged it back into the hole for dinner or a late-night snack.

"Ahhhhh, he must not be hungry. He's gonna save it for later."
Carlin moaned, then kicked a rock out from under his left foot.

Serpentine recalled being secretly glad that she didn't have to
watch the spider eat. She felt sorry for the poor ant. He was
probably happy, living his life, minding his business, and now he
was gone.

"**I** saw you on the news earlier at the hotel. You were great," Carlin said to garner her attention again. "I thought about calling the
station, but didn't know how you'd respond. When I saw you at
the club tonight, I knew this was meant to be."

"Taking me to dinner was meant to be?" she asked dryly.

"No, my apology was meant to be," he clarified. "I'm really
sorry."

The smell of jerk chicken floated across the room as their
waiter delivered hot meals to a nearby table. She sat and stared at
the man across from her, wondering why she had agreed to come.

"Can you forgive me?" Carlin asked.

"I don't know, maybe," Serpentine answered. "I'll have to
think about it. I do need to thank you for helping me get an 'A' in
my vertebrate zoology class in college."

"I helped you get an 'A'?" Carlin asked, surprised.

"I never could have studied the life and behavior of snakes,
if I hadn't been your bug hunting assistant that summer," she
explained.

The waiter brought out their drinks and hurried away.

"So how're your mother and father?" Carlin asked, taking a
gulp of his water.

"They're good. And yours?"

"Pop is retired now, and Mom still works over at Wheatley
Hospital."

"That's good."

"You always said you wanted to be on TV; and here you are, a
reporter in the Windy City. Are you happy, Serpentine?"

Serpentine shrugged. "I guess I am," she said. "How about
you? I heard you were going to medical school."

"I quit, dropped out, was kicked out; it depends on who's

telling the story. The bottom line is that I looked around and realized I was miserable. I'm interviewing for a research position with Dow Chemical here in Chicago." Carlin waited for a response that never came, then continued. "I've been substitute-teaching fifth-grade science and I love the kids, so I'm not sure I want to leave them. I might get my teaching certificate and try it full-time."

"Teaching is an important profession, especially for a positive black man. Daddy loved it. They need people like you in the classroom desperately."

"Did you just call me positive?" Carlin teased.

"Don't get too excited. It was just a figure of speech," Serpentine told him between sips of her iced tea.

"I really think it was fate seeing you in that club tonight, Serpentine."

She didn't respond. She sat thinking that Carlin had been a cute boy back then and now he'd become a very good-looking man. She felt warm inside, but shook that feeling off.

Carlin kept talking. "That summer when we met was wonderful. Sometimes I'll be skimming through a book or watching something on television, and a memory of you will pop into my head. You were my best friend and I was too dumb to realize it. I've missed having you in my life."

Serpentine rolled her eyes at him just as their food arrived with the steam drifting upward from the plates.

He *was* dumb, at least he had that right!

They were best friends that summer. Serpentine went to a morning writing camp; then she spent almost every afternoon with Carlin. Sometimes they'd sit on Serpentine's porch and read the afternoon away, or play kickball in the middle of the street until the sun went down.

She and Carlin started at Central together, and that was when their friendship crumbled. They were scheduled for different classes and different lunch periods. In the beginning, they tried to steal a few minutes between classes or after lunch, but after a few months, Carlin started to simply wave and pass her by.

He made new friends quickly, unlike Serpentine. When she

tried to see him after school, he was usually too busy with football practice, homework, or his new buddies, so she eventually retreated back into her comfortable shell.

As Serpentine remembered it now, that was when weight first became a major issue in her life. Especially when she started to see Carlin and Daphne together. The first time she heard rumors that they were boyfriend and girlfriend she got out her mother's recipe for marshmallow cream fudge and made a large, oblong pan full. In a couple of days, she had eaten most of it by herself.

She got into fried-pork-chop-eating contests with her sister and enjoyed mounds of greasy french fries that her father deep-fried in Crisco. Serpentine gained twenty pounds that year. She was still cute, with an average chest, but healthy hips were forming and she no longer needed that diaper pin for her cousin's hand-me-downs.

One afternoon as she rushed out of her history class, trying to catch her bus, she accidentally bumped into Daphne who was huddled with several friends at the end of the hall.

"Damn, watch it!" Daphne yelled at her.

"Sorry," Serpentine muttered, barely looking up. She continued past the group as quickly as possible.

"You should be sorry," Daphne called after her, then turned to her entourage and spoke loudly so that Serpentine would hear: "You have to admit that fat ass was really moving!"

Serpentine stopped when she heard the insult followed by laughter. She turned and stared Daphne dead in her face. Serpentine's eyes narrowed and her lips tightened as she readied herself to do battle. Then suddenly, Serpentine dropped her eyes to the floor and ran away. She raced out of the building and didn't stop running until she reached her front porch. There she flopped down on the steps and sobbed because Carlin was standing beside Daphne, and he was laughing too.

By the end of the evening, Serpentine was surprised to find herself smiling at Carlin's silly stories and laughing at his stale jokes. His buoyant charm was still enticing.

They talked for hours on the phone about everything. Carlin

didn't get the job in Chicago, so he decided to go after his teaching certificate and continue his true passion full-time. She loved to hear about how he was making a difference in his students' lives. He had taken the time to get to know the parents, sponsored after-school tutoring sessions, and was including self-esteem affirmations in his classes every day.

One evening, he told her how upset he was when he caught some of the kids teasing an overweight student on the playground.

"I need to say I'm sorry again, Serpentine, because it made me realize what you must have gone through that day," he said sincerely.

"Kids are cruel," Serpentine told him.

"I'm rescheduling my lesson plans for the week to help them understand the value of difference."

Serpentine shifted the phone from her left ear to her right. "That might make the girl feel even worse, if she thinks it's because of her."

"I'm covering it up by talking about different cultures, religions, and skin colors. I plan to sneak in body types. I even found a game they can play exploring differences like dark and light skin, good and bad hair, blue and brown eyes, smart and not-so-smart."

After just two months, it was hard to believe, but Serpentine found herself falling for Carlin all over again.

Perfection

There's really no such thing as perfection, only the illusion of it. I realize that I've spent a great deal of my life creating that illusion. Some would say my education, my career, even my life in general have been close to perfect. But underneath the illusion there have always been issues like self-esteem, love, stress, and, of course, weight to deal with.

Today, when I asked myself the same question for the umpteenth time, I wasn't expecting an answer. Why have I been able to do everything in life I've wanted to do except control my weight? And when the answer came I was shocked because it was so simple: Everything else that I've ever cared about doing, I've done. So, it soon became painfully obvious that I really don't care about losing this weight.

What I care about is how society treats me differently because I'm not a size eight. What I care about is how I've been shamed, embarrassed, forced, hustled, guilted, tricked, pushed, bullied, and even frightened into trying to be who society wants me to be. Whenever I've lost weight I didn't lose it for me. I lost it for society; to fit in; to be called cute or pretty; to catch a man.

It feels good to finally admit that. When I told Aunt Regina about my revelation she laughed and said it was about time. She told me that my next step should be to move away from perfection and accept being human. Aunt Regina's favorite saying is "The measure of a person's life is not what size they are, it's how well they live." And my aunt Regina has lived very well!

ౚ ౚ ౚ

South Elizabeth, number 11512, jumped the last Friday of each month. For the past six years, Regina Bentley had hosted her bid-whist club's ritual bash. Two folding card tables were set up in the center of her living room, with two different decks of cards on each table. The two decks, Serpentine soon learned, were necessary to keep the game moving: As one player dealt, the next dealer in line shuffled the second deck to save time.

When Serpentine first moved to Chicago, she stayed with her aunt Regina for six months until she could save up enough money to get her own place. She should have been Regina's child, because she was much closer to her aunt than to her mother. They had a lot of values, attitudes, and beliefs in common. They also looked very much alike, with broad football-player shoulders, a large supple chest, no waistline, and a voluptuous behind.

The dinette table was overloaded with tasty treats, from chips and dips to fried chicken wings and potato salad. No hard liquor was allowed, because Regina was a God-fearing woman. Her late husband Samuel had been an alcoholic, so she refused to aid in the destruction of other souls. However, a limited amount of wine or beer was available upon request. The limit was two cans of beer or two glasses of wine. Those people who wanted to get drunk were forced to show up that way.

Serpentine had rarely attended the Friday night card festivities since she moved out, but tonight she wanted to see her aunt. They hadn't spent much time together, lately, and she needed a "dose of Regina" to motivate her periodically. About nine o'clock that night the first guests began to arrive and soon the party was under way. Food was being eaten, cards were being slammed, and lies were being told.

The game was always "rise and fly," which meant if you or your partner bid and didn't make the bid, your opponents would get the score. If you won every book it was called "going to Boston" and a trip to Boston always cleared the board.

"I said five no trump," Aaron shouted over the head of his nemesis.

"Please! You think that sorry bid's gonna walk? My partner's gonna eat that shit up," Regina said, pushing her new shoulder-length braids behind her left shoulder.

"Eat it up with what? My fingers, 'cause I sure don't have a knife, fork, or spoon in this hand," Sonja replied.

"It would be nice if you two could stop talking across the board and bid," Aaron's partner Shawn complained.

Sonja laid her cards facedown on the table. "I can't do nothing but pass," she said, shifting her large, pear-shaped bottom in the chair.

"Damn, Sonja, you didn't hear me or what?" Regina yelled, bouncing up and down.

"I heard you, but if I got nothing, I can't bid nothing," Sonja shot back, folding her arms across her heaving chest.

"We five on, girl. I'd rather lose that five trying to win than let them go out on us," Regina explained.

Shawn slid the kitty over toward her partner. "Well, I pass, so you coming up or down, partner?"

"I think down is the right choice," Aaron replied, then picked up the six cards from his kitty and began sorting through his hand.

Serpentine went into the kitchen to get a glass of water and noticed that the door to the basement was cracked open. She walked to the top of the stairs and leaned over the banister. She was surprised to see a crap game in full swing. The smoke-filled room seemed to wobble as she squinted at the circle of men. The one whose face she could see was tall and lanky. He looked like a black version of Walker, Texas Ranger. One of the other guys called him Pee Jay as he blew on the dice and rolled them past piles of money.

"Don't start no shit, won't be no shit, Pee Jay," hissed a guy with a Band-Aid on his arm.

"Throw the damn dice, man, and shut the hell up," Pee Jay instructed with an attitude.

"Niggah, just 'cause you been to prison, ain't nobody scared," Band-Aid replied.

Serpentine eased back into the living room, wondering what the hell was going on. She walked over to the card game, but decided to wait until Regina's game was over.

"You sure better have some cards to stop 'em or I'm gonna whup your ass," Regina joked with Sonja.

Aaron started the game by throwing out the ace of spades.

Sonja tossed the little joker on top, then turned to Shawn and twisted her mouth. "Did you hear what she said to me? She said she's gonna whup my ass. Can you believe that? I don't think she can whup my ass, do you?"

Shawn played the big joker before she spoke. "I don't see how she could miss it, as big as it is."

All eyes turned to Sonja, who flashed Shawn a hurt look but didn't reply right away.

Regina stirred the embers. "Damn, Shawn, you didn't have to go there. Your ass is just as big as hers." She slapped down the jack of spades.

"Shawn, stop talking garbage," Aaron added. "Make yourself useful and pick up the book."

"Sonja knows I was just kidding," Shawn said, flashing a phony smile. She patted Sonja on the back of her hand, then pulled the cards into a pile in front of her. "Sonja's my girl."

Sonja glared at Shawn.

"Well, I ain't kidding when I say bring me back some baked beans 'cause somebody's going to Boston!" Aaron suddenly shouted and slammed down the three of spades.

Regina frowned and shook her head. "You're so corny, Aaron. You ain't sending nobody no further than Walgreen's on Forty-fifth Street to get some toilet paper to wipe up that shit you talking."

Aaron put the rest of his cards in a pile facedown and laid his head on the table.

"Just tell me when to play," he said. " 'Cause it don't matter no more!"

Shawn took her cue. "Okay, partner; play," she told him.

Without looking up, Aaron turned over each card and flipped it onto the center of the table. The others played in turn. "Who was that talking about whuppin' some ass earlier? 'Cause I got a can of whup ass, right here, and I'm just about to open it up on ya'll!"

As Shawn raked the next-to-the-last book into a pile, Regina shot an "I told you so" look at Sonja. "You gonna stop this Boston, or what?" she screamed.

"Hell no, she ain't stopping nothing!" Aaron shouted.

He slapped his last card, an ace of diamonds, onto the table. "See ya!"

Shawn smacked the outstretched palms of her partner. "Boston!" she yelled.

"Come on. Get on the love train, ladies!" Aaron continued, boasting.

"You see what I'm talking about? We were five on," Regina fussed at Sonja. "That's why you don't let them have the bid, especially a no-trump. Now I got to hear this fool's mouth all night long."

"You know I'll always love you, Gina baby," Aaron said, giving her a big hug.

"Don't even try it," Regina replied, pushing him away playfully.

"What do I always tell you?" Aaron teased. "No guts, no glory!"

Regina ducked into the kitchen and Serpentine followed.

"Can I help with something?" she asked, glancing at the basement door.

"Yeah, get me a bowl out of the cabinet," Regina ordered.

"Auntie, who are those people shooting craps in the basement?" Serpentine asked.

"That's Pee Jay. You'll get to meet him pretty soon. Today's his birthday," Regina answered with a grin, then grabbed several snack bags for the food table.

Serpentine glanced at the basement door and followed her aunt back to the living room. "But who is he?" she asked again.

Regina was just about to speak as Pee Jay sauntered into the living room. When he spotted Regina, they went into what looked like a well-developed routine.

"Where's my beautiful Big Mama?" Pee Jay bellowed across the room.

Regina turned immediately with the sound of his voice, and threw on her widest smile.

"Hey, Daddy Pee Jay," she answered.

They walked slowly toward each other in a seductive dance until they met in the middle of the room. Pee Jay took Regina's arm and twirled her around. All eyes were glued to their performance.

Serpentine was flabbergasted. How embarrassing to have this man calling her Big Mama in public! Serpentine wanted to crawl up under the bed and hide.

Regina and Pee Jay spun around the floor. He pulled her close and they swayed tightly together to Bobby Womack's classic "That's the Way I Feel About Cha." Pee Jay sang along with Bobby into Regina's ear.

When the song ended Regina pulled away reluctantly and hurried into the kitchen. Pee Jay's crap shooting buddies had made their way upstairs and were holding up the walls. Serpentine stood and watched the festivities. She didn't like these people and they seemed to be too at home in her aunt's place.

She especially didn't like Pee Jay. He had to be the reason she and Regina had not met for their weekly lunches or talked on the phone late at night like they used to. She made note of every fault. He was crude, straight out of the ghetto. As he rocked Regina in his tight Jordache blue jeans and brown velour pullover shirt, she could tell that he thought he was nickel-ass slick. Even worse the man was an ex-convict.

Regina returned with a large chocolate birthday cake holding five flickering candles. Each candle represented ten years of Pee Jay's life. Everybody clapped and sang Stevie Wonder's version of "Happy Birthday." She set the cake on the card table in front of Pee Jay and kissed him gently on the forehead. "Make a wish, Daddy," she said. "And I'll make it come true."

The room was silent as Pee Jay closed his eyes and thought for a moment. Then he opened his eyes and blew out the candles. Pee Jay shoved his left hand into the cake and pulled out a hunk. He held it toward Regina and she took a bite, sensuously licking his finger. He winked at her, then stuffed the rest into his own mouth.

Serpentine grimaced. What kind of asshole would dig into the cake with his hand like that? What was wrong with her aunt to tolerate this mess?

Regina grabbed a napkin and wiped at Pee Jay's mouth, then dabbed her own. She cut around the hole he'd dug out and sliced the rest of the cake for the guests.

Soon Pee Jay had returned to his basement crap game and others started to leave, so Serpentine slipped into the kitchen to help Regina clean up.

"Why didn't you tell me about Pee Jay before?" Serpentine asked.

"Tell you what?" Regina replied.

Serpentine tossed the paper cups and plates she'd gathered into the trash. "I mean, who is he? Where'd he come from?" she asked, cautiously.

Regina wrapped the last two pieces of cake in foil. "He's a friend, a good friend," she replied, almost as if she anticipated the question.

Serpentine turned her nose up into the air. "What could you possibly see in somebody like him, Aunt Regina?"

Regina turned to face her niece. "What do you not see in him?" she asked, bluntly.

Serpentine wiped at the cabinet top as she spoke: "To be honest, he doesn't seem good enough for you."

"And how do you know what's good enough for me?"

"He's so different from Uncle Samuel."

Regina turned on the hot water and tossed dishes into the sink. "Of course he's different from Samuel. But Pee Jay is a good man, just the same."

"He's got a crap game going on in your basement!"

"And I go out on the riverboat and do the same thing two or three times a month. What's your point?" Regina asked irritably.

"I guess I'm just worried about you," Serpentine mumbled. She picked up a towel and started drying.

"No need for worry. I can handle me," Regina told her, pulling the dishrag from the soapy water. "You never have been a very good judge of people," she added.

"Auntie, having these kinds of people in your house is dangerous. Folks who rob you have usually been in your house and know what you got."

Regina snorted. "I trust Pee Jay. He wouldn't bring anybody into my home that would harm me. Besides, I let the Lord handle those kinds of things."

"The Lord wants you to help yourself. You shouldn't take this so lightly, Auntie. It really is a terrible world," Serpentine warned. "I've been thinking about buying a gun for protection, things are so crazy."

Regina stared at her niece. "You don't need a gun, Serpentine, and I want you to promise me you won't buy one," she pleaded.

Serpentine backed down. "I was just thinking about it, that's all."

"The real discussion we need to have is about this new fella of yours," Regina blurted out. "LaJune says he was quite the ladies' man."

Serpentine gave her aunt a surprised look. "LaJune has a big mouth. But Carlin's really wonderful. I think he's exactly what I need in my life right now."

Regina chuckled. "Well, maybe I've got the man I need in *my* life right now, too."

Serpentine sat down at the kitchen table. "Touché," she said.

Just then, Pee Jay came out of the basement, strutted over to Regina, grabbed her from behind, and kissed her on the neck.

Regina kissed him back, quickly, then pulled him toward Serpentine. "Pee Jay, I want you to officially meet my niece Serpentine. Serpentine, this is my Pee Jay."

Serpentine nodded and held out her hand. "Hi," she said.

Pee Jay took the outstretched hand and yanked her out of her seat. "I don't want no handshake, girl," he said, giving her a big bear hug.

"Boy, you sure look a lot like your auntie," Pee Jay continued. "Two pretty women this close to me is something to sure enough give thanks to God for on Sunday."

Serpentine dropped back down. "How did you two meet?" she asked.

"I'm gonna let you tell her the story. I've got to go to the little girls' room," Regina purred.

Pee Jay grabbed a cup from the cabinet and poured black coffee into it, watching Regina leave the room. "I met Big Mama up at Muddy River when I was doing some time for a stupid scam. She came up to visit me with my cousin Reverend Middleton at Mount Glory Baptist. That aunt of yours saw through my hustle and took me into her heart. I'm gonna tell you something: She is truly a godsend. Ain't nothing in the world I wouldn't do for her."

Serpentine sat and watched him carefully. She didn't like the way he twisted his head as he spoke, or the tone of his voice when it shot downward at the end of each sentence.

Pee Jay noticed her intense stare and shifted nervously over toward the doorway. "I was blessed when your aunt opened her heart to me," he concluded.

When Regina brushed past Pee Jay in the doorway, Serpentine caught a glimpse of his hand stroking her behind. She also noticed that her aunt's eyes seemed brighter and her smile wider. Pee Jay kissed Regina one more time, then shuffled back down to his crap game.

Regina smiled at Serpentine almost as if she could read her thoughts. "Pee Jay is a nice guy with a kind heart and I believe in him, honey." She dropped her hand to her hip. "On a good night, he'll come into the bedroom after his poker game and wake me up by tucking two or three hundred-dollar bills into my bosom. And on a bad night, he'll come into the bedroom and make sweet love to me as if I'm the only game in town. When his straight pushes past my ace in the hole, I go flush. He's my king and I'm his queen, baby. I hope you're lucky enough to find this kind of happiness one day."

Serpentine hesitated, then stood up and gave her aunt a long hug. "I guess I should get on out of here," she said.

"It's so late. Why don't you stay tonight rather than be out on that road alone," Regina suggested.

"I got an early day at work tomorrow. I need to get on home."

As Serpentine walked through the living room toward the front door she noticed for the first time that the pictures of her uncle Samuel that usually sat on the front mantel were gone. Two wedding pictures, a few general snapshots, and an Easter portrait of the two of them that had been removed from the frame.

Yo-Yo Blues

All my life I've been singing the yo-yo blues:

I got me this fat gene that won't leave me alone.
My waist it done left me. It's just up and gone.
I exercise and try to eat right, but I tell you it ain't fair.
If people bought fat at a penny a pound, I'd be a millionaire.
I got the blues, the low-down yo-yo blues! (Repeat)

Serpentine sometimes spent her mornings in the public library before going to work. She thumbed through books and magazines that caught her attention, searching for new story ideas. She enjoyed library research, which, thanks to the new Internet craze that seemed to be taking over newsrooms, almost seemed like a lost art.

As she fingered through an article on full-figured fun in *Belle* magazine that Thursday morning, she noticed the same guy walk past her table for the third time. She tried to ignore him. She had very little time left before she needed to get to the station. On his fourth pass the guy finally stopped his slender frame beside her chair.

"Can I help you?" Serpentine asked, trying not to sound too annoyed. She knew this was part of the job, people recognizing her and wanting autographs.

"You're Serpentine Williamson from WXYZ, aren't you?" he asked with excitement.

Serpentine nodded and managed a quick smile, then dropped her head back down into the magazine. But she realized immediately that he wasn't going to accept her "too busy" hint, so she looked up at him again, hoping that he would just ask for an autograph and go away.

"I know you're real busy, but could I just ask you a couple of quick questions?" he continued nervously.

Serpentine took a deep breath, trying to get her attitude together.

"I was just wondering . . . I mean, I travel a lot, and everywhere I go, especially big cities, I see sisters out of control," he said, shifting what little weight he had from his left leg to his right.

Serpentine panicked inside, because this wasn't a quick conversation as far as she was concerned. "What do you mean 'out of control?' " she asked.

"I mean I'm tired of seeing huge behinds, fat ankles, double chins, and big stomachs on beautiful black women. It's sickening."

Serpentine looked the thin, obnoxious man up and down for a moment. She really wanted to curse him out, but her professionalism took over.

"I'm sorry, but this is not a discussion I want to have right now with you. Do you mind?" she said icily.

"I don't mean to offend you, but you're one of my favorite TV people and when I see you gaining weight, too, things have gone too far."

Serpentine was visibly shocked. She stared down at the scratched-up wooden table in front of her and counted to ten in her head. Who the hell did he think he was? She knew she was gaining weight and she sure didn't need him or anybody else to tell her that shit.

"I don't know what to tell you, Mister," Serpentine finally replied. "Maybe I'll do a report about weight gain and explain it to everyone." She turned back to her magazine, satisfied that her response had been strong yet tactful.

He nodded, then continued his inquisition. "I don't mean to insult you, Ms. Williamson. It is 'Ms.,' isn't it?"

"Yes," Serpentine responded sharply.

The man pulled out the chair across from her and sat down as he spoke. "I don't mean to upset you, but you're way too pretty to let yourself go like you have. Black women have forgotten that they're the queens of this earth. How do you feel when you see white women out there running and exercising to keep themselves in shape?"

Serpentine couldn't respond right away because she was thinking about the nerve this guy had to sit his ass down in the chair across from her. "Well, Mr.—" she started.

"Mr. Jacob," he said, holding out his hand.

Serpentine didn't oblige him. "Mr. Jacob, I couldn't possibly speak for all black women. As for myself, I don't think anything about white women keeping in shape. More power to them. You have to understand that losing weight is not as easy as you seem to think it is."

Mr. Jacob sat in front of her fingering a pile of magazines. "That's actually not true, Ms. Williamson. Losing weight is very simple. Tonight, you go to the store and buy a piece of fatback. Take it home, put it in the oven at two hundred degrees for thirty minutes, and pour the grease off into an empty container."

Serpentine watched as he rubbed his stubbled chin between sentences. She still couldn't believe this skinny man who had probably never had a weight problem in his life, was telling her about her situation.

Mr. Jacob continued. "Now, you put that same piece of fatback back into the oven, and turn the oven up this time, to four hundred degrees. After the same thirty minutes, pour that grease into a different container."

Serpentine shut the magazine and looked into his aging face. "What are you trying to say, Mr. Jacob?" she hissed.

"When you compare the two, you'll see that there's a difference. The grease represents the pounds that have melted off. The more exercise you do, the more heat you generate, the more fat you burn, and the more weight you lose."

Serpentine cleared her throat. He might as well have said get up off your fat ass, you lazy cow! Maybe if she did that report she'd include his fatback story. That was just what plus-sized women needed to hear. If losing weight were that easy there wouldn't be a major weight problem in this country.

When Serpentine finally spoke, it was in a nice-nasty tone. "I'm so glad you have it all figured out, Mr. Jacob. Thank you for sharing."

But Mr. Jacob was on a roll now and he didn't show any signs of leaving it alone. "My wife is a good example," he continued. "She comes home from work and sits around the house watching that damn boob tube all night, eating ice cream and drinking beer, and then she complains about how big her behind is getting. What does she expect?"

Serpentine couldn't contain herself any longer. "Maybe she's tired from working all goddamn day! Have you thought about that, Mr. Jacob?" she spat out. "Maybe she needs to eat just to put up with your bullshit!"

Mr. Jacob stood up, suddenly acknowledging her rage. "It's just sad, Ms. Williamson, that's all I'm saying. I love black women and I hate to see this happening to them. They're supposed to be our beautiful black queens."

Furious, Serpentine stood across from him and dropped her hand to her hip. "You know, the problem could also be your limited definition of 'beautiful,' Mr. Jacob," she said sternly. "If you'd been raised in a society where skinny women were considered puny and ugly, you'd probably be talking about them right now. This struggle is about a lot more than putting some fatback in the oven, and until you understand that, you need to get out of my face, because a village somewhere is obviously missing its idiot!"

Mr. Jacobs looked at Serpentine with a blank expression on his face.

"I'm sorry you feel that way," he said, then turned and strolled away.

No longer able to concentrate, Serpentine packed up her things and headed to the car. She didn't really feel like going to work. She thought about calling in sick, then going home to her bed and her remote control. But she had an editing session scheduled to work on her story about improving student reading scores and she needed to finish it.

She drove out of the parking lot and down Randolph Street, tuning the radio to one of her favorite talk shows, Bonnie B on WVOT. Serpentine held her breath when she heard what Bonnie's topic was that morning.

"We're talking about the full-figure revolution. Get on the phone and call me at 1-800-978-TALK. Do you think things are getting better for the full-figured woman, or worse? Are people more accepting of larger bodies or not? I also want to remind you that our guest today is Dr. Dora Penn, a weight counselor and nutritionist in the Chicago area. Dora, what do you think about this full-figure revolution?" Bonnie B asked.

Dora audibly swallowed, then spoke. "I'm excited about it,

Bonnie. I think it's about time black people stopped buying into the media hype. We are a beautiful people in all shapes and colors, and we need to recognize that."

"I agree. Okay, let's go to the phone lines and talk to some callers. Marlon, you're on the air."

"Hi, Bonnie, and hello to your guest. I think we need to be honest. We can use all the nice words we want, but obese is not beautiful or healthy."

"What?" Serpentine groaned out loud.

Bonnie jumped in. "Well, Marlon, there is a segment of our society that fits somewhere in between skinny and obese. Those are the women we're talking about today."

"I'm sorry, but I can't agree, Bonnie," Marlon continued. "I was in Europe recently and I couldn't believe how beautiful those women were. You could tell they take good care of themselves, and black women need to do the same here in America."

"Screw you!" Serpentine screamed.

"Thank you, Marlon, for your comments, but we need to move on to our next caller," Bonnie purred.

"Remember, we're not talking about obese or unhealthy here, we're talking about women with some weight on them. Do you want to respond, Dr. Dora?"

"His comment hits at the heart of the matter, Bonnie. We have bought into the hype and stopped loving ourselves just the way we are."

"We'll talk to Andrea next."

"Good afternoon, Bonnie and Dr. Dora. I'm calling because I'm a full-figured woman and my husband wants me to lose weight, but I haven't been able to do it. I'm really frustrated."

Serpentine was so engrossed in the conversation that she didn't notice the traffic light had turned red. She slammed on her brakes, stopping about an inch away from the car in front of her.

"The first problem is that you can't do it for your husband, Andrea. You have to want to lose weight for yourself," Bonnie replied.

"That's true," Dr. Dora agreed. "What exactly did your husband say to you, Andrea?"

"He said he didn't marry a fat woman and he doesn't want to live with a fat woman."

"Whoa!" Bonnie interjected. "Some strong words. What do you think that means, Dr. Dora?"

"I think that Andrea has to be careful, because a statement like that comes dangerously close to saying that his love for her is limited. If loving her is dependent upon the issue of weight, then he doesn't love her for who she is, and that's sad."

"You might have to kick him to the curb, girl. Thanks, Andrea. Next on the line is Bill."

"Hi, Bonnie. I just want to say that I love full-figured women and I think they're beautiful. I think all black women are beautiful."

"Thank you, my brother. I'm sure black women love you, too. If you haven't already been caught, give my producer your number and we'll hook you up for our next dating show. We need some good brothers up in here. Thanks! Okay, Jeremy has been waiting patiently to talk to us."

"Hey, Bonnie. We need to get back to the topic of health and weight, because I work in a hospital and I see firsthand what those extra pounds can do to people. Too many black folks, especially women, are fat, and research tells us it's not healthy."

"Well, as I said earlier, Jeremy, we're not advocating weight at the expense of health in this show," Bonnie replied.

"I'd also like to caution Jeremy against reading too much into most of the research out there," Dr. Dora jumped in. "Black body structures are different. Many of us carry more weight. Also, much of the research done in this country is not focused on black people. As a matter of fact, most of those studies include very few black participants, if any. So be careful, because you can put too much emphasis on statistics that don't fit."

"Thank you!" Serpentine added.

"The thing I've noticed, Dr. Dora, is that we've had very few women call in and talk about this topic. Give us a call, ladies, and let us know how you feel; 1-800-978-TALK."

"Bonnie, women are probably not calling in because this is a difficult situation. Those who find themselves dealing with weight issues are bombarded from all sides with inconsistent ideas and conflicting attitudes. That's why I always suggest to my clients that they follow their own hearts and their own minds. Nobody can tell you what's best for you," Dr. Dora concluded.

Serpentine turned in to the television station's parking lot. She was sick of being emotionally pulled into contradictory places. One week she would feel blissful and the next week depressed. She could be energetic, then turn lethargic, all in the same day. Her spirit sometimes grew heavy and then light again, in a matter of minutes. She sat and listened for a few more minutes before turning the show off and heading inside.

Darkness

A walk in the dark was comforting tonight. It's hard to see the rolls of fat in the dark. I feel safe and acceptable in the dark. The darkness always reminds me of the first time I made love to Carlin.

As he gently felt his way across my full torso, I was worried; sometimes the imagination can be worse than reality. Soft, honey-colored fingers slid down my stomach and I cringed. I held my breath, hoping he wouldn't jump up and run for the door. Hoping that he wasn't just out to get a quick piece and dump me. Hoping he could see beyond the surface and recognize the wonderful person I was inside.

I slowly let my breath go as his hands continued past my belly button and down to my legs. With no hesitation he reached upward and caressed the sweetness that rested between my shivering thighs. Carlin moved through the darkness like water moves through a tube, molding his strong powerful body to mine. When he lifted himself up and shifted his chest down against my waiting breasts, I thanked God for Carlin that night.

In the weeks that passed, Serpentine continued to worry about her aunt's relationship with Pee Jay, her weight gain, and even her renewed feelings for Carlin. She prayed that the little happiness she had would not be drained away by something or someone.

A heavy snow had started around midnight and continued all through the next day. Weathercasters warned viewers that the first snow of the season was going to be a heavy one, with seven to ten inches expected. She left work early planning a nice quiet evening alone.

Serpentine had closed on her house almost two years ago, but she still got excited every time she put her key in the lock of the three-bedroom ranch. One bedroom was her office. She had bought a new Macintosh computer, fax machine, and two file cabinets that were mainly filled with high school and college memorabilia.

In the living room, she had arranged three beautiful ivies across the front window ledge. They were pieces of her grand-mother's ivy that she'd clipped years ago before Mamaw died. Serpentine had nurtured those gifts for almost ten years as a testament to her love.

The kitchen was large, with built-in everything, including a skylight that allowed the sun and moonlight to filter inside.

The master bedroom had its own bath, along with Serpentine's favorite piece of furniture: a king-size brass bed that she polished at least once a month.

Finally, the den hosted a mini-fitness center. Over the years, Serpentine had bought so many exercise machines that she didn't need to join a gym. For the last five Christmases her gift to herself had been a new piece of equipment. She vowed each year to use the space-saver treadmill, ski machine, rower, step machine, and bicycle for a healthier lifestyle, but the room represented those resolutions that she'd failed to keep.

Serpentine was just getting comfortable in front of the television when she heard someone outside honking like crazy. She glanced out her front, plate-glass window to see Carlin's silver Range Rover sitting in the driveway. She slipped her parka on and headed toward the car.

"Hey, what are you doing here? I wasn't expecting you until Friday," she said, leaning over into the driver's window to give him a quick kiss.

"I came to get you," he said matter-of-factly.

Serpentine looked at the thick flakes of snow that fell all around her. "There's a snowstorm going on, you know," she reminded him.

"I want you to see a miracle," Carlin told her, flashing his dimpled smile.

Serpentine grinned, then ran back into the house, got her purse, and locked up.

Once she had slipped into the passenger seat, Carlin drove away so fast that she could feel the wheels spinning underneath them.

"So what kind of miracle is it?" she asked as they drove toward the freeway.

"The best kind," he replied.

They hummed along with the sounds of Kirk Franklin's hit song "Stomp," passing neighborhoods filled with Halloween images. Witches, jack-o'-lanterns, and ghosts decorated many of the houses, office buildings, and street lamps that flew by.

They drove about forty minutes out of the city down I-80 West. At the Joliet exit, Carlin slowed down and turned off. He drove up a long gravel road and stopped at the bottom of a steep hill. They sat surrounded by snow, scattered trees, and a wire fence. Carlin jumped out of the car and opened the trunk.

Serpentine unsnapped her seat belt, but before she could open the door, Carlin was there, left arm extended. In his right hand he carried a big, flattened cardboard box.

"What in the world are you doing?" Serpentine asked as she walked with him to the fence.

"Just follow me," he said with an intriguing laugh. He tossed the box over the fence. Then he put on his gloves and pushed the top two rows of wire as far down as he could.

Serpentine carefully stepped over the fence. Once she was safely on the other side, Carlin pushed down again and jumped the fence as easily as a quarter horse at the Nation's Cup competition.

With Serpentine close behind, Carlin dragged the flattened box twenty feet to the top of a large hill. He sat down on the cardboard and motioned for Serpentine to join him.

"You must be crazy," she said. "Where's the miracle?"

"You're supposed to trust me," Carlin coaxed.

"You bring me out during a snowstorm to an empty field in the country to ride on a piece of cardboard, and you want me to trust you?" she asked, wiping flakes of snow from her nose.

"Take this leap of faith with me, baby."

Serpentine hesitated, but finally sat down on the cardboard in front of Carlin. He wrapped his arms tightly around her waist and gave the cardboard a slight push with his right foot.

Their two bodies suddenly moved in sync with the wind. Fresh white snowflakes blew across their faces and the flood of excitement in Serpentine's chest caused her to scream with delight as they slid faster and faster down the hill. When the board hit a bump, they both fell off and rolled down to the bottom.

Carlin stood up, laughing. "Come on, it's over here," he said, running and waving her over toward an old barn.

Serpentine followed him, but stopped to pick up a handful of snow. She packed it tightly together and threw it at him. The snowball hit Carlin in the back of the head and he turned to see that she was busy making another one.

Carlin quickly reached down and scooped up his own batch of snow, ducking her second snowball. He threw one and hit her in the arm, but she didn't feel anything through her fleece-lined coat. Carlin ran as fast as he could until he reached the barn, and Serpentine chased him inside. When she rushed through the open door, Carlin tackled her and they shared a warm embrace.

"What about the miracle?" Serpentine asked.

He answered with a kiss, then led her over to a stall in the back of the barn. Serpentine peaked inside and saw a tiny baby foal wobbling next to his contented mother.

"It's wonderful, Carlin. Where are we? Whose barn is this?"

"This is my mare and my foal."

"Seriously?"

"Yeah. This is my uncle's place, and he keeps the mare for me. I've had her for about four years now," he explained. "She was artificially inseminated this time last year, because they normally don't breed in the winter."

Serpentine allowed her smile to spread even wider.

"So what do you think about my miracle?" Carlin asked.

"It's beautiful," she answered, throwing her arms around his neck, and kissing him sensually.

Carlin pulled Serpentine down into a nearby pile of hay. He rolled over on his back, twisting her on top of him. Warm, tender kisses ignited her soul, and she enjoyed the merging of hot skin until their passion burst.

The storm stopped as the sun triumphantly set in the west. Carlin shook the hay out of his coat and Serpentine slipped on her pants. As he held her hand, pulling her back toward the car, he stopped to survey the span of perfect white snow covering everything.

"Isn't this a gorgeous sight?" he asked. "I have a lot of great childhood memories here: cardboard sleds, horseback riding, snow angels."

Suddenly, without warning, Carlin dropped down on his knees and turned over on his back. He lay flat, spreading his arms and legs out as far as they would go. He slid his limbs back and forth across the snow, creating one of the most perfect snow angels Serpentine had ever seen.

For their four-month anniversary, Carlin sent a single yellow rose and a card that read, "My place this weekend." Serpentine flew to Kansas City not knowing what to expect. When she entered his apartment, she was met by soft candlelight illuminating a Kente tablecloth spread over the middle of the floor. On it were bowls of apples, oranges, pineapple, mango, and strawberries peeled and cut into bite-sized pieces.

"See how much I missed you?" Carlin asked as he carried her bag into the bedroom.

"I see," Serpentine replied. Chills immediately stirred inside her.

"I spent most of the week planning this celebration," Carlin explained as he entered the kitchen and washed his hands in the sink.

Serpentine moved closer. "It looks wonderful," she said. "Can I do anything?"

He took her hand and guided her to the center of the room. "Just sit down right here and open up your mind for me. That's all I need for you to do."

Serpentine sat and listened to the sounds from the kitchen. Ice trays were being emptied; ice cubes were dropped into a container, glasses clinked, and there was the pop of a cork hitting the ceiling. She slipped off her black pumps and slid them under the end table behind her.

"I wanted tonight to be really special," Carlin called from the kitchen. "After tonight, there should be no more doubts about my love for you."

Serpentine felt her lips parting longingly as he spoke. She trusted him now, but that inkling of doubt was still wedged into her soul. The man was almost too thoughtful and too understanding. Lately, she had been praying that nothing would go wrong.

Carlin entered the room carrying an ice bucket with a bottle of white Zinfandel and two wineglasses. "I have something to ask you," he said as he handed Serpentine her glass. "I hope you'll say yes."

"What?" she asked nervously. It was much too soon for the question to involve marriage.

Carlin dropped down beside her and filled her glass. "Have you noticed my theme for tonight?" he asked, pointing to the fruit picnic.

Serpentine looked around the room and across the floor, but couldn't come up with a theme, so she shook her head.

"I wanted tonight to mark a new level for us, Serpentine: complete trust."

He picked up the bowl of sliced apples in front of them. "This celebration is about truly letting go of our inhibitions from the past."

Serpentine focused on his soft tan lips as he spoke.

Carlin continued. "Every piece of fruit in front of you is bare. It has no covering. That's the theme."

Her eyes suddenly darted downward and she squirmed. She hoped he wasn't saying what she thought he was saying.

Carlin stood up with a sly smile and began to undress.

"I know you're self-conscious about your weight, and that's why we always make love in the dark. But your weight is not an issue for me, Serpentine, and I need for you to believe that."

Serpentine watched in horror as Carlin took off his shirt and then his pants. She panicked. What was he asking her to do? How could he even suggest something so cruel? She couldn't be comfortable naked in front of him with all the lights on, not tonight, not ever.

As Carlin ceremoniously removed his red boxer shorts and stood in front of her in all his glory, Serpentine hopped up and sped toward the door.

She stopped just in front of it. "I can't, Carlin," she stammered, her mind spinning back to the fact that this was the same man who had laughed about her weight years ago.

"Don't say you can't," Carlin pleaded. "Remember faith? You've got to have it, too."

The doorknob waited for her touch, but she didn't oblige.

Carlin walked up behind her and put his hands on her shoulders, pressing firmly. "You've got to trust me, baby. I love you," he said.

Serpentine closed her eyes. She wanted to trust him. There he stood totally exposed, with two small love handles and a tiny tummy. She couldn't imagine what he would think about her if she took off her clothes. Yet, if they were going to move forward, he was right: she had to trust him. She had to believe that he loved her for who she was no matter what.

"Okay, you can do it," she mumbled.

Carlin shook his head. "I can't do it for you, Serpentine," he told her. "You have to feel free enough to show me who you are with the lights on."

Serpentine twisted her head and stared directly into his eyes. This man was either a devil or an angel: she wasn't sure which. She closed her eyes and swallowed, then pulled off her black suit jacket. Next, she unbuttoned her red blouse and slowly removed it. She kept her eyes on the floor as she reached around to unsnap her bra, and stood very still as she watched the ivory lace fall to the floor. She gingerly unzipped her suit skirt and let it slip down to her ankles. Then she pulled down her beige ivory lace panties and stepped out of them.

Serpentine couldn't look up into Carlin's face. At that moment, her doubts and fears were overwhelming. She stood perfectly still, feeling silly, awkward, and even stupid. She wanted to grab her clothes and run out of the apartment, but she also wanted to stay and prove that she loved him too.

Carlin took her hand and led her back over to the picnic area. They stood in front of each other in flickering candlelight that seemed as bright to Serpentine as a sunny day. She glanced up at his face and was startled by the tears that flowed.

"You're beautiful, Serpentine," he whispered. "I'm going to help you believe that someday."

It was the most special evening of her life. Feeding each other passion fruit, sipping wine, and when she crawled into bed beside Carlin that night, they made love, for the first time, with the lights on.

He held her face in his hands and kissed her softly on the lips. "I love kissing you," he said.

They kissed over and over with a passion that had been building for many years.

"How do you feel?" he asked as he caressed her bare shoulders.

"Do you really love me, Carlin?" Serpentine had to ask.

"I fell in love with you that summer, at eleven years old, but I needed to grow up to understand what it meant."

Serpentine smiled. "I have to admit I've wondered over the years about us together."

Carlin chuckled. "I've had a few wet dreams on that topic myself."

His fingers massaged her inner thighs and created an electric current that she couldn't shut off.

"You love me?" Carlin asked, lifting himself on top of her.

"Very much."

"That's all I need to hear," Carlin said, before his lips sparked a desire that they both wanted to fulfill.

Soul Food

Wouldn't it be nice to eat like they did in that movie Soul Food *and still look like Vanessa Williams, Vivica Fox, or Nia Long?*
  Let the church say AMEN!

Serpentine shifted sideways in seat 14A in an attempt to find some comfort. It seemed that the seats on airplanes got smaller each time she flew. As she unbuckled the tight seat belt from around her waist, she wondered how somebody larger than she was could fly at all.

The plane twisted to the left, then jerked to the right, and Serpentine's head slid off the small flat pillow. The movement abruptly pushed her forehead into the scratched-up plastic window. "Ouch. Damn," she mumbled.

The "Fasten Seat Belt" sign lit up and the captain's voice leaped from the overhead speakers to apologize for the turbulence. Serpentine took a deep breath, forcing herself to yawn, then waited for the pop as her ears unplugged. The pressure subsided and she could hear clearly again for a minute or two.

LaJune woke up as the plane began its descent, but pulled the blanket up over her shoulders, and closed her eyes again.

"June, are you okay? You look green," Serpentine said.

LaJune opened one eye. "Hell no, I'm not okay. I'm sick as a dog." LaJune sat up and snatched the barf bag from the front pocket to make a deposit.

"What's wrong with you?" Serpentine asked.

"You're not gonna believe this, but girl, I'm pregnant," LaJune answered.

"Pregnant!" Serpentine shouted. "Why didn't you tell me?"

"I just found out myself when the doctor confirmed it yesterday. I'm not sure I can get through nine months of feeling like this."

"Parren's last trip home must have been a good one."

"That depends on your definition of 'good.' "

"How far along are you?"

"Next April. Don't tell mama yet, okay?"

Serpentine nodded as the wings of the plane suddenly began shifting like a teeter-totter, up and down, left then right in the strong wind. The wheels hit the runway and the plane bounced for a while before coming to a steady roll. While the plane taxied to the gate, fellow passengers sat poised like track stars waiting for the starting pistol to fire. Once the wheels pulled into the assigned spot, the jetway was attached, and the pilot turned off the "Fasten Seat Belt" sign, there was a frenzy of pulling, twisting, yanking, and ripping bags from the tiny compartments above and the tiny seats below.

Serpentine and LaJune sat and watched the madness until the aisle seat beside them cleared. They pulled their totes from beneath the seats in front of them and scooted toward the aisle. During a break in the line they thrust their bodies forward with the rest of the group and marched out of the side door of the Boeing 747.

Thanksgiving in Kansas City was always the same. Family in and out, more food than anyone could possibly eat, and the television blasting football games all day and night. Serpentine, Regina, LaJune, and Kendrick sat watching the Detroit Lions beat the Minnesota Vikings twenty to seven, when Nolita entered the room that afternoon.

"Serpentine, you need to go downstairs and look in those boxes on the table and see if you want that stuff. I'm going to start my cleaning right after the holiday, and anything that's left here when you leave goes in the garbage," Nolita said.

"Okay, Mama," Serpentine replied.

"LaJune, you've got some things down there, too."

"Sure, Mama," LaJune answered. "I'll get it."

Nolita stood near the basement door, waiting for somebody to move. Nobody did. "If you guys forget and I throw your things away don't say nothing to me," she added, then huffed back into the kitchen.

Serpentine took in a deep breath, trying to ignore her mother, but she finally exhaled deeply, got up, and stomped downstairs.

LaJune did the opposite. She put her feet up on the footstool and leaned across the arm of the couch as if she were burrowing in for the winter.

Serpentine flipped on the switch with a vicious force and brought light to the dark basement. Nolita always got to her. La-June didn't jump up and run downstairs, but Serpentine, as usual, had cracked. She turned on the radio to KPRS—the Kolored People's Radio Station, as they used to call it in high school.

She pulled a box to the edge of the table, sat down, and opened the vanilla folder on top. Serpentine stared at the eight by ten picture of her ROTC unit. She laughed, remembering that summer between her junior and senior years when she thought about join-ing the military. She blew the dust from the photo and held it closer to the light.

"Ummm, ummm, ummm," she moaned. In that picture she was probably as thin as she'd ever been in her life. During that six-week Air Force camp, she'd lost weight she didn't even know she had.

Serpentine and Marleen drifted apart during their junior year in college. Marleen pledged a popular sorority, while Serpentine put on a uniform and joined the campus ROTC.

Serpentine was amazed at how similar their experiences turned out to be. In Air Force camp, she was forced to march in line with her unit, just like Marleen walked in line with her fel-low Pyramids. At five in the morning, the bugle would blow and each recruit was expected to be in formation in thirty minutes. At five in the morning, the phone would ring and each pledge was expected to gather in the designated dorm room in thirty minutes.

They were both punished with extra chores, exercise, or other challenges if they made mistakes. Serpentine spent most of her Saturday afternoons washing military cars or cleaning govern-ment offices. Marleen spent her weekends writing apology letters, cleaning big sisters' cars, and washing dirty dishes.

Each morning at inspection, Serpentine's hangers were checked to make sure they were spaced exactly one inch apart throughout the closet. Her bed was supposed to be three inches away from the wall, a distance measured with a three-inch wooden block. Marleen and her line mates were blindfolded and their hands were guided into the toilet to squeeze a banana that they were told was human excrement.

There was one major difference in the girls' experiences that summer. According to military weight guidelines, Serpentine was forty-one pounds too heavy. She was placed on a strict one-thousand-calorie diet and involuntarily registered in an evening exercise program. By the end of the first week, she felt she was going to die of starvation. The dry meat patty, carrot sticks, salad, and Jell-O that became her mainstays quickly got sickening. But after the fourth week, when she saw the stubborn pounds leaving, her complaining stopped.

The sixth and last week of camp, Serpentine was called into Captain Hampton's office. She marched into the too-small room and stood at attention in front of his too-big desk.

"At ease, Williamson," Captain Hampton barked.

Serpentine parted her feet in a more relaxed position and crossed her hands in front of her stomach.

"Williamson, you seem to have adjusted very well to the military," Captain Hampton said with his chest stuck out. "I made a bet that you would be one of the first candidates to give up and go home, but I lost, and I'm glad I lost."

Serpentine stood stiffly and listened to his well-crafted speech.

"I'd like to offer you a spot as a first lieutenant in the United States Air Force next year when you graduate."

Serpentine didn't respond. She had learned that protocol meant she should wait for her cue.

Papers flapped in Captain Hampton's hands. "So what do you think, Williamson? I have the paperwork right here. Do you have the stamina to become a member of the United States Air Force?"

Serpentine shifted her feet. She hadn't really thought that far ahead. She'd joined the ROTC to give her life some structure, some consistency. Not to mention the fact that she was one of twelve women among sixty-eight men. She'd thought it might be interesting to check out ROTC and camp, but she didn't know if she was ready to make a major commitment like this.

Serpentine cleared her throat. "Can I be honest, sir?" she finally asked.

Captain Hampton nodded and set the papers back down on his desk.

"I'd like to thank the captain immensely for his offer, but I don't think I can agree to join anything a year from now. I don't know where my head might be when I graduate. I could decide to go to law or business school, fall in love, get married, and even get pregnant in the next year. Who knows?"

He sat down with a pained look on his face. "You know, Serpentine, we're making this offer even though you are still twelve pounds over our weight standards. There are a limited number of spots, and once they're filled you won't get a second chance."

Serpentine winced when she thought about losing twelve more pounds to fit into an Air Force weight chart. She had looked in the mirror that morning and saw a thinner body than she ever dreamed possible. But if she lost any more weight, she'd look like a drugged-out zombie. Her eyes already looked sunken in and her shoulder bones protruded awkwardly.

Serpentine cleared her throat. "Sir, I don't know if I could ever get down to where your weight charts say I should be. Maybe those charts need to be updated, and made more realistic for women today. And as far as the offer, sir, thank you very much, but I've still got to decline."

The smile on Captain Hampton's face dissolved as he listened. "Are you sure, Williamson?"

Serpentine searched his floor for specks of dirt, especially since she was the one who cleaned on Saturday. "Yes, sir, I'm sure."

"Okay then, you can go, Williamson," he barked.

"Thank you, sir." She took a sharp military turn, marched out the door and around the corner.

Serpentine had to chuckle when she remembered that senior-year transformation. She returned to school and was immediately released from her ROTC unit. But her twenty-nine-pound weight loss meant that she could live again. Serpentine dug deep in the back of her closet and pulled out clothes that she hadn't worn since her freshman year. A pair of blue jeans, size twelve, fit nicely around her shrunken, shapely hips, and her size-fourteen sequined-silk skirt set hung just right, showing off one of her best features: her big, curvy legs.

She flirted with, teased, and tortured various interested men that year. Bryan took her to dinner a number of times and even brought flowers for Sweetest Day, but he didn't thrill her. Lloyd was her science partner, and he wanted to explore human physiology together, but Serpentine wasn't interested. Warren was an impressive business major until the first date when she immediately had to cut the egomaniac loose.

Marleen warned her that she was being too hard on men. She suggested that Serpentine compromise a little bit more. Serpentine laughed at the suggestion. She was now a Rolls-Royce and she planned to drive like she owned the road.

At the bottom of the box, Serpentine found a wrinkled piece of paper that also brought back memories.

" 'The amazing seaweed wrap,' " she read out loud. " 'Imagine yourself 20 pounds thinner in just two weeks! That's the miracle of this product. If you commit two hours a day for the next 14 days, we guarantee you will see the results you're looking for. This wonderful product will literally melt the pounds away right before your eyes. Simply mix one packet of the pounds-away solution with water each day, thoroughly wet the seaweed wrap with the mixture, and twist the plastic around the problem areas of your body. Let the wrap stay on for a minimum of 60 minutes or a maximum of 120 minutes. The longer the wrap stays on, the quicker the weight will disappear. You have just made the most important purchase of your life, and we are pleased that our product can help you lose the weight you desire.' "

In high school, each month had meant a new fad diet, and each failure meant more desperation to find the answer. At five-feet-eight inches Serpentine weighed about one hundred and seventy-six pounds. She wasn't skinny, but she was a long way from fat.

Yet something was wrong, because she couldn't accept herself and the normal growth of her body.

The girls in high school who had it going on were the ones the boys slobbered all over and followed around. They were much smaller than Serpentine, with tiny waistlines emphasizing well-rounded bottoms.

She had always envied those girls. She wanted boys to look at her with that same interested smile. She often wished she could be like the models in magazines and on television, who seemed to have no weight problem at all. They were gorgeous and society loved them.

She would usually start a new diet on Monday morning, and by Friday it would be history. The seaweed wrap was one of her craziest efforts. Serpentine remembered that day clearly. When she got home from school she grabbed the box from the porch and rushed into the house.

"Mama, Mama, it's here!" she screamed, dropping her bookbag on the kitchen table. She sat and examined the sealed brown package that had taken four to six weeks to arrive.

Nolita came out of the bedroom with a red-and-yellow checkered scarf wrapped around her head and a limp dust rag gripped under her right arm.

"What are you screaming about, Teenie?"

"It's finally here, Mama, come on."

"I'm dusting the bedroom. Give me a few minutes to finish."

"I can't wait a few minutes," Serpentine begged as she tore the brown paper cover from the white box.

"Get things started and I'll be there in a minute," Nolita said.

Serpentine practically skipped into the bathroom. Following the directions on the package, she pulled a small red bucket from the linen closet, filled it with lukewarm water, tore open a package of the pounds-away magic powder, and dumped it inside.

"Okay, Mama, I'm ready," she called, stirring the mixture.

"In a minute!" Nolita shouted back.

Serpentine hurried into her bedroom and snatched off all her clothes. She threw on an orange terry cloth bathrobe and appeared back at the bathroom door at the same time as her mother.

"Now, what do we need to do?" Nolita asked, shaking her head.

"I already mixed the stuff, so now I'll get in the tub and you can dip the plastic in the mixture and wrap it around my body."

Filled with an irrepressible hope, Serpentine hung her bathrobe on the silver hook behind the bathroom door and stepped into the white porcelain tub.

Nolita knelt beside the bucket and pulled a long piece of plastic seaweed wrap from the box. She dipped it into the liquid mixture and slowly began covering Serpentine's body. She twisted the wet sticky plastic around Serpentine's arms, her chest, her waist, her butt, and her thighs.

Just when Serpentine was covered completely, LaJune burst into the bathroom, looked at her big sister, pointed, and laughed.

"Get out of here, stupid!" Serpentine yelled.

"You the stupid one. You look like a piece of Mama's day-old fried chicken when it's wrapped in the 'frigerator. Yum, yum, eat 'em up," LaJune teased, rubbing on her stomach.

"Mama, would you tell her to leave, please?"

"LaJune, go on to your room and change out of your school clothes," Nolita told her.

LaJune headed for the door, then turned back around. "I'm hungry, Mama, we got any fried chicken in the 'frigerator?" she asked, flashed a wide grin at her sister, then dashed out the door.

Serpentine chose the maximum time to lose the maximum amount of weight. For two hours she stood stiffly in the center of the tub, practically mummified. Nolita used a sponge to rewet the plastic with the magic mixture every fifteen minutes until the phone rang.

"Mama, telephone for you—it's Daddy!" LaJune yelled from the kitchen.

"I'll be right back, Teenie. Try to stand still."

When Nolita left, Serpentine waited patiently for her return. It was the itch just above her right eye that finally forced her to move. She tried but couldn't bend her arm to reach it, and her head wouldn't move far enough to let her rub the irritation against her shoulder. The more Serpentine tried not to think about the itch, the worse it got.

"LaJune, come here a minute," Serpentine finally called out and listened for her sister's footsteps. LaJune appeared in the doorway with a bed pillow in her hands. "What?"

Serpentine wrinkled her nose. "Could you do me a favor and scratch this spot above my right eye?"

LaJune dropped the pillow on the floor. "Why should I help you?"

"Girl, stop playing and come on, it itches," Serpentine pleaded.

"What do I get if I help you?" LaJune asked, keeping her distance.

"My undying gratitude or a butt-whuppin', take your pick."

"I don't want either. Thank you very much," LaJune responded, turning to walk away.

"Okay, okay, how about a dollar?"

LaJune walked over to the tub. "You have to swear you're going to really give me a dollar."

"Come on, LaJune, I swear," Serpentine whined.

With that oath, LaJune climbed onto the edge of the tub and scratched at the top of Serpentine's eye, but as she tried to step down her hand slipped. LaJune reached up and grabbed Serpentine's shoulder with one hand and tried to find a spot on the side wall to hold on to with the other. The motion knocked Serpentine off balance and she fell hard against the back wall. She struggled to stand upright again, but failed.

"Damn, LaJune, you always messing shit up!" Serpentine scolded, trying to push herself upright without success.

"I'm telling Mama you cursed," LaJune told her, and took off running.

"I don't care what you tell. I ain't givin' you no dollar either," Serpentine shouted.

"Mama, come here a minute!"

Serpentine heard the door open. "Mama, LaJune made me fall over. I need—" Serpentine stopped talking when she saw it wasn't her mother.

It was LaJune grinning with a camera held up to her face. "Say cheesy noodles!" she yelled, and snapped the picture.

"LaJune, don't!" Serpentine screamed as the flash went off.

Days later, she paid LaJune the dollar she owed her, plus another five as blackmail money to get the picture and negative destroyed.

By the end of the first week, Serpentine had not lost a pound; instead she had gained two. She tossed the remaining miracle seaweed wrap into the trash and began a grapefruit diet the following Monday morning.

Serpentine carried the box upstairs and set it next to her suitcase. These were memories she wasn't quite ready to part with. The house smelled good. Nolita had cooked a ham and turkey for Thanksgiving dinner, along with the trimmings: dressing, macaroni and cheese, candied yams, broccoli, and homemade cornbread.

After dinner, bowls of peach cobbler and ice cream waited on the kitchen counter. The line formed as relatives claimed their bowls. When Serpentine walked into the kitchen, Nolita watched her out of the corner of her eye. As soon as she picked up one of the prepared bowls off the cabinet, Nolita spoke.

"You sure you want that much, honey? I made a smaller one, especially for you," Nolita said, handing her a cup of pie and ice cream.

Serpentine was devastated. She looked around as LaJune, Kendrick, and other relatives stared in her direction. "Damn, Mama, why don't you leave me alone!" she cried. She snatched the cup away from Nolita and dumped the contents on top of the bowl she already held. "I don't need you always on my back, judging me!" Serpentine tossed the empty cup into the sink where it broke, then stormed into her old bedroom and slammed the door.

She gulped down the cobbler and ice cream, then defiantly went back to the kitchen for more. Serpentine ate so much that night she made herself sick. She lay in bed suffering until she couldn't stand it anymore. She finally went into the bathroom, knelt in front of the stark white toilet bowl, and summoned the courage to put her finger down her throat. Her stomach erupted like an active volcano.

Serpentine threw up mounds of cobbler and vanilla ice cream the first time. The second time, she could see pieces of macaroni and cheese, ham, and even broccoli floating in the water as well. She sat and stared at the mixture for a moment, lost in guilt, and then she flushed it all away. She rinsed her mouth with mouthwash and crawled back into bed.

The Tales a Tree Can Tell

*It's been so long since I've taken the time to enjoy the little things
in life. But today, everything, even the trees seem to be telling me
about their unique and purposeful existence.*

*Each one reaches deep into the sun-bright sky, showing off its
shape and texture. One leans to the right, like a charming old man
tipping his hat. One stands straight and tall, like a military hero at
roll call. One sports a jagged trunk, with pieces of shredded bark in-
terwoven like Grandma's patchwork quilt. One has a long, smooth
trunk that shimmers like the belly of a cobra.*

*I admit that I was afraid, caught up between my overactive mind
and my underactive body. Fear takes over when we sit down and accept. It can only be overcome if we get up and act.*

The newly renovated Blue Room on Eighteenth Street was a historic legacy of Kansas City's heyday in the 1940s and 1950s. It was located near the famous Twelfth Street and Vine where you could find the best jazz, blues, baseball, and barbecue. Local talent like the Kings of Rhythm, Lester Young, Count Basie, and Charlie "Bird" Parker could be heard in clubs up and down the block. The 1924 National Negro League world champion Kansas City Monarchs had an office down the street. And right around the corner was the hangout of a popular black motorcycle group called the Zodiac Club, along with Konner's Menswear Store where a "Buy one, get one free" suit meant one pant leg or sleeve was probably shorter than the other.

The first thing Serpentine noticed when she entered the club that Friday night, was that Carlin knew a lot of the people there. She stopped to read the flyers on the bulletin board while he shared a joke with one guy and a handshake with another. The band they had come to see was called Fusion Soul, Featuring Shalay. Serpentine had heard of the group. They'd recently released their first CD and the single, "Loving My Life," was climbing up the *Billboard* charts.

The picture on the flyer wasn't clear, but Serpentine could see that the group consisted of three men and a woman. The woman was beautiful. She was small, with a nose that was perfectly centered in the middle of her oval face. She wore her hair in short waves slicked down against her rounded head. In the picture, she managed a dark, sultry look with eyes that seemed sad and funny all at once. She stood in the middle of the three band members with her left leg kicked up behind her and her right arm raised victoriously in the air.

"This is nice," Serpentine told Carlin as he joined her and they found an empty table.

Carlin took her coat, and draped it over her chair, while she sat down. "I knew you'd like it," he replied.

"I missed you yesterday. Thanksgiving is usually a day you spend with loved ones," Serpentine whispered, leaning closer to him.

Carlin shifted in his seat. "I missed you, too, but I had to check on an investment up in St. Louis."

Serpentine rested her chin in her hand. "What kind of investment?" she asked.

"It's a surprise," he replied, and winked.

Serpentine looked around at the twenty to twenty-five tables. Most of them were filled. A small dance floor was positioned on the right side of the long wooden bar.

"Okay, I'll leave it alone, for now," she teased. "Have you heard this band before?"

"Yeah, they're very good. This time next year they'll probably take off like Hootie and the Blowfish or the Spice Girls."

"They must be taking a break," Serpentine said, motioning toward the empty stage area, where a keyboard, bass, and drums waited to be played.

Carlin nodded. "You're going to love this group. They can really blow," he said, bobbing his head to the beat of a jazz tune from the jukebox.

Serpentine relaxed her knee against his leg and faced the tiny stage. She noticed the single spotlight that hit the standing microphone, then she glanced over at Carlin, who was looking around as if he were expecting somebody.

"Is everything okay?" she asked, slipping her black beaded purse on the table in front of her.

"Sure. How about a drink?" Carlin answered, still tense.

"A Long Island iced tea," Serpentine replied.

Carlin jumped up before she could finish and rushed off to the bar, right past a waitress who was headed their way.

Serpentine watched as he flirted with the female bartender making their drinks. The bartender pointed toward the back of the room, and Serpentine turned to look in that direction, but she didn't see anything.

Her eyes halted on the couple at the table next to them. They were older, probably her mother and father's age, caught up in the bluesy tune that vibrated across the room.

Carlin returned with the drinks. He patted his coat pockets before sitting down.

"Is something wrong, Carlin?" Serpentine asked.

Carlin shook his head no. "Hey, this is a jam," he added quickly, as "Stairway to Heaven" by the O'Jays came on. "You got to give me this dance."

Serpentine stood up and followed Carlin to the dance floor. He held her close, humming the tune. The older couple joined them and started an X-rated performance, grinding finer than Colombian coffee. Serpentine watched as the woman's rounded thighs seemed to embrace his small pelvis the way a well-worn chair fits a familiar bottom.

Serpentine focused on a long black scar down the woman's arm and was reminded of a similar scar on her knee.

"You remember the first day of school, when I fell down and scraped up my knee?" she asked.

Carlin chuckled. "Sure. You looked really funny."

"It wasn't funny, Carlin Dumont," Serpentine protested. "I was trying to impress you with my new outfit and red tights."

"I *was* impressed, baby," he replied. "You were like Buzz Lightyear from that movie *Toy Story,* falling in style."

"You know, I still have that scar on my knee," Serpentine pouted.

"I know, but it's a beautiful scar," Carlin joked, kissing his hand and tapping the kiss onto her knee.

The record ended and Carlin led Serpentine back to their seats just before the lights went down, and the owner of the club trotted up onstage.

"Good evening, folks," he yelled unnecessarily into the microphone. "I'm Tommy Cahill. This is the place to be, and the people in the world who matter are the people who are here right now. Give yourselves a big round of applause!"

The audience clapped while Cahill loosened the microphone stand and dropped it down about three inches. "I want to introduce, for your listening pleasure, one of the best groups in the city. Their first single, 'Loving My Life,' is burning up the charts: Fusion Soul, Featuring Shalay."

The three male musicians took their places onstage and the audience applauded. When the ovation died, Shalay appeared from the back of the room and the applause started all over again.

Shalay wore a long white sequined gown that highlighted her smooth, chestnut skin. The spaghetti straps fell loosely off her shoulders, exposing an ample bust for her tiny frame. She looked different from the picture on the flyer; younger and smaller.

Carlin stared at Shalay while hot, fluent vocals mesmerized him along with the rest of the audience. She sang sad, distressing love songs, along with happy, party down songs, and when she recognized Carlin, she sang her own version of "My Funny Valentine" directly to him.

Carlin nervously pulled at his tie as Shalay's haunting voice echoed through the room. His eyes didn't leave the stage; he was lost in her melody. Serpentine started to feel uncomfortable, but she couldn't explain why.

The group played eight songs. Serpentine counted each one. When they finally finished the set, she was ready to go home. However, as soon as Shalay disappeared in the back room, Carlin vanished too.

"Excuse me a minute, I'll be right back," he told Serpentine, then hopped up before she could get a word of protest out of her mouth. Other couples stood up, put on their coats, and scurried out into the cold, while Serpentine sat and waited.

Fifteen minutes later, Carlin came back to the table with Shalay on his arm.

"Serpentine, I want you to meet Shalay. Shalay, this is my girl, Serpentine," he said.

"Hi," Serpentine replied, barely managing a smile.

Shalay's voice practically sang. "Hello."

"Shalay's a very good friend. We've known each other a long time," Carlin continued.

Serpentine forced a smile, then stood up and stared at Carlin. "Can we go now?"

"Just a minute," Carlin replied, turning his attention back to Shalay. "You sang beautifully tonight, as always," he told her.

"Thanks, baby," Shalay purred, playing with his mustache. "This man will always be my heart. You're a very lucky woman."

Serpentine found it difficult not to slap Shalay's hand away from Carlin's lips. She counted to ten silently.

"Oh, stop it," Carlin moaned with a stupid grin on his face that Serpentine wanted to knock off.

Her temperature steadily rose, as Shalay wrapped her arms around Carlin again and he returned the embrace. Serpentine had to get out of there before she exploded. She snatched her coat off the back of the chair and slid it on. Who the hell *was* this woman hanging all over Carlin like that? And *why* the hell was he grinning all up in her face?

She steadied herself. "I'm ready to go, Carlin," she said, with an obvious attitude.

"I'd love for you guys to come to the after-set at my apartment tonight," Shalay said, handing Carlin a small piece of paper. "Please, try to come?" she purred in his ear, then kissed him gently on the lips. "It was nice meeting you," she told Serpentine in a syrupy-sweet tone and hurried back to her dressing room.

Serpentine grabbed her purse off the table and stormed away.

Carlin followed. "What's wrong with you?" he asked.

"What the hell is wrong with *you*?" Serpentine answered as she reached the front door. "What makes you think I want to sit and watch you drooling all over some other woman? You ain't all that, Carlin!"

"That's just how Shalay is. It didn't mean nothing," he explained, struggling to slide his arm into his coat sleeve.

Serpentine spun around. "That was totally humiliating, Carlin!"

"There's nothing going on between me and Shalay."

She looked him directly in the eyes. "Can you honestly stand there and tell me you've never slept with that woman?" she asked.

Carlin hesitated. "No," he answered. "But I *can* honestly tell you that what we had is over."

Serpentine slipped her hands into the pockets of her black wool coat and burst out the front door. "You may think it's over, but that's not what she thinks."

Carlin continued to defend himself. "You're being paranoid. Shalay don't want me, she wants to be a star."

"Carlin, why did you bring me here tonight?" Serpentine asked.

"I wanted to hear Shalay sing, and I didn't want to come alone." He stepped around to the driver's side of the car.

"You could have brought a buddy."

"I wanted *you* with me, Serpentine, because you're the woman in my life now."

Carlin unlocked the doors, but Serpentine stood and waited. She normally would have opened the door herself, but he was going to show her some respect tonight. It took a moment for Carlin to realize what was going on. When he did, he rushed back around to her side, opened the door, and shut it behind her.

As Carlin started the car and drove off, he kept glancing at Serpentine, but she refused to look at him. Instead, she focused straight ahead, thinking about the enormity of her fears at that moment and wondering why her dreams never came true.

Shopping

You know, shopping is shopping. It doesn't matter if you're shopping for a new dress or a new man; the strategies are the same.

For example, some women are "bargain hunters." They're usually looking for something for nothing, and nothing is often what they get.

The "greener grass gambler" can find exactly what she wants at her first stop, whether it's a man or a pair of shoes, but she can't bring herself to commit until she's checked around to be sure there's nothing better out there.

In her search for perfection, the "loyal label lover" is only interested in the surface, the man's title is more important than his heart.

The "passive purchaser" is a pushover for any smooth-talking salesman who comes along. If he says the right things at the right times, she'll follow him anywhere.

The "window shopper" is what most men would call a tease or a flirt. She enjoys the interaction and attention, but she's not interested in anything permanent.

The "secondhand hustler" can always find treasure in someone else's trash. She likes married or committed men.

The "choosy changer" gets something new only to change it. Maybe it's the buttons on a new dress that don't really look right, or the man who would be a great catch, if he had a different line of work.

I figure if we understand our shopping strategies better, we might be able to actually get what we want, or at least have a clearer idea of what we're getting and why.

ဏ ဏ ဏ

The Christmas Eve sickle-cell telethon needed a host; Serpentine applied and got the assignment. She hated shopping for clothes more than anything else in the world, but the occasion called for a flashy new outfit.

She called her sister because LaJune always helped to take the sting out of a shopping trip. She was surprised when a man answered.

"Hello," the man said cheerfully.

Serpentine hesitated, because her sister's husband was supposed to be out to sea. "Hi?" she replied cautiously.

"Hey, what's up, Serpentine?"

She suddenly recognized Parren's voice and relaxed. "Hey, Parren. I didn't realize it was you," she said.

"Who else would it be? Is there some other man answering my baby's phone?"

"No, of course not. I just didn't know you were home."

"Took a red-eye so I could kiss my baby when the sun came up this morning."

Serpentine chuckled. "So, how are you, Parren?"

"Just fine. I put on some pounds. Been lifting weights on the ship. Girl, you won't recognize me, I'm so buff."

Serpentine laughed to herself. She couldn't imagine Parren as anything other than a tall, thin toothpick of a man.

"By the way, congratulations, Papa."

"Thanks. It's the best news I've had in a long time. Hey, how's my man Carlin?"

"Carlin is a man, what more can I say. And you know me, all work and no play makes Serpentine a dull girl."

"You can whistle for the wind, and it will come if you want it," Parren told her.

"What?" Serpentine asked. She wasn't in the mood to try and figure out one of Parren's riddles at that moment.

Parren repeated slowly: "You can whistle for the wind and it will come if you want it. It means Carlin could be the guy, but you have to know what you want first, or you'll never be satisfied."

"Yeah, sure, Parren, whatever. Is June in?" she asked, dismissing his words of wisdom.

"I'll get her."

Serpentine heard loud shuffling noises in the background, the sound of Parren's laughter, and finally LaJune's soothing voice saying hello.

"You seem to be occupied," Serpentine told her.

"Yeah, girl, Parren got a one-month shore leave. He flew in to surprise me. Ain't that sweet? I could just eat him up."

"Well, I'll let you get back to doing whatever you two were doing."

"No. It's not a really bad time. An hour ago we wouldn't even have answered the phone," LaJune explained between giggles.

"You better get all you can now, 'cause when the baby comes no more spontaneity," Serpentine warned.

LaJune chuckled. "I'll just bring the baby to her aunt Serpentine when we want to get a little freaky."

Serpentine noticed the sound of something sizzling in the background. "Sounds like you're actually trying to cook something," she said.

"Parren went out and bought bacon and eggs, girl. He said that's what he had the taste for."

"And he's letting you cook 'em?"

"I can cook when I want to."

Serpentine moaned. "Poor thing. He's been out to sea much too long."

"You're very funny."

"But honestly, there is one question I need to ask."

"What?"

Serpentine chuckled. "Why are you cooking breakfast at eight o'clock at night?"

LaJune hesitated, then responded sharply. "We didn't eat breakfast or lunch, either, if you must know! We were busy doing other things, Ms. Smart-ass!"

"I may be smart but it ain't got nothing to do with my ass." She laughed, remembering the childhood line. She stacked her bed pillows on top of each other and leaned back against them. "Well, you and Mr. Parren have a good evening."

"Did you want something or did you call just to meddle in my business?"

"I did call for a reason, but your business is so much more interesting."

"Well, speak now or forever hold your peace."

"I wanted you to do me a little favor and go shopping with me tomorrow to get something to wear for this telethon."

"Oh, Lord, shopping with your picky ass. That's a *big* favor."

"Come on, June, I need you."

"I guess I'll be nice this time. I'll meet you at your place around ten, tomorrow."

"Thanks. I owe you."

"Don't worry, I'll collect one of these days! Bye, bye," LaJune said, hanging up the phone before Serpentine could remove the receiver from her ear.

Their excursion started out badly, with what Serpentine labeled an SCWA, a skinny clerk with attitude. She noticed right away when they entered the shop that the sales clerk smirked in their direction.

The shop was called Fashion Boutique. LaJune had passed it a number of times and wanted to go inside. The clerk's eyebrows rose when she saw LaJune's slightly pregnant belly, then her eyes swept over Serpentine's larger body. She didn't bother to ask if they needed help. Serpentine soon confirmed that she was in the wrong place—the largest size in the store was a ten.

LaJune dragged Serpentine across town from mall to mall until they ended up at River Oaks in Calumet City. There were several shops for plus-sized women: The Avenue, The Answer, Lane Bryant, and Ashley Stewart for Women, but Serpentine was still not happy.

One store carried no clothes for dressing up, just pants and tops for everyday wear. Another store had a single rack in the back with special occasion outfits in sizes ranging from sixteen to twenty-four—but there was only one outfit in each size. Serpentine took the twenty-two and the twenty-four into the dressing room to try them on.

The twenty-four fit okay, but it was a bright, canary yellow that reminded her of Big Bird. She decided to not even try on the twenty-two because it lacked pizzazz. It looked like something somebody's grandma would wear with big pink flowers with bumblebees buzzing around.

At their next stop, stylish choices were also limited. Serpentine tried on a black-and-white empire-waist dress.

"That's not bad," LaJune commented when she came out of her dressing room and stood in front of the three-way mirror.

"No way," Serpentine shot back. "This makes me look more pregnant than you."

LaJune shoved a full purple-and-gold swing skirt with matching jacket over the dressing room door. "How about this?" she asked.

Serpentine pulled the outfit into the room and tried it on. She liked the design of the fabric: the gold lines faded in and out of the purple cloth elegantly. But when she pulled the skirt up over her hips, it was much too tight: size twenty.

"Do they have it in a bigger size, LaJune?" Serpentine asked.

LaJune motioned to the salesclerk. "Do you have a size twenty-two or twenty-four in this one?" she asked, pointing at the rack.

The clerk shook her head. "I'm sorry, we only got one of each size, and the bigger sizes sold earlier in the week."

"That makes a lot of sense doesn't it?" Serpentine grumbled. "A large-women's store and the pickin's are still slim."

She tried on another outfit that had some potential: a black wrap jacket with a shawl collar over a matching textured skirt. She wasn't thrilled, but maybe she'd come back if she didn't find anything else.

She put her jeans and sweater back on, ready to give up, but LaJune convinced her to try the plus-size section at Diamonds Department Store at the far end of the mall.

"I hate this shit," Serpentine said as they walked to their next destination.

LaJune put her arm around her big sister to comfort her. "Maybe we should try again tomorrow," she said. "Maybe you'll have a better attitude."

Serpentine stopped to look at the slender, plastic underwear models in the Victoria's Secret window. "I'm not going to feel any different tomorrow."

"I want a Pepsi," LaJune said, stopping at the walkway vendor.

"No soda, June, unless it's caffeine free. Get an orange juice and bring me one, too," Serpentine ordered, sitting down on a nearby bench. LaJune joined her, carrying the two juices.

Serpentine scowled as she took the lid off her cup. "Did you see *The Steve Harvey Show* last night? I hate the way he teases Regina by calling her piggy. Last night she called herself that horrible name!"

"I can't imagine hooking up with somebody who picked on me as a kid because I was fat. What would he do if they got married, and she had a baby, and gained the weight back?" LaJune added.

Serpentine shrugged, taking a swig from the cup. "You know what? I'm doing the same thing, June. Carlin laughed at me, along with everybody else when we were kids, so why am I with him now?"

"Good sex," LaJune joked.

"Great sex! But that's not it. I've never had anybody understand me the way he seems to understand me. It's almost scary, how in tune we are."

"At least Carlin's not laughing now. Steve Harvey is still calling her Piggy and trying to get all up in her drawers at the same time," LaJune complained.

Serpentine stood up. "I've been thinking, maybe I should move back to Kansas City."

"Move! Girl, you can't leave me! What would I do in Chicago without you?"

"Maybe if I were around more, this Carlin and Shalay feeling would go away."

"That's a big step, to move back to Kansas City for a man who might be playing on you."

"I honestly don't know what to do anymore."

Serpentine shook her head and shuffled slowly toward Diamonds as if she didn't really want to get there, and LaJune followed.

"And why is it still so difficult to find decent clothes for larger sizes?" Serpentine complained.

"Because thin is in, sis, and I don't think that's going to change in our lifetime," LaJune replied.

Serpentine covered a yawn with her palm. "I wish I could open up my own shop. I could design some great clothes for a larger frame like mine," she bragged.

LaJune patted her hips and laughed. "Well, get on it. Now that I'm carrying these childbearing hips, I could use a more flattering style myself."

"I guess there is a positive side to all of this. Shopping is actually not the horror it used to be. I remember when there were no plus-size stores out here. Progress is being made, but it's much too slow," Serpentine admitted as they entered the department store.

"This way," LaJune said, dragging Serpentine over to the large red-and-white plus-size sign on the back wall.

They made a sharp left turn and found the formal dress rack. Serpentine sorted through several possibilities. "Look at this garbage," she complained after thumbing past an ugly, hot-pink skirt set, a blue sequined dress, and a black knit skirt set with big purple and green flowers. She looked at a cotton blue-jean jumper, then held up a striped two-piece silk skirt set. "Everybody knows that stripes going across the body make you look bigger. What the hell is wrong with these designers?"

LaJune giggled. "They're obviously not in touch with half the female population in this country."

Serpentine stomped about eight feet over to the misses' section and snatched out a long simple burgundy crepe dress with a stylish matching cover-up jacket. "Size eight, now why can't they make something like this in my size? This would look good on a big woman. But what do we get? Damn barnyard designs."

LaJune's giggle became a full-fledged laugh. Serpentine turned and gave her a dirty look.

"I'm sorry," LaJune finally said. "I'm not laughing at you. I'm laughing with you. Check this out."

LaJune lifted up a mauve cotton vest with a big pink pig embroidered across the back. They both whooped so hard that La-June almost coughed up juice all over the floor.

They left the offensive vest swinging on the rack and headed for the exit.

"Why not have Aunt Regina sew something for you?" LaJune asked as they reached the car.

"Please, you know Aunt Regina's taste. She likes loud colors and bold fabrics," Serpentine replied. "That's fine for her, but I'd end up feeling like Bozo's sistah."

"You want to try anyplace else?" LaJune asked.

"No, let's go home. I'll wear my faithful black silk tuxedo suit."

"Please don't!"

"Why not? Most people won't know it's old," Serpentine rationalized.

"But you will," LaJune replied.

Celebrity Pounds

I just finished Sinbad's book, Guide to Life. *I had to laugh at his jokes about dieting. He said he was addicted to a chocolate spray, with a full-bottle-a-day habit, and he found funky success on a colon-cleansing diet.*

Right on, Denene Millner, Sistah's Rules *says it all. "Rule #1: Celebrate the power of the booty; be proud to be you!"*

Sometimes I think about Phyllis Hyman's struggle with weight and how it helped to push her into committing suicide. She was a woman who had the things we all dream of—beauty, talent, and success—yet life was somehow still not worth living.

And of course I can't talk about celebrity weight loss and not include Oprah. She's been my hero for so long, I can't remember when she wasn't on television. But, I have to admit that I'm one of those conflicted fans who both hated and loved to see her lose the weight. I hated it because she was no longer a tormented soul like me—she'd overcome. I loved it for the same reason.

Serpentine picked up her tuxedo suit from the cleaners on the way to the studio. Even though it was Christmas Eve, she was excited about hosting WXYZ's Sickle-Cell Anemia Telethon. Waiting for the stoplight to turn green, she glanced at the pamphlet she'd received in the mail. The taping directions included a long list of dos and don'ts, which nobody in the industry paid attention to anymore:

Please follow these important guidelines:
NO large prints or patterns
NO black-and-white or shiny fabrics
NO overwhelming scarves or ties
NO noisy or shiny jewelry
NO loose change in pockets
NO hats with wide brims

YES solid colors (bright or subdued)
YES makeup (men and women)
YES usual eyeglasses
YES pastel shades or off-white

DO be on time
DO listen carefully to all directions
DO assume, once program begins, that you're on the air
DO talk normally

DON'T make unnecessary movements or noises
DON'T slouch, or get too casual
DON'T cover your mouth with your hand as you speak

Her shining silk suit and dangling earrings violated at least two of the guidelines.

This was a great opportunity for Serpentine. It was the first time she'd been allowed to stretch out and do something different. She was anxious to show the "powers that be" that she was versatile.

When she arrived on the set that evening, Serpentine headed for the green room. She grabbed a bagel from the snack tray, spreading honey-walnut cream cheese on it. She checked her watch and zipped down the hall to the doorway of her cohost, Elese Holly, a popular jazz singer.

"It's wonderful to have this opportunity to work with you, Ms. Holly," Serpentine told the five-foot-six, two-hundred-pound woman who stood regally in front of her. "I know this is a line that everybody uses, but I'm truly a fan."

"I admit, I hear it a lot, but to be honest with you, I can't hear it enough," Elese told her with a grin.

Serpentine looked down at her bagel. "Would you like me to get you one of these from the green room?"

"Honey, I might as well rub that bread and cream cheese all over my ass, because that's exactly where it'll end up," Elese prophesied.

They laughed together for a few minutes until Serpentine checked her watch again, and rushed to her dressing room to get ready.

By six o'clock Serpentine was standing on her assigned spot in front of the camera. Behind her were five rows of tables. Each table held ten phones and ten volunteers to answer the phones. On the right was a large money board to display the total amount collected, and off to the left was a stage area set up for the various singing, dancing, comedy, and magic acts that were scheduled to appear.

"Stand by, five, four, three, two, one," the director said, then pointed his finger at Serpentine.

"Good evening and welcome to the Third Annual WXYZ Sickle-Cell Anemia Telethon. I'm your host, Serpentine Williamson, and my cohost, who we'll hear from in just a minute, is one of today's true divas, Elese Holly."

As Serpentine read from the TelePrompTer, she glanced over at Elese, who was preparing for her song. Serpentine smiled, thinking about the bread-and-cream-cheese joke. Then she continued to read: "Tonight we have some great entertainment for you. Legends like Frankie Beverly and Maze, actress and comedian Kim Coles from *Living Single*, popular gospel singer John P. Kee, and a fast-rising group, Fusion Soul, Featuring Shalay—" Serpentine stopped reading and stared at the TelePrompTer in shock.

The director stood up and waved frantically until she finally caught herself and continued: ". . . a video message from superstar Michael Jordan, jazz sensation Kirk Whalum, and many other surprises, so stay tuned. We want you to sit back and enjoy the show, but first pick up your phone and call in your pledge. The number is at the bottom of the screen: 1-800-4-ANEMIA. Call now. We're going to start tonight's festivities with a song from my marvelous cohost, Elese Holly."

The director switched from camera one, on Serpentine, to camera two, on Elese, as the stage lights faded down and the spotlight faded up. Elese stood in her assigned place and sang her current hit, "Always."

"What's going on?" the director whispered loudly to Serpentine.

"Nothing, I'm fine," she replied. "It's okay."

The phones lit up and volunteers started taking pledges. A production assistant brought out two stools for Serpentine and Elese to sit on as Kirk Whalum blew his saxophone. Serpentine spent a few minutes talking to the director, then sat and waited for her cue. The director pointed and she spoke again.

"I know the news about sickle-cell has died down these days with so many other major diseases on the rise, but that doesn't mean it's been conquered. Thousands of black people every year are dying from this killer. Call now: 1-800-4-ANEMIA."

The director cut over to the Michael Jordan tape, giving everyone the clear signal. When the doors swung open and Shalay stepped into the studio their eyes met, and Serpentine held her breath.

"Is something wrong?" Elese asked, noticing the tension.

Serpentine shook her head. "Let's just say I have a brief history with that woman over there."

"I bet it involves a man, doesn't it?" Elese added. "It always does."

Serpentine pretended to read the note cards in her hand.

"So, are you going to tell me what happened, or what?" Elese prodded.

Serpentine silently counted to ten to relieve the pressure.

"She's my boyfriend's ex," she finally said.

"Is she trying to get him back or something?" Elese continued to probe.

"Carlin assures me I have nothing to worry about, but I can't seem to stop worrying," Serpentine admitted.

"I know it don't help that she's a skinny little thing, either," Elese spat out.

Serpentine was glad to get the cue from the director. She watched the next act, a local one, "Mr. and Mrs. Magic." They did some simple tricks, with seven or eight kids sitting around ooh-ing and ah-ing. They were especially good at making things disappear and reappear: a silver dollar, a scarf, and a hamster. Serpentine wondered if she could get them to work their magic on Shalay.

As she waited for her next segment, a production assistant handed Serpentine a note. She unfolded the piece of paper and read it.

"She wants to see you, right?" Elese asked.

Serpentine frowned. "How did you know that?"

"Please, this threesome is right out of *The Young and the Restless,* Callie, Olivia, and Malcolm."

Serpentine moaned. "That's the problem. I can't handle a daytime drama in my life right now."

"You've got to deal with it, girl. Women like her don't just go away," Elese warned.

The director gave them the "Ready" signal and they both sat up straight on their stools.

"Welcome back," Serpentine read. "This is truly a wonderful cause, and we need each of you to get involved."

The TelePrompTer switched to Elese. "Sickle-cell is a hereditary disease characterized by abnormal, sickle-shaped blood cells. The sickle-shaped cells are unable to pass through blood vessels, which leads to blood clots and possible death."

The director cut back to Serpentine: "You can help. Call the number on the screen and pledge ten dollars, fifty dollars, one hundred dollars, or one thousand dollars. Do it right now! Up next, comedy by Kim Coles. She's gonna tell you all about *Living Single* with her popular book, *I'm Free, But It'll Cost You.*"

Elese agreed to handle the next segment alone, so Serpentine told the director she'd be in the back for a minute or two. She slowly trudged down the hall and knocked on the door of dressing room B.

"Come in," Shalay called out.

Serpentine opened the door and stepped inside.

"Hi, Serpentine. Thanks for coming. I was glad to see you out there, because we really need to talk."

"I don't have much time. What do you want?" Serpentine asked, making the chip on her shoulder obvious.

"Look, I just want you to understand the relationship Carlin and I have," Shalay told her.

"Carlin says you two don't have a relationship anymore," Serpentine replied curtly.

Shalay pulled off her robe and stepped into her red sequined dress. "Of course he's going to tell you that. I've known Carlin for the last eight years, and believe me, I know him very well."

Serpentine rolled her eyes. "What do you want, Shalay?" she repeated.

"Carlin loves you, Serpentine. I don't deny that."

"Yeah, he loves me, and you obviously love him, so get to the point, I don't have time for this bullshit."

"You know, I was hoping you had more sense than his last bimbo."

"I'm outta here." Serpentine turned to leave.

"Look, I'm trying to give you the inside track," Shalay said, then lit up an unfiltered cigarette.

"There's no smoking in here," Serpentine informed her, pointing toward the sign.

Shalay ignored her. "Carlin is a wonderful man and I want to see him happy." She inhaled another large dose of nicotine. "Carlin wants a family with marriage and kids. That's not for me."

Serpentine was suddenly pissed. She marched over, snatched the cigarette out of Shalay's hand, dropped it to the floor, and mashed it out viciously. "I said, there's no smoking in here, dammit!"

Shalay looked at her defiantly. "What I'm trying to say is that you can have all that traditional stuff with Carlin, but he's an itch and I've got to scratch. That shouldn't be hard for you to understand."

Serpentine became even more annoyed, if that were possible. "Look, I don't give a damn about you itching and scratching."

"Serpentine, let me break it down for you. I'm going to be a success in my singing career. I don't want the traditional wife-and-mother thing. I'm just suggesting we sidestep the dumb shit and be honest. We could both get what we want out of this."

Serpentine looked at Shalay the way a lion would look at a rabbit who just smacked him in the face. "What the hell are you talking about?"

Shalay sat down in front of the large mirror and smeared fire red lipstick on her puckered lips. "Carlin is one of those men who can't stick with one woman. He loves you, Serpentine, but he also loves me. You could give him the marriage, house, and kids he wants. I'm just asking for a little bit of his time, say one weekend a month."

Serpentine almost gagged. "You're kidding, right?" she asked, two octaves above her normal voice.

Shalay shot her a confident look. "Don't be naïve, Serpentine. Ninety percent of all women share their man at some time or another; they just don't know it."

Serpentine couldn't respond. The woman was serious. She sat in front of that mirror lining her eyes and talking as if she had just said, "Let's share some popcorn at a movie."

Shalay continued. "Be honest, there aren't a lot of men like Carlin out there, especially for somebody like you. And you can't compete with me, so a compromise would be best. Don't you think?"

"You and Carlin can both go to hell!" Serpentine screamed and yanked open the door.

"You should be realistic," Shalay added. "Your only choice is to share and get something out of the deal, because whenever I call, Carlin *will* come running. Now, we need to wrap this discussion up before the show is over, because I have to go straight to my concert at Lincoln Theater after this."

"We can wrap it up right now, Shalay," Serpentine snapped. "Fuck you and Carlin, if he wants you!" She slammed the door, and hurried back to the studio.

As Serpentine waited at her assigned spot, Elese finished talking with several people who were suffering from sickle-cell. Serpentine felt like she was having an out-of-body experience. It was as if somebody else had taken over and was finishing the show for her.

The director cut to a videotaped message from TLC's T-Boz who talked about her experience growing up with sickle-cell and becoming a star. Next, he gave Serpentine her cue. "We have some truly wonderful talent on our show tonight, especially my cohost, Elese Holly," Serpentine read.

Elese took over: "I'm glad to be here for this important cause. Sickle-cell is a disease that affects too many African Americans, and we need to wipe it out for good."

Serpentine continued: "That's why you should call: 1-800-4-ANEMIA right now and make your pledge. You can make a difference."

Elese couldn't wait to get the scoop when the cameras were off them. "So what did she say?" she asked. "You two gonna do battle over this man, or what?"

"Actually, her offer was the opposite." Serpentine turned one side of her mouth downward for emphasis.

Elese didn't hide her agitation. "What do you mean, 'opposite'?"

"She wants to share him. She said I can marry him and have the traditional kids and the house with the white picket fence, but she wants to screw him one weekend a month."

Elese looked closely at Serpentine, waiting for her to admit that she was kidding. When she realized Serpentine was serious, her mouth flew open. "Damn!" Elese said. "You got to admit the woman has game. Men been doing that shit for years. You gonna give it any thought?"

"Elese, you must be as loony as she is," Serpentine replied. "I ain't sharing a man with nobody. I ain't that damn desperate. If Carlin wants to be with Shalay, he can take his happy ass on down the road."

The program continued. Whenever the phones were slow Serpentine and Elese would encourage more calls. When the phones were all lit up, they would introduce the next segment.

"Let's look at our total board," Serpentine told the camera. "Two hundred and five thousand dollars is our total so far. But we need more than that. Our goal is five hundred thousand dollars. Grab that telephone and call now. What are you waiting for? The number is 1-800-4-ANEMIA."

Elese followed her cue: "This next group is so very talented, and they've been around almost as long as I have. Put your hands together for Frankie Beverly and Maze."

"You're worried about the man going back to her, aren't you?" Elese asked Serpentine as they bounced with the beat, waiting for the performance to end.

"I wish I could get this weight issue out of my head," Serpentine mumbled. "If I were smaller maybe it wouldn't bother me."

"Girl, if it isn't weight, it's something else. Color, age, even my refusal to get up onstage and show my behind years ago when a director wanted to see it has impacted my life. Racism, sexism, ageism, and weightism are all battles that we have to fight."

The director cut to the general manager who gave a brief speech about WXYZ's interest in the community.

"Shalay doesn't seem to think I can compete with her because of my size," Serpentine told Elese.

"That's a bluff. If she wasn't worried about you, she wouldn't be proposing a compromise."

"You think so?" The thought made Serpentine feel somewhat better.

"I know so," Elese answered.

The red light came on in front of their camera. Serpentine looked into the TelePrompTer and spoke. "Let's go over to the total board again." She strolled to the board and the camera followed, then the director cut to a closeup of the board.

"Three hundred and ninety-two thousand dollars!" Serpentine shouted excitedly. "We're almost there. If you haven't made your pledge yet, do it now. 1-800-4-ANEMIA. Let's go over to Elese, who's with a couple of local organizations making their pledge."

"I'm here with Calvin Banks from the Chicago Black Gentlemen's Association," Elese said, handing Calvin the microphone.

"On behalf of the Chicago Black Gentlemen's Association, I want to make this pledge of one thousand dollars to the Sickle-Cell Telethon," Calvin said nervously, then handed the microphone back.

"Thank you so much," Elese said.

"This is what we need: for everybody to get involved, get in the spirit, and pick up the phone right now!" Elese almost sang the words. "We also have with us a representative from the Brownies Troop 459 in Highland Park. This is ten-year-old Ava Innis." She held the microphone in the child's face.

"One of our troop members has sickle-cell, so we sold candy as a fund-raiser and made two hundred and thirty dollars," Ava said proudly.

Elese hugged the little girl. "Thank you both very much," she said. "Now here's a group that has been burning up the charts: Fusion Soul, Featuring Shalay."

Serpentine rushed out of the studio and into the women's restroom when she heard the name. As she leaned over the sink she could hear the haunting voice singing a familiar melody.

She stayed in the restroom until she was sure Shalay had finished her song and left the stage. Serpentine hurried back to the studio just before the telethon ended.

"Let's check the total one more time," she said, walking over to the board. "Five-hundred and seven-thousand dollars is our final total. Thank you so much for helping us meet our goal. You can still continue to call. The phones will be open for another thirty minutes."

The director cut to Elese. "We want to thank all of our guests tonight for their assistance in this very worthwhile cause. Progress is being made in the treatment of sickle-cell anemia, but we haven't won yet."

Joining Elese at the center of the set Serpentine concluded, "Thank you for helping us to fight the good fight against this terrible disease, and good night." The credits rolled.

Serpentine walked with Elese back to her dressing room.

"You gonna be okay?" Elese asked.

"I'll be fine," Serpentine replied, secretly praying for it to be true.

Elese winked at her. "Just don't be like me, honey," she warned. "Crying at your wedding because you *didn't* marry the *best* man."

Sometimes You Feel Like a Nut . . .

On Christmas Day, I did something different. Instead of watching the programs on television, for about an hour I focused on the commercials. Now I see why this is a confused society.

Did somebody say McDonald's? It's not delivery, it's DiGiorno. Velveeta: It's a hunka hunka melted love. I was getting married and I was fat: Slim Fast. Got milk? Get your burger's worth at Burger King. Yo quiero Taco Bell. Equal: No Calories, No Guilt. 1-800-45-JENNY. You know you want it, so have it: Kraft Lite Macaroni and Cheese. Time to start the New Year's diet: Kellogg's Special K, lose the holiday fat. Let's make everything big: Little Caesar's. Snackwells Peanut Butter Cookies: passion, desire, and devotion, it goes way beyond that. 1, 2, 3, success from Weight Watchers.

In order to sort through the conflicting messages you need to use six senses: touch, taste, sight, smell, hearing, and common.

The holiday meant a skeleton crew at the station, and on top of that, three people had called in sick with the flu, so Serpentine spent most of her day in the editing room tagging footage for a number of different stories. Despite years of doing it, she still couldn't believe it was Christmas and she was at work just like any other day. That was the hardest lesson to learn about working in the media. Radio and television stations broadcast on holidays and newspapers publish as well. She remembered her first year at WXYZ, when she'd naïvely asked Terry about getting Christmas off and he laughed her out of his office.

She finished logging her third video; a press conference with the district attorney about the upcoming trial of a twelve-year-old accused of killing an eleven-year-old, and began shuffling through the pile of tapes looking for something less depressing. She picked up a video labeled "Fusion Soul, Featuring Shalay at Lincoln Theater."

She checked the date; it was yesterday, the same day as the telethon. Serpentine took the half-inch videotape out of the case and fast-forwarded through the maze of images. She stopped for a few minutes to listen to the beauty of Shalay's voice. It was hard to hate someone who had such a wonderful talent.

About the middle of the tape, the cameraman started shooting cutaways of the audience, the lights, and the band. Serpentine watched the drummer pounding his cadence and the keyboard player's fingers massaging the ivory keys; the guitarist was tickling his nickel-plated steel strings with Shalay's voice declaring itself the most powerful instrument of all. Suddenly, Serpentine stopped the tape and rewound it for several seconds. She pushed the Play button, and there he was.

Carlin was standing backstage, just to the left of the curtains. Serpentine froze the tape on his image and stared at the small screen. She slammed her fist onto the table and cursed out loud. "Damn him!"

She lifted her thumb up to her mouth and chewed on the edge of the nail. Carlin had been in Chicago and he hadn't called. Even worse, he'd been here to see Shalay. Serpentine felt like such a fool. He was probably waiting for Shalay in her hotel room when she appeared on the telethon and made Serpentine that proposition. He probably came up with the idea!

She snatched a blank tape out of the cabinet and dubbed Carlin's image onto it. Then, she had to get out of the room; the building. Outside, she squinted in the harsh light. The icy wind pushed and pulled against her brown wool coat, sneaking into all available cracks and crevices. A silver Range Rover drove by just as she got to her car. She searched for Carlin's face in the driver's seat and was relieved not to see him. Serpentine was resentful, short of breath, and angry. Her neck felt stiff and sore, her eyes were heavy and half-closed, her soul overwhelmed.

She sat in her car and took in the brilliant winter colors. Traces of windswept snow blew vigorously down the sidewalk as her heart swelled with a mixture of hate, fear, hurt, and love. She checked to make sure no one was around, then howled like a wolf caught in a trap in the woods. Wrapping both arms around her shoulders, Serpentine drew them closer and closer together. With each pull she released an intense sob.

Five minutes was all she needed. After a minute or so, the sobbing turned into moaning. Another minute or two, and the moaning turned into whimpering. One more minute and the whimpering became muted anguish.

Serpentine pulled herself together and went back into the building. The situation with Shalay and Carlin weighed heavily on her mind all afternoon. She had trusted Carlin, believed him when he said he loved her and that things with Shalay were over, but he had to be lying all along.

At six-thirty, she gathered up her notes and marched into the conference room, where a special story meeting had already started.

"Okay, what are we thinking about today?" Terry asked.

Trina raised her hand. "I've been hearing rumors down at the courthouse that there's a problem with the jury in the Vaught embezzlement trial. There's a possibility of a mistrial, but we won't know until after the holidays."

"You have any more details?" Terry asked, leaning forward.

"Something about a juror complaining that two of the other jurors have shown prejudice because the defendant is gay," added Trina. "I don't know exactly what happened yet. I have a call in to one of my sources, but you know it's Christmas."

"Sounds good, stay on it."

"I think it's time we did another story on AIDS. An update on research, along with maybe a personal piece about someone living with the disease," Benton said in his gruff voice.

Terry cocked his head. "It would have to be somebody who's doing more than sitting around and waiting to die, and not someone who's out helping other AIDS victims. Those stories have been done to death."

"I have the perfect person," Trina offered. "A guy in my building found out he was HIV-positive last year, and he's not wasting his time. He's been to Disneyland twice, gone deep-sea fishing, bungee jumping, and he just bought a ticket to go on an African safari this summer."

"Yes! That's exactly the angle we need," Terry exclaimed. "You think he'd talk to Benton?"

"I'll set something up," Trina replied, crossing her legs confidently.

"What about you, Serpentine?" Terry asked, suddenly realizing how quiet she'd been.

Serpentine jerked her mind back into the room. She threw out the first idea that came to her.

"I've come across a small but growing group of folks who are using God to conquer their weight problems. I've been thinking about exploring that for a potential story. I could tie it into the Christmas season," she offered.

"What does that mean, using God?" Terry asked.

"They meet on a weekly basis, like a Weight Watchers group, except they talk about Scripture and how it deals with food and weight. They pray together about losing weight and try to maintain the faith that their success will come through Jesus."

"Praying about it won't do any good if they keep pigging out and don't exercise," Trina tossed out in a sarcastic tone.

"You'd be surprised what the power of prayer can do," Serpentine informed her.

"Praise the Lord!" Trina joked, "and pass the double-chocolate, caramel, nutty-fudge ice cream!"

Serpentine cut her eyes at Trina, then around the room to stop the snickers and giggles. It soon became quiet as Terry let the tension die down.

He glanced over at Serpentine. "I like the idea, but let's table it for now until you get more details. We'll cut this meeting short today. Have a good Christmas. What's left of it."

Back at her desk, Serpentine returned a couple of messages, then she dialed Carlin's number. She quickly hung up when the answering machine clicked on. She hurt all over and there was nothing that could stop the pain. She couldn't let Carlin back into her life after what he'd done, and she knew losing him would make her truly ill.

When she left the station, Serpentine drove straight to the post office and parked in the snow-plowed lot. She hurried inside and pulled a Priority Mail envelope out of the glass case. She wrote Carlin's name and address on the envelope and slipped the tape inside. She found a crisp five-dollar bill for the postage machine, stuck the three-dollar Priority stamp on the box, and dropped the package into the mail chute.

Serpentine drove home slowly. She cried all the way. Once again she had trusted this man. And once again she had lost. She knew it was too perfect; the way he dropped into her life, won her heart, and promised to be there forever.

When she turned the corner and drove onto her block, a red Mustang passed in the opposite direction and the horn blew. Serpentine forced a smile and waved back. That car belonged to her neighbors, Zoe and Nadine, two women who had given up on men completely. She'd gone to dinner at their house several times and they always seemed like a very happy couple. Serpentine wasn't ready to move in that direction, but she was quickly losing faith in the traditional option. She pulled up into her driveway, pushed the remote, and watched the garage-door rise.

When she stepped into the house she couldn't shake the chill that followed her inside. She had cared too much and been let down too often. The phone rang, but she didn't answer it. Instead she stretched out on the couch and tried to figure out who was to blame for this mess that black men and women found themselves in. Maybe it was her fault. Maybe black women don't do all they can to make relationships work. Maybe it was Carlin's fault. Maybe black men give up on black women too easily; maybe they don't try hard enough. Maybe it was society's fault. Gender roles were changing and everyone seemed to be confused. Maybe it was the media's fault. The unrealistic images they perpetuate tell people who's acceptable and who's not. Maybe it was nobody's fault. Maybe this was just the way it had to be.

Happy New Year

To BALL is truly wonderful. Everybody should try it sometime. It helps the body to relax as never before, and the mind becomes alert and energized. When I first saw the term I had to get my mind out of the gutter. BALL is an acronym for "believe, accept, love, and live."

I went to a lecture today at Northwestern about spiritual rejuvenation. The presenter was excellent and her message was simple. She said instead of waiting for someone to believe in us or accept us or love us, we have to believe in ourselves, accept ourselves, and love ourselves in order to live.

The words are easy to say, but the action is much harder to do. To BALL is probably the most difficult thing I've ever tried to do in my life and the funny thing is, it shouldn't be. If I could learn to believe in myself, accept myself, and love myself, maybe I could finally live and this would be a happy new year after all.

Serpentine drove back and forth in front of Donut World three times before she finally pulled in and came to a stop. She sat very still, wanting to restart her dirty car and drive off, but nothing. She didn't move. The car didn't move.

She lifted her right thumb to her mouth and chewed on the cuticle uncontrollably. She didn't need this. She could ignore the urges. She could say no if she wanted to. Serpentine slid her hand into the door handle, but hesitated when she thought about her two large thighs that rubbed together when she walked, her two heavy arms that she was ashamed to show in public, and her double chin that seemed to be building a third layer.

A rush of fear spread across her face. Here she was again in the same place; in the same abyss. She couldn't even say how she got here or explain why she hadn't seen it coming. It was as if her whole life was simply moving around in a perverse circle.

She took a deep breath and sucked in her stomach. So what if the weight was back again. The hundred extra pounds that clung to her medium frame was like a massive malignant tumor. She knew it needed to be removed, but nobody had perfected the technique yet.

Serpentine found herself sinking deep into a personal hell. The devil whispered sweet nothings in her left ear, while God screamed his commandments into her right. The issue of weight was like a dandelion weed that came back no matter how many times she tore it out of her heart by the roots.

What made the experience of eating so soothing? How could the act be so satisfying, yet so destructive? Serpentine had vowed a zillion times to give up sweets, limit fats, and eat more vegetables. And she actually succeeded many times, until the rain came, followed by the sun, then more rain, and that pretty, destructive weed would grow stronger, taller, and bolder.

As she swung her left leg out of the car, a cold wind brushed past her thick calf, and she looked around for its origin. It blew from the south, past Lake Michigan, across the right side of her face. It was strong enough to move the brightly colored streamers that hung above the shop's front door in honor of that night's New Year's Eve celebration. Twenty footsteps and seven deep breaths later, Serpentine found herself at the counter, pulling out a ten-dollar bill to pay for the half-dozen glazed donuts she'd ordered.

Once back in the car she pulled a donut out of the bag and bit into it slowly, deeply. She inhaled the aroma and savored the sugary taste. She took steady deliberate bites, chewing carefully to extract all possible flavor. She put the key in the ignition, started the car, and began the short drive home. This was about control. It was about anybody, even herself, having the nerve to say no, off-limits, forbidden. Serpentine had sworn as a child that once she was grown, she would do *what* she wanted, *when* she wanted, and *how* she wanted. Well, this was what she wanted!

She made a right turn at the light and slowed down to let a couple of kids jaywalk in front of her while she licked the excess glaze off her fingers from the second donut. "So what?" she finally screamed in anguish. It was her body! It was her life!

As she pushed the remote control, her garage door rose slowly. She inched the car inside, pushing the button again. With the garage door closed, she scooted herself out of the driver's seat and opened the back door of the car. She grabbed her purse, the donut sack, and two plastic bags of groceries to take inside.

Serpentine was maneuvering the key with one hand and clutching the packages with the other when the phone rang. She slid the key into the lock on the second ring, turned the knob, and opened the door on the third. She dropped her bags on the floor on the fourth, and hustled to the phone by the fifth ring.

"Hello," she said into the receiver, straining for breath.

"Hi. Is Serpentine Williamson in, please?"

"This is she."

"I'm Jill, Dr. Clark's receptionist, and I'm very sorry, but Dr.

Clark has had a personal emergency and we will need to reschedule your appointment next week."

Serpentine's face dropped. She squeezed her eyes tightly, gritting her teeth.

"Ms. Williamson, can we reschedule for the middle of January?"

Serpentine didn't respond right away. She concentrated instead on managing the panic that suddenly seized her soul.

"Ms. Williamson, we can do this at your convenience."

Serpentine hesitated. "That's fine," she replied, leaning her head against the textured beige wall.

"We apologize for the inconvenience."

Serpentine hung up the phone and moved slowly back through the hallway. She didn't know if she could wait another week or two to talk to somebody. She had been trying to hold it together for the three weeks it took to get this appointment.

Calling a psychologist had been her final attempt to grab on to something. When LaJune first mentioned a therapist, Serpentine wasn't sure it would help. But LaJune got Dr. Clark's number from a colleague at work and the crumpled business card remained in Serpentine's purse for several days before she had actually called.

She picked up her packages and carried everything into the kitchen, moving slowly like a snail. The decision to see a psychologist made her sad. It confirmed the fact that she'd failed to succeed in her own life. She was a loser. No matter how hard she tried to live like a normal human being and be happy, it was impossible. All of her experiences were intricately connected like a dog that has to pee on every tree he passes. At that moment, Serpentine felt so drained, so tired, so consumed, so frazzled, so sad, and so hopeless.

She set the groceries on the kitchen counter, tossed her purse on the couch, and went into her bedroom. Serpentine spread the white comforter over her unmade bed and lay across the end, very still.

"It's okay," she told herself out loud. "You can handle this." She closed her eyes and took a few deep, cleansing breaths. Then she picked up the phone and dialed.

"LaJune Thompson, please."

The soprano voice on the other end told her that LaJune had left work already. Serpentine dialed LaJune's home number, but there was no answer.

Serpentine got undressed. She carefully removed her black panty hose, then peeled off her lavender skirt suit and hung it in the closet. She stood for a moment, admiring her organizational skills. Her shoes, belts, earrings, and other personal items were on the left side neatly arranged on six shelves. Her clothes hung on the right side; dresses, pants, and skirts together, blouses and sweaters next, followed by jackets. She tossed a brightly colored, African-patterned caftan over her head and slipped on her gold-braided house shoes.

In the kitchen, Serpentine hit the Play button on her answering machine, then put the groceries away. The answering machine started almost immediately.

"Hi, Teenie. Oh, I'm sorry, I keep forgetting that you don't want to be called that anymore. Sweetie, I'm calling to report in. Lord, I gained two pounds since Thanksgiving. How are you doing? You know how hard it is to diet when your father is constantly cooking his deep-fried delicacies. Are you still using your treadmill? What's your New Year's goal? I'm gonna try and lose fifteen pounds. Dad says hi. We love you."

Serpentine grunted as she took a box of melting ice cream sandwiches out of her grocery sack and pushed them into the freezer. She slid two cans of tuna fish into the bottom cabinet, tossed a loaf of whole wheat bread onto the tabletop, and shoved the plastic grocery sack into a drawer below.

She pulled another donut out of the sack and gulped it down quickly.

"Hey, Serpentine, call me, please. I wish you'd at least let me explain this tape. How many times do I have to say it? Nothing happened. It was just a concert. I miss you, sugar. If I didn't love you, I wouldn't call your machine and beg like this. Call me, please."

Serpentine threw a half-eaten donut across the room at the machine. How dare that asshole act like everything was supposed to be okay!

"Well, Carlin, you want the skinny bitch, have her and be happy!" she yelled.

Serpentine leaned against the counter and allowed Carlin's voice to circulate through her mind for a moment. He always knew the right things to say to coax people over to his side. But this time, it was about action, not words. It was about respect, not that bullshit he wanted to substitute for it. What would he do the next time Shalay shook her skinny ass in his face? Serpentine stomped into the dining room, pulled a photo album off the bookcase, and opened it.

Carlin's crooked brown lips were quickly frozen in her memory. She yanked the pictures from Six Flags Astro World out of the book. They had taken one in front of the Ultra Twister where the track dove down over ninety feet, then made a three-hundred-and-sixty-degree turn in midair. Another one showed her precious Carlin standing next to a six-foot-tall Bugs Bunny.

She stopped to remember that day. She thought she'd finally found the man who truly loved her. Their relationship had passed almost every test. She had purposely worked through each level at a snail's pace. They'd talked over the phone for hours, getting to know each other. They didn't sleep together until after the lust period was over. And she'd even made sure not to tell him she loved him until he'd said it first.

She figured part of the problem had to be his friends. He listened when they bragged about their fine young hotties; thin and perfect according to society's unrealistic standards. Carlin wouldn't admit it, but he believed the hype. Women who looked anorexic, their clothes hanging off their bodies, their bones protruding through their skin, were the women to desire.

So, of course, when Shalay offered up her smaller pussy, he couldn't refuse. He had to take it, enjoy it, and use it until he was sure it was his any time he wanted. Then, once he was secure again, he'd show up on her doorstep begging to get back in.

"Well, that's too goddamn bad, Carlin!" she screamed at the picture. "Things will never be okay again!"

Serpentine slammed the photo album shut. What would she do without Carlin? He was so safe and comfortable. With him in her heart, she could go to a nightclub with Marleen, and it was okay if she wasn't asked to dance. With him in her heart, she could watch a love story on the big screen and believe that she, too, had that kind of happiness.

She grabbed another donut and shoved it into her mouth, whole.

The machine beeped through several hang ups and a third message began.

"Serpentine, this is Constance. I got your demo tape and I've checked around in Kansas City like you asked, but this is a bad time for you to move. There's not much out there right now. As your agent and your friend, I also have to be honest with you. That demo doesn't do much for you. The weight gain is too obvious. My advice is to take six months and get on some kind of diet and exercise program. Drop some pounds and reshoot the demo. Maybe by then the market will open up. Give me a call if you have questions. Take care!"

Serpentine snatched the bag with two donuts left and dumped it into the trashcan. Then she clicked on the living room television and flipped quickly through the channels. She wasn't really looking for anything in particular. She didn't want to see any of the New Year's Eve celebrations. She wasn't happy, and in her own home she didn't have to pretend. She finally stopped when a talk show caught her attention. There were two teams of obese people, and they were playing a game: bobbing for Twinkies.

Serpentine sat paralyzed as several participants from a group calling themselves Obese Incorporated bent over big plastic tubs filled with water, grabbing as many bags of Hostess Twinkies with their mouths as they could in the allotted time. While huge behinds were tilted up in the air, the sounds of mooing cows and grunting pigs were intermixed with audience laughter.

In the second part of the contest, each team tore open the bags of wet Twinkies they'd retrieved and in an exaggerated manner shoved them into their mouths one after another until their cheeks puffed out from gluttony. All the while the song "Whoop. There It Is" played in the background. Serpentine couldn't hold back the tears. They flowed continuously, earnestly, and helplessly.

She turned off the television, walked into the kitchen, and pulled the donut sack out of the trash. She sat at the dining room table, eating the fifth donut with a glass of milk, in silence. She was tired: tired of struggling, tired of fighting, tired of losing, and tired of crying.

The dying fire inside consumed her. It corroded everything she tried to do. When it burned hot, it was like the radiant heat from the sun, generating an energy she couldn't contain. When it flickered warm, it was like the cool blue water from the ocean, stabilizing her spirit. But now it was dying.

She checked the cherry-finished wood clock that hung against the wall. It was five minutes until midnight. Serpentine surveyed her favorite room in the house. She loved the cherrywood table and chairs and the matching mirrored cabinet that held her grandmother's best china on display.

She wrote a quick note on the pad by the phone, and grabbed the last donut from the bag on the kitchen cabinet. She took a faded blue blanket out of the linen closet and went into the garage, shutting the door behind her. Serpentine walked around the car rolling down all the windows, first the back and then the front. She opened the car door, slid into the driver's seat, and slipped the key into the ignition. She shut her eyes tightly and started the car.

Serpentine wrapped herself up in the light cotton blanket and took a large bite out of the last donut. She apologized to God for letting Him down and asked Him to allow her into heaven. Then she closed her eyes and counted: five, four, three, two, one. Happy New Year! She lay back against the molded leather seat, waiting for a permanent sleep to come.

THE END

(This Spring)

Waiting

Waiting is probably one of the worst situations that human beings are forced to endure.

The anxiety is deadening.

The fear is chilling.

The need is overwhelming.

Inside my head I scream: Hurry up! What the hell is wrong with you? It must take you two hours to watch Sixty Minutes! *Please! Please! Please! Get on with it! Get out of my way, asshole! Do you need to see the Wizard for a brain, or what? Move it! Move it! Move it!*

But I don't dare say those things out loud. Instead, I sit and wait.

Dr. Greeley didn't respond to Serpentine's account right away. He waited, allowing her to struggle with her conflicted feelings, then he stood up, got a box of tissues from his bookshelf, and handed it to her.

"How do you feel about all of that now?" he asked, almost in a whisper.

She took the tissue and blew her nose. "Truthfully, Doc, I still wish I had died that day."

Dr. Greeley leaned forward, with a concerned look on his face. "Why, Serpentine?" he asked. "Why do you still prefer death?"

Serpentine sat up and pulled her purse onto her lap. "My life hasn't changed. I've been wanting things to change, praying that things would change, but everything is still screwed up, maybe even more than before," she said.

"Do you think you could really do it?" Dr. Greeley asked, in what sounded like his textbook-training voice.

Serpentine thought for a moment then reached inside her purse and slid out a .380 Colt Pony handgun. She held the metal weapon gingerly in her right hand as she spoke: "I've been thinking that this time I would do it right," she said with fierce determination.

Dr. Greeley stood and took a couple of steps toward her, then stopped to check her reaction. He looked relieved when she didn't jump.

She sat and watched Dr. Greeley carefully. Despair surged through her veins. She didn't really want to die, but she didn't want to live either. She waited, allowing precious moments to pass. She wished things could be different. She didn't want to let Dr. Greeley down. He had tried hard to help her. But why should she stay around to suffer?

Dr. Greeley summoned his courage and pushed out his right hand. "Why don't you give me the gun, Serpentine?" he asked firmly.

Serpentine locked her eyes on him. He still didn't have a clue. She stood up, waving the gun in the air.

"You know, Doc, I don't get it. You of all people should understand now. You know everything! I don't really have a choice here. I wanted to be thin, honestly I did. I wanted to fit into society's idea of beauty. I'd like to know what it feels like to smile widely when I look into a mirror or compare myself to another woman. But those things are not going to happen for me. I'm never going to be thin! I'm never going to be beautiful! I'm never going to be happy!"

Dr. Greeley stood stiffly in front of her, mapping out his next move in his head. "You *will* find happiness, Serpentine," he promised. "But it takes time. That gun is *not* the answer. Death is *not* the answer."

Serpentine paced across the room. "How do you know?" she shouted as her fleshy arms slid back and forth against her rotund body. She waved the silver gun out in front of her.

"What difference would time make?" she asked, not really wanting to hear his answer. "Nothing's going to change, not my job, not my mother, not my luck with men, not even my weight. Why shouldn't I just get the hell out of this messed up place?"

Dr. Greeley walked slowly in her direction. "Giving it more time could make all the difference in the world, Serpentine. You've come so far already. You're no longer that depressed, self-destructive person I met in the hospital several months ago. You know you can survive the job, the Creightons and Carlins, your mother, and even your size issues."

Serpentine wanted to believe him. She turned his words over and over in her mind, but her foreboding doubt was relentless, forcing her to move forward. She held the barrel of the gun up to her temple.

"Serpentine, listen to me," Dr. Greeley urged. "Maybe other people and events in your life haven't changed, but something has changed. *You've* changed. Think about it, Serpentine, you can make things better."

She lowered her head for a moment. It felt like such a strain to hold it up. She thought about Dr. Greeley's words as she prayed for the piercing pain that crippled her entire body to stop. She wanted to believe him. She needed to believe him. Anything to make life worth living again.

She searched for that fire that usually guided her. She had followed it to the University of Iowa, where she earned her bachelor's degree in journalism. She had followed it to her dream job as a television news reporter in Chicago. She had followed it when she stood up to Nolita and when she dumped Carlin. She would follow it now, wherever it led.

Serpentine looked up at the man who knew most of her deepest feelings, and prayed for that fire to guide her one more time. When she felt it at first, it was minuscule, then it slowly grew warmer and brighter until it burned flagrantly in her heart. The fire took control, igniting her exhausted spirit, and she collapsed through impassioned tears.

Dr. Greeley walked over to Serpentine as she slid down the wall, and wrapped his arms around her trembling body. He carefully pulled the gun away and clicked the safety on. Once the gun was safely in his desk drawer, he hurried back to Serpentine. When he knelt down in front of her, she surrendered, allowing him to gently pull her head onto his waiting shoulder.

Move Something

For some reason, I lost my mind this morning and attended a nine a.m. step-aerobics class at the YWCA. Tiny-waisted women (any waist smaller than mine) twisted, bounced, and jumped off beat. It was painful and embarrassing, and I'll never do it again. I tried it because a voice in the back of my head said that walking is not enough.

The voice told me that walking is okay for those who are just trying to lose a few pounds or those who want to maintain their weight, but for someone like me, serious exercise is necessary. Halfway through the one-hour session I swear I heard Susan Powter yelling: "Stop the insanity!"

I know better. All I have to do is move one foot in front of the other, take one step at a time, and I can be healthy. And that's the real deal, health. When I walk, it not only speeds up my heart rate, but also reduces my stress level. It gives me time to think, to relax, and to plan. And even more important, I enjoy walking. After walking, I feel good; not exhausted, not sore, not angry, not embarrassed, just good.

Serpentine looked for Provident Hospital as she turned the corner onto Fifty-first Street. She checked her rearview mirror, then changed lanes. She thought briefly about the hospital's history. Dr. Daniel Hale Williams established the first Provident Hospital at Dearborn and Twenty-fifth Street in the 1800s. Just two years later, he made history as the first surgeon to successfully close a wound in the human heart. Pride welled up in Serpentine's soul whenever she thought about people like him. African Americans had overcome tremendous odds to survive.

The idea of spending her Saturday afternoon with a bunch of other people in group therapy did not make her happy, but Dr. Greeley had convinced her to try it. She hurried inside the entrance doors, taking the elevator up to the second floor to room 245.

There were five women and a man sitting in the room. Serpentine claimed the nearest empty chair just before Dr. Greeley arrived.

"Sorry I'm late," he said, hustling into the room. "I will spare you my excuses. Let's go ahead and get started by introducing ourselves to a potential new member—Serpentine." He pointed in her direction. "She's visiting with us for this one session to see if she likes it, so let's make her feel welcome."

Noreen was an average size, maybe a twelve or fourteen. She seemed very nervous to Serpentine; her movements were jerky and stiff when she spoke. "Hi, I'm Noreen. Born and raised right here in Chicago."

"Lonnie," the tiny girl sitting next to Noreen said quickly. She was young, in her twenties, and very thin. She didn't even look like she had a weight problem.

Marsha was about five-foot-three and she looked as big around as she was tall. "I'm Marsha," she said, struggling to get comfortable in the tiny chair. "As you can tell, food is my best friend."

"Myrna and Cecile are sisters from Seattle," Dr. Greeley said, nodding for them to continue.

Both women were short and dumpy, in their fifties, with bright red freckles on pale white faces. Cecile had twice as many freckles as Myrna, but Myrna had a great sense of humor. "Hi," they chimed together.

"You'll soon find out that I'm the one with all the problems around here," the lone man of the group joked. "Perry is my name." Perry was of medium build, with a large beer belly that made him look like he was pregnant.

Dr. Greeley began the evening's conversation. "Let's talk tonight about diets; what they do and don't do. I'm sure we've all experienced the dreaded diet."

"I probably start Weight Watchers every couple of years," Perry admitted. "It's the only diet I can honestly say I've lost weight on and kept it off for a significant period of time."

"I lost weight on Weight Watchers and Slim Fast, too," Marsha jumped in. "But I've never kept it off."

"Do either of you know why you put the weight back on?" Dr. Greeley asked.

"I stop following the plan and go back to my old eating habits," Perry replied. "I'm a pancakes-and-milk-in-the-morning and steak-and-beer-at-night kind of guy."

Marsha nodded. "I have to cook to feed the kids, and when I cook I eat."

"How about you, Serpentine?" Dr. Greeley asked.

Serpentine smacked her lips irritably, before she spoke. "I refuse to diet anymore," she said in a low but defiant voice.

"That's smart," Noreen agreed. "Diets don't work, anyway."

"Unfortunately, scientists didn't find that out until it was too late. My metabolism was already shot to hell," Serpentine added.

"Lonnie, let's hear from you," Dr. Greeley suggested.

"I drive a cab, so fast food is my mainstay. I know I have to do something about that, but there's not much I can do right now."

"Excuse me, but can I ask what your weight issue is, because you look great! Exactly like they say everybody is suppose to look," Serpentine blurted out.

Lonnie smiled. "Sure I look like this now, but I was on Fen-Phen for almost two years. I lost ninety-four pounds in all. But with that report about possible damage to the heart and lungs, I can't take the drugs any more." Lonnie choked back tears. "I've gained back six pounds in three months and I don't know what I'm going to do. I just can't go back to being fat again."

Everyone was silent for a moment. Noreen handed Lonnie several tissues.

"Wouldn't you want them to take something off the market that could kill you?" Noreen asked.

Lonnie shook her head. "It's like cigarette smokers, I should be able to take my chances, too."

"Not me. I don't want to lose anything that bad," Marsha said. "The women in my family have always been big boned, so I get it honestly."

"I stay hungry," Myrna admitted.

"Me too," Cecile followed. "If I want a chocolate cupcake and I try to substitute something else, I will eat and eat and keep on eating because I haven't satisfied that taste."

"That's true," Myrna added with a chuckle. "I tell her all the time, eat the goddamn cupcake and be through with it!"

Perry shifted in his seat. "You guys probably won't believe this, but I got bigger than my wife when she was pregnant. She's slimmed back down now, and I can't seem to get motivated."

Dr. Greeley crossed his legs, resting his hands on his right knee. "I'd like for each of you to imagine your weight problem going away and tell me how you'd like for it to happen," he said. "Let's start with you, Serpentine."

Serpentine frowned. This was another of his dumb questions. "I'd like for it to all melt off in the next three days," she tossed out.

"Okay, let's take a look at that wish," Dr. Greeley said. "What does that wish tell us about Serpentine?"

Perry started. "She wants the weight to just melt off, which suggests that she might not be willing to work hard at losing it. She likes things to come easy. I know, because that's my problem, too."

"Very good, Perry. What else?" Dr. Greeley continued.

"She's not being realistic about the time period," Marsha added. "The weight didn't show up in three days and it is not going to leave in that amount of time, either."

"At least she's not in my situation, eating just to throw it back up again," Noreen said.

"That is really a disgusting practice," Perry complained, shaking his whole body.

Noreen bristled in her chair. "Maybe, but I don't have that gut you have. It only hurts for a minute or so, then I feel fine."

"I'd wish away my emotional ties to food," Lonnie said. "For years, I would eat every time my husband came home late from one of his so-called business meetings. Not because I was hungry, but because I was pissed."

As Lonnie spoke, Serpentine looked around the room and allowed her mind to drift for a while. She didn't really want to talk about her weight in front of these people, and it didn't matter that they were experiencing similar struggles. It became clear very quickly that each person in that room hated him- or herself. They had all experienced countless failures and inside their heavy bodies were seriously heavy hearts.

"Serpentine, what's on your mind?" Dr. Greeley asked, breaking her concentration.

Serpentine selected her words carefully. "I don't know. I guess the bottom line is that I've been blaming society for this struggle, and not looking at myself. I've worried too much about what other people think of me and the focus has to be on what I think of myself."

Dr. Greeley smiled. "It's a very good point. So, how do you stop worrying about what other people think of you?"

Serpentine twisted her neck until she heard the stress-relieving pop. "If I knew that, I wouldn't be here," she replied sarcastically.

Serpentine again drifted in and out of the conversation once she realized that none of them, probably not even Dr. Greeley, knew the answer. Weight was a daily struggle for all of them, and it had been that way for a long time. The situation wasn't simply about their flabby bodies, but their flabby minds.

"My minister told me once that there's something about the act of eating that's spiritually necessary," Marsha said.

"At times, it takes over the mind, body, and soul," Lonnie agreed.

Noreen cleared her throat. "I remember when McDonald's first started their 'two for one' burger sales. The whole time I stood in line, I thought about how small the burgers probably were. So, when I finally stepped up to the counter, I ordered four, and super-sized everything else."

"Did you eat all that?" Cecile asked.

"Sure did," Noreen answered. "I ate it so fast that I didn't even taste it. An hour later I was in the restroom barfing it up."

"People do crazy things concerning food," Perry interjected. "It's almost like I'm a split personality, my ego wants to lose the weight, but my id tells me I have a right to eat whatever I want!"

"That's the truth," Myrna added. "I attended an Overeaters Summit about a year ago. It was a one-day conference with workshops on health, nutrition, and stuff like that. I went with this group of people from my apartment complex." Myrna leaned back. "We spent all day attending sessions and getting information on health and diets; then we left the convention center and went to the Shakey's all-you-can-eat buffet and pigged out!"

The laughter echoed around the room.

"My aunt is always talking about counting calories. But whenever we go to this popular barbecue place in Kansas City, she orders two slabs of ribs and a diet Coke!" Serpentine contributed.

The group laughed harder. It was a profound, penetrating laughter; a laughter they understood, since they had all been there at one time or another. Serpentine's attitude eventually softened. Group therapy was a mass cleansing effort, in which everyone could let their doubts and fears float out into the air and mingle among kindred spirits. They were allowed to unleash their demons and find comfort for a little while.

As the hour drew to a close, Dr. Greeley began to wrap up. "Food is different for everybody," he said. "Let's throw out a few solutions before we go."

"I don't think it's what I eat, or even how much I eat. My problem is when I eat. I get the munchies late at night, real bad," Noreen said.

Myrna shook her head. "I've got to find a way around this starve-yourself mentality. It just doesn't work for me. I know I can't starve my body without starving my soul."

"I still believe I have a thyroid problem that the doctors can't seem to find," Perry joked, "but seriously, I probably need to eat more vegetables."

"I've tried other outlets, but there's nothing like a Sara Lee pound cake when you're feeling down and out," Lonnie told them. "I'm learning to talk through my feelings instead of eating through them."

"To move something," Serpentine blurted out. "Instead of sitting around watching television and eating anything in sight, I need to get up and move."

"If we know what the solutions are, but we still can't do it, what does that say about us?" Cecile asked nobody in particular.

Serpentine took a deep breath. "I think my aunt Regina would say, 'It means we're human and that's okay.' "

Beautiful Babies

Babies are so wonderful! They come into this world with no baggage, naïve and happy. Then society starts to work on their tiny mental psyches. Little girls should cook and clean. Little boys should wrestle and fight. Little girls should be sensitive, helpful, and quiet. Little boys should be macho and cool; and no matter what, no crying. Things are changing. Today, men wear two earrings and women have landed top management positions, but for all the progress we've made, many of the old myths remain too powerful.

I thought I was dealing with this kind of bullshit in the best possible way. I would sweep it to the side and keep on moving. I wouldn't even stop to get my hands dirty. But when my niece, Micah, was born, I realized that sweeping it to the side wasn't the answer. Sweeping it to the side only meant that it would still be there for her to step in when she gets older. I realized that I have to remove the bullshit, get rid of it completely. So now, I carry a shovel everywhere I go.

Serpentine whipped into the only parallel parking spot on Ellis Street; two blocks away from her destination, Columbia Michael Reese Hospital. The front end of her Geo Prism hit the curb and her tail end stuck out almost two feet into the street.

Serpentine hopped out of her car and rushed down to the corner. She winced as she stepped into a puddle of black mud left from yesterday's spring rain. She crossed the street and hurried through the double glass doors to the information desk.

"I need to find LaJune Thompson's room, please," she told the clerk behind the desk.

The clerk looked through several pages while twirling her red-streaked hair. She finally responded, twisting her mouth as if it hurt. "She's in Maternity, room 451, upstairs, fourth floor." She pointed to the elevator without looking up.

Serpentine didn't bother to thank the woman for her rude assistance. She hustled onto the elevator. It was still hard to believe that her baby sister was about to have a baby. They had just finished the last pre-birth class a week ago. She stood paralyzed in the elevator for a moment, realizing that if her suicide attempt had been successful she wouldn't have seen this wondrous day.

Serpentine checked her watch. It was eleven-thirty. She'd had to do some serious driving to get there in forty minutes. She chuckled thinking about the fact that she had been one of those drivers whom she usually cursed out. She'd cut people off, jumped in and out of lanes, and run yellow-red lights just to arrive a few minutes sooner.

LaJune had called the television station at seven with the news that her water had broken. Serpentine didn't believe LaJune could actually get dressed and drive herself to the hospital, but she was waiting patiently in a birth suite when Serpentine arrived.

Serpentine rushed into the room, pulled off her tan pleated jacket, and tossed it over the nearest chair.

LaJune lay on the hospital bed with a *Parenting* magazine in one hand and a Pepsi in the other.

"How are you doing?" Serpentine asked.

"This ain't so bad, I'm ready to get it over with, though," LaJune announced to her big sister, laying the magazine down.

Serpentine walked over to the bed and took the soda out of La-June's hand. "This poor baby truly needs me," she said.

LaJune frowned. "If anything happened to me, I know you'd take good care of her."

"Stop talking like that," Serpentine warned. "You need anything?"

LaJune rolled her eyes in Serpentine's direction. "I need my Pepsi back," she told her.

"It ain't going to happen," Serpentine said sternly. "You know, caffeine is not good for baby."

LaJune scowled. "Then just sit your ass down and relax till I need you," she muttered under her breath.

Serpentine stood next to LaJune's bed and gulped down the rest of the soda.

LaJune picked up her magazine and threw it at Serpentine. It hit her on the arm and landed in the middle of the floor

Serpentine shook her head. "Where are your contractions now?"

"About twenty minutes apart. The nurses say I got plenty of time."

"You scared?" Serpentine asked, dropping onto the recliner next to the bed.

"A little," LaJune mumbled.

Several unnerving screams suddenly seeped into the room from down the hall, and the sisters looked at each other with apprehension.

"A lot," LaJune added.

"It's going to be all right," Serpentine assured her.

"She doesn't sound like she's having a very good time."

"Don't worry about her. You come from good, strong, African stock. Our ancestors were survivors."

"I already told my doctor when the pain gets bad I want drugs," LaJune said confidently.

"So what does the pain feel like now?"

"Like monthly cramps. Irritating, but bearable."

"Too bad your tolerance for pain is so pathetic. You could've done natural childbirth," Serpentine joked.

"Girl, please, I'm not one of those women who needs to suffer—wait—" LaJune stopped talking. She closed her eyes and took several deep breaths until the pain passed, then continued, "to know it's good."

"Mom and Dad on their way?"

"Yeah, they should be here in about four hours."

"What about Parren? Should I call somebody?"

"I already did. I called the naval office. They're supposed to get a message to him out on the ship. Hey, feel this."

Serpentine laid her hand on the right side of LaJune's stomach and felt the strong, forceful jabs of a tiny foot or elbow. She wiped the tears that rushed from her eyes, smearing her mascara.

"What's wrong with you, I'm the one in pain," LaJune complained.

"This is so wonderful, June, you're having a baby."

"I'm still not sure if I'm ready yet."

"Parren would have a fit if he heard you say that."

"I know. He thinks he created this miracle all by himself."

"He did, didn't he?"

"He ain't did nothing but knocked him off a piece. This is God's miracle."

"It's a shame Parren can't be here to see his child born."

"He had the nerve to ask me to make a videotape," LaJune snorted. "Ain't nobody gonna put my coochie on tape. I don't care if it *is* a miracle."

Serpentine laughed. "It would take a miracle for somebody to want your coochie on tape."

LaJune laughed, then frowned, concentrating on another contraction. "Wow, that one was stronger," she moaned.

"What do you want me to do?" Serpentine asked.

"I really need another Pepsi," LaJune whined. "I'm so desperate, I'll drink caffeine free."

"How about an apple juice?"

"Yuck," LaJune said.

"Milk?"

LaJune rolled her eyes. "Give me my remote," she ordered.

Serpentine tossed the remote to her sister and checked her watch again. It was close to midnight, and she could feel the stress of wanting to get some sleep, even though she needed to stay awake for LaJune.

"You think I have time to catch a nap?" Serpentine asked with her eyes already closed.

LaJune glanced at her sister and answered sarcastically: "Sure, Teenie. I'll just deal with my pain quietly so as not to wake you up."

Serpentine shifted her hips in the chair. "Get a grip, June. I'm here, ain't I? I just need a quick twenty minutes."

LaJune lifted the right side of her behind and allowed a loud fart to pop out. "Excuse me," she giggled.

"That's so vulgar," Serpentine grumbled, and held her sleeve over her nose.

"That's the thing I'm going to miss most about being pregnant. You can just let 'em rip and blame it on the baby."

"You should still be embarrassed."

"When you're lugging around an extra forty pounds, you don't have the energy to care what other people think."

"Well, I'm embarrassed for you, especially last week when you did that all loud in the grocery store and had the nerve to stick out your chest and tell that man, 'I'm pregnant!' "

Their laughter mingled with the canned laughter on a rerun of *Living Single.*

"I *am* pregnant!" LaJune said proudly. Her eyes glued to the television where Sinclaire was giving Khadijah a big hug and saying her famous, "Woo, woo, woo."

It had been a long day and Serpentine was fading fast. It seemed like she had just drifted off, when LaJune screamed so loud she was forced to wake back up.

"June, you okay?" Serpentine asked, jumping up.

"I don't know!" LaJune cried. "Get somebody!"

As Serpentine rang for the nurse, she caught sight of her watch. She had slept for more than an hour.

The nurse hurried into the room to check on LaJune, but she was still only two centimeters dilated. Another hard pain hit just as the nurse finished her examination. LaJune grabbed onto the rails of her bed.

"I think I need something for the pain now," she timidly told the nurse.

The nurse stopped in the doorway. "I'm sorry, but you must be at least three centimeters dilated for medication. It slows down the process. I'll check on you in another thirty minutes."

"Thirty minutes!" LaJune screeched in disgust. "I can't wait thirty minutes, you've got to do something now! Call my doctor!"

The nurse left the room just as another pain took control of La-June's entire body. She twisted and screamed.

"Breathe," Serpentine told her, rushing over from the chair and standing beside the bed. "Remember the breathing techniques."

"I *am* breathing, goddammit! It ain't working! Where's my doctor? I need drugs!" LaJune wailed.

Serpentine helped LaJune turn over on her side. During the next incoming pain she massaged her sister's lower back, exactly the way they'd practiced in class. But it didn't have the same effect. LaJune anticipated each building pain and couldn't relax.

Like clockwork, thirty minutes later, the nurse returned, and notified LaJune that she was finally three centimeters dilated. The shot of Demerol helped LaJune to drift into a comfortable, numbing high. With the edge off, she found herself laughing in between contractions.

"You're a good reporter, Serpentine, stop worrying," LaJune told her after hearing for the umpteenth time about Evan and the focus groups.

"I know I'm good, but it doesn't seem to matter. Everything seems to be working against me," Serpentine said.

"Is Evan the one you have to interview with?"

"No. Mr. Marshall."

"Well, he likes you, right?"

"He doesn't really know me. I'm sure Evan has filled his head with all kinds of junk."

"Stop worrying," LaJune continued. "Wait until there's something to worry about."

Suddenly, a severe pain brought the first tears. "Oh, Lord. I'm gonna be so happy when this child is outta here," LaJune cried. "I want my body back." The medication was wearing off, and the pain had simultaneously mutated. LaJune gnashed her teeth and fought the discomfort that tortured her. "That one was much worse, Serpentine. Get the nurse."

Ten minutes later, when the nurse made it back into the room, LaJune was frantic again. "I need another shot," she cried out from behind the tears. "This stuff ain't working anymore."

The nurse checked LaJune's cervix. She had jumped from four to six centimeters. The seemingly distant and uncaring nurse suddenly panicked and rushed out of the room to call the doctor. Then she scurried around the room, like a cockroach on speed, to prepare for the baby's arrival.

When the white wool sweater, cotton dress, and leather shoes stopped to toss out a word of assurance, LaJune repeated her plea for more drugs. The nurse turned abruptly. "Oh, I'm sorry, Mrs. Thompson, but it's too late to give you anything else now. The baby's too close," she said with a practiced sympathetic look.

LaJune's jaw fell open and her hands began to shake. "What the hell do you mean it's too late!" she screamed. "I told my doctor I wanted drugs. You've got to stop this pain!"

"It's okay, June. You can do this." Serpentine tried to quiet her sister down while wiping the sweat that rolled from her forehead into her eyes.

LaJune rocked back and forth, moaning as the pains grew stronger and came more often. She jerked forward with a pain that shot through her belly so hard, it probably shook her intestines loose. "I can't do this, Serpentine. I feel like I'm gonna die," LaJune moaned. "Please make 'em help me!"

Serpentine watched her sister in agony, realizing she wasn't prepared for this. No matter how many times she'd seen it on television or in the movies, the real thing was very different. The real thing was frightening even in a safe, comfortable hospital room.

"Oh, Lord, help me, please, help me! Help me, Lord Jesus, help me please! I need you Jesus, Lord, help me, please!" LaJune shouted. Her face distorted. She strained, with every muscle pushing downward.

"Something's happening!" she spit out between contractions.

Serpentine darted out of the room, but by the time she got back with the nurse, the baby's head had already crowned. The doctor bolted in after them, slid on his plastic gloves, and took his place at the foot of the bed.

"Okay, Mrs. Thompson, I need for you to push as hard as you can for me," he said in a cheerful voice that irritated LaJune.

"What the hell you think I been doing?" she shot back at him, then grunted, moaned, and screamed all at the same time.

Serpentine watched as LaJune's body shook each time she pushed. "Help me, please Lord Jesus, help me! Oh Lord! Help me please!" LaJune yelled.

While her sister prayed, Serpentine inched down to the end of the bed and peeked over the doctor's shoulders. She was mesmerized when LaJune thrust her pelvis forward with a loud scream and the baby's full head popped out.

"It's the head, June, her head just came out!" Serpentine exclaimed, clapping and jumping.

"This ain't no damn game show!" LaJune snapped.

"You're doing great, Mrs. Thompson. Keep pushing," the doctor said, bringing LaJune back to focus.

Serpentine moved up to the side of the bed and cupped both her hands over LaJune's clenched fist. "Come on, girl. It's almost over."

LaJune tried to find her smile, but it was lost inside the intense pain. She braced herself again as an accelerated contraction moved deeper inside her. After several strong pushes, the baby's shoulders emerged, followed by the rest of the body. The nurse laid the crying baby on LaJune's stomach while the doctor cut the umbilical cord.

"You did it, girl. Look, June, she's here!" Serpentine told her sister between hugs and tears. "She's beautiful."

LaJune glanced down, but she couldn't see beauty at that moment. All she saw was a little grayish-brown lump that had caused too much pain. The baby girl cried and kicked as her body was wiped and wrapped in a blanket, then taken to a warmer near the bed.

"This really is a miracle, June. Another human being came out of your stomach. Girl, that's too deep!"

"Yeah, deep," was all the vocabulary LaJune could muster. She closed her eyes and slept as the doctor disposed of the placenta.

Serpentine gently pulled her hand away from the moist fingers of the sleeping mother and tiptoed over to the warmer to get a better look at this girl-child. As she studied the innocent face she couldn't help but worry. Her soul was happy, but her heart was sad. This new life was wonderful, exciting, a miracle, but what kind of future would she have in the increasingly hostile world Serpentine reported on everyday?

Small streaks of red blood were still visible on the tiny multicolored body. Her legs and arms flailed frantically at the newness of life. Serpentine vowed to do the best she could to make the world a better place because this little person deserved that.

Eat Your Broccoli First

I don't like broccoli. But when I was growing up, we had broccoli at least once a week. I thought for a long time that my mother just wanted to torture me, but it was simpler than that. She liked broccoli. It had vitamins and minerals we needed, so we had to eat it!

In Mama's house we also had to clean our plates because kids in Africa and other parts of the world were starving. Every time one of those public service announcements came on television asking people to pledge seventy cents a day to save a child, my mother would call LaJune and me into the room. She'd say, "See, look at that poor baby. It's a sin the amount of food we waste in America."

These memories have good and bad implications for me. The bad is that I learned to keep on eating even when I was full. The good is that I learned to eat my broccoli first. I would focus on the green, lumpy pile, chewing it quickly and just enough to get it down my throat. Then I'd enjoy the good stuff that was left on my plate.

Serpentine stepped on her treadmill, determined to walk for at least thirty minutes. The dull ache in her left knee was back. It always showed up when she avoided walking for more than two weeks. She straddled the walkway and turned on the machine at level 2. When it slowly started to move she stepped on and merged with the flow, concentrating on the rhythm from Erykah Badu's latest CD.

After a couple of minutes, she felt comfortable enough to turn the machine higher. She stopped at level 4 and took longer, more confident strides. Suddenly her left knee twisted and a sharp piercing pain shot up into her thigh. Serpentine grabbed hold of the bar to balance herself and ripped out the safety key. The treadmill slowed, then stopped. Serpentine limped over to a chair in the corner of the room and sat down. She massaged the injured knee for a while before calling her chiropractor for an appointment. This was a constant dilemma in her life: the battle of wills between her mind and her body.

LaJune and her two-day-old baby, Micah, had come came home from the hospital that morning. Nolita and Kendrick picked them up. Serpentine limped into LaJune's apartment about two o'clock in the afternoon.

"What happened to your leg?" Nolita asked as Serpentine eased herself down into the beige chair next to the door.

"I twisted my knee on the treadmill this morning," she replied.

"Good to know you're still trying to exercise, sugar. You can get that weight off, if you just stick to it," Nolita pushed.

Serpentine closed her eyes and imagined her mother as an alien with a big water head, four tentacles sticking out of her chest, and a green gooey substance dripping from her mouth. "Get off my planet!" she silently screamed. She was surprised that it worked. She laughed as she tiptoed into LaJune's room to tell her. She stopped in the doorway and watched the new mother and baby sleeping. LaJune's head leaned to the side of the bed and a low rumble came from her throat. Micah was resting comfortably in her last-minute, on-sale pink canopy bed.

Serpentine changed directions and moved into the den to hang out with her dad. She'd have to endure whatever sporting event he had on television. Fly-fishing was the sport of the hour. They watched as a middle-aged white man stood in the middle of a tiny boat in the middle of a huge lake and cast his line into the middle of the calm liquid.

Just as a huge bass grabbed the line and yanked the pole forward, LaJune entered the den with Micah in her arms.

"Hey, baby," Nolita cooed at the tiny bundle in LaJune's arms, rushing into the room to collect her first grandchild.

LaJune reluctantly handed the child over.

"Do you need anything?" Kendrick asked LaJune as he got up to go into the kitchen.

"No, not right now, Daddy," LaJune replied, not taking her eyes off Nolita and Micah.

Serpentine sat still in the chair. "How you feeling, June?" she asked.

"I'm better. The doctor says I'll be sore for a while," she explained.

Nolita sat down on the couch and slid her finger into Micah's palm. Micah held on tightly. "Hi, Micah," she purred. "I love your name, Micah. You're going to be a modern-day prophet, aren't you?"

When the doorbell rang, Kendrick answered it, and Aunt Regina hurried in.

"Where's my great-niece?" she asked in her booming voice. Regina walked straight over to Nolita, scooping the baby out of her arms. "Come here to your great-auntie," she said, smothering the child in her hefty bosom.

"I'm doing just fine, Auntie," LaJune said mockingly. "Thank you for asking."

"I know you're okay, girl. It's this precious little lady I'm interested in," she replied sharply.

LaJune frowned. "You know grown folks have germs that they can pass on to little babies. Everybody can't be breathing all over her."

Regina rolled her eyes, sat down on the couch, and reestablished her connection with Micah. "You and Serpentine both survived my germs. What makes you think Micah won't? Ain't that right, baby? Your mama is so silly, isn't she?"

Kendrick entered the room with a bowl of beef stew and a spoon.

"How do you like your old sorry granny?" Regina asked the bundle in her arms. "Remember, she's your example of who not to be like."

"I told you I don't want to be called no damn granny," Nolita said forcefully. "Madear is what she's going to call me."

"Your grandma got a bad attitude, Micah," Regina whispered to the baby.

Then Regina fell silent. After a few moments, she spoke very softly. "A new baby is such a wonderful occasion for us all to be together," she said. She didn't say anything else; she didn't have to. They all knew what she was thinking. Regina had lost her only child, Samuel's child. The baby boy had lived only a few days because of complications with the development of his lungs, and Regina never got pregnant again, even though she and Samuel tried. Several years later, Samuel died of cirrhosis of the liver.

As Serpentine sat and watched her aunt, she felt bad. There were so many terrible mothers who shouldn't have babies, while Regina, who would have been a great mother, wasn't blessed with a child. Regina would probably never have made her kids eat broccoli.

"Kendrick, what's in the bowl?" Regina asked.

Kendrick finished a bite and smacked his lips before he spoke. "I made some great beef stew. You should try it."

"I'm going to get some. You want me to get you a bowl, Aunt Regina?" Serpentine asked.

"Sure, baby."

Serpentine disappeared into the kitchen for a minute, then returned and set Regina's bowl on the coffee table.

Kendrick finished his last spoonful and stood up. "I'll take my grandbaby so you can eat," he ordered.

Regina held the baby up. "I'm gonna let you spend a moment with your grandpa. Be nice to him. Remember, he can't help it that he's funny-looking," she told the baby, then kissed her fingers.

Serpentine got herself a bowl of stew and sat at the dining room table to eat it.

"You get that diet I sent you last week, Serpentine?" Nolita asked.

Serpentine rolled her eyes up into her head. "Yeah, I got it, Mom," she mumbled. "I threw it in the trash."

"Leave her alone about a diet," Regina spoke up. "Ain't nothing wrong with her size. She's an African queen and her body comes direct from the motherland."

"You'd better be careful because you're spreading all over the place, too," Nolita warned her sister.

Regina stuck her chest out. "My baby, Pee Jay, don't complain. He loves what I got, so your opinion is not important, is it? You need to put some meat on those puny bones of yours, so Kendrick can have something to grab hold to." Regina winked at Serpentine.

"Kendrick likes me as I am, don't you, baby?" Nolita asked.

"Everybody looks fine, so let's drop it," Kendrick answered, abruptly.

Nolita snorted. "Who is this Pee Jay, anyway?"

"He's my honey. You'll meet him later. I invited him over," Regina responded.

"Nice of you to inform me that you have someone coming by," Nolita said, eyeing her sister. "How long you been seeing him?"

"Long enough," Regina replied, sharply.

Nolita seemed agitated. "Well, tell me something about the man!" she demanded.

"Serpentine's met him. She can fill you in," Regina said with a smile.

All eyes were now on Serpentine, who looked back and forth between her mother and Regina, then spoke: "He's a nice guy, kind of country, but okay."

Regina winked. "Now, are you satisfied?"

LaJune shifted in her chair in obvious pain.

"How you feeling, June?" Kendrick asked.

"I'm okay, Dad. Thanks for caring. Nobody else seems to," La-June pouted.

"Girl, you ain't the baby no more. So you might as well get used to it. This little angel done changed everything," Nolita told her.

Kendrick looked into his granddaughter's half-closed eyes. "She's beautiful, June," he said. "Just beautiful."

"She looks like her aunt Serpentine," Serpentine teased.

"Yeah, right. You wish you looked that good," LaJune snapped back. "My baby could be a Gerber baby."

"Y'all need glasses—this baby is the spitting image of me," Regina concluded.

"I think I should head to the restroom. I feel a need coming on," LaJune announced, pulling herself up and out of the chair slowly.

Nolita watched LaJune leave the room and shook her head. "June, your hips have really spread," she observed out loud.

Before LaJune could respond, Serpentine exploded. "Damn, Mama! She just had a baby! Why do you always have to focus on people's weight? Would you give it a rest?"

"What did I say except the truth?" Nolita asked in her defense.

"Well, nobody wants to hear that shit!" Serpentine replied angrily. "Her hips are part of the miracle of childbirth. They should be revered as a national treasure."

"I don't know why you always get so bent out of shape, Serpentine. I can't help it that I'm an honest soul and I speak my mind."

"Here, Nolita," Kendrick said, standing up. "Take your grand-baby and be quiet. We ain't been here but a couple of days and you already got everybody upset. I'm going to get some coffee. Anybody else want anything?"

"Daddy, could you bring me a Pepsi?" LaJune asked as she ducked into the bathroom.

"Nolita, you want anything?" Kendrick asked.

"Is it okay for me to speak now?" she replied in an annoyed tone.

"Only to answer this one question," Kendrick teased.

Nolita rocked back and forth with Micah. "Nothing, I don't want nothing," she said.

LaJune and Micah were soon back in bed, while Kendrick dozed in the big gold chair. Serpentine napped on a comfortable pallet on the floor. Nolita and Regina sat on the couch and watched a rerun of *Barney Miller*.

"Whenever I see these reruns, I always think of Samuel," Regina told her sister nostalgically.

"Samuel always talked about *Barney Miller*," Nolita replied. "There was that one episode he laughed about all the time. Remember the stockbroker who lost his job on Wall Street and became a bum begging on the street? He used to laugh so hard tears would come to his eyes."

Regina lay her head on her sister's shoulder. "My Samuel was a character, wasn't he?"

"Remember that family reunion in Oklahoma when Samuel needed to use the restroom?" Kendrick asked with one eye open.

Serpentine chuckled as Regina started the story. "He injured his kidneys in a tank accident in the army. So when he had to go, he had to go."

Nolita continued: "He tried to ask one of the grocery store clerks where the restroom was, but the boy ignored him and just walked away."

"Poor Samuel," Regina jumped in.

"He was trying to make it outside, but he couldn't, so he whipped it out in aisle fifteen and pissed all down the canned goods, from the asparagus to the peas!"

LaJune entered the room as it filled with a deep, full laughter.

"I was waiting at the checkout lane," Kendrick added, "when he flew past me, heading for the car. He didn't say a word about it until we got back to the house. I went back to the store to get pictures, otherwise nobody would've believed me. Are those pictures still in the photo album, Nolita?"

"Yes, Kendrick," Nolita groaned.

The doorbell chimed and Serpentine got up to answer it.

She opened the door and there stood Pee Jay on the other side in all his splendor. He wore a big brown cowboy hat with his tight jeans and a blue-and-beige checkered shirt.

"Hey, Pee Jay." Serpentine looked him up and down. He was definitely country as hell, but kind of cute, now that she took a good look, with long curly eyelashes.

"What's up, Serpentine?" Pee Jay bellowed.

"Not much. Everybody's in the den. Follow me."

Serpentine snickered. She hoped Regina had prepared Pee Jay for Nolita, because she knew Nolita wasn't prepared for him.

Regina grabbed Pee Jay's arm as soon as he entered the room. "I want you guys to meet Pee Jay."

Kendrick stood up and offered a handshake.

Nolita nodded. "Hello."

Regina cut her eyes in Nolita's direction.

"It's great to meet you good people. Big Mama has talked so much about you that I feel like family already."

Nolita frowned when she heard her sister referred to as Big Mama. Serpentine snickered as she watched her mother's response.

"Well, Pee Jay, what do you do?" Kendrick asked the question that was on everybody's mind.

"I'm working at Mount Glory right now, cleaning up and other odds and ends. But I'll probably be driving a limo for Harvey's Limos, downtown, starting next month."

"I'm retired. Taught math for thirty-five years."

Pee Jay took a seat on the couch next to Regina. "Teaching is a good job. When I was up at Muddy River I knew a guy who had all kinds of degrees—B.A., M.A., Ph.D.—even had a law degree, I think. Income tax fraud. He said he planned to teach when he got out."

Nolita's frown grew broader as Pee Jay spoke. She excused herself and disappeared into the kitchen.

"You hungry, Pee Jay? There's beef stew," Regina offered.

"I'd love to try some, if it's not too much trouble," he answered.

Regina went into the kitchen, got a bowl out of the cabinet, and began to scoop out the stew.

"I'm gonna get some water. Anybody want anything?" Serpentine asked as she followed Regina.

"Where in the world did you find this one?" Nolita asked sarcastically as Regina entered the kitchen.

"You got something to say, say it," Regina replied.

"Where did you even meet such a character?" Nolita continued.

"At the prison, if you must know. He's Reverend Middleton's cousin."

Nolita cocked her head to the side. "That explains it. You'll do anything for that reverend of yours, including pick his cousin up out of the gutter."

"Get a grip, Nolita."

Serpentine stood still watching the fireworks.

"I just wish you would find somebody nice to replace Samuel, Regina. It seems each one is worse than the last," Nolita complained.

"How do you know he's not as good as Samuel? He recently joined Glory and he asked me to marry him," Regina shot back.

Nolita grimaced. "Marry him? The man's a jailbird. Lord, Regina! You can't be that desperate!"

Regina laughed at her baby sister. "Desperate like when you got pregnant by Kendrick to make him marry you?"

Nolita rolled her eyes. "You know I didn't do that on purpose."

"Other people have lives, Nolita, and even though they don't fit in with what *you* think is best, you have to let us live them."

"So, I'm not suppose to care about my family?" Nolita asked.

Regina grabbed the paperback dictionary from the cabinet where LaJune sat each morning and worked on her crossword puzzles—the only habit she and Nolita shared. Regina tossed the dictionary to her sister. "Look up the word caring, then look up the word meddling. They're not the same thing."

Nolita caught the book.

"You'd better get it together before you run everybody who cares about you out of your life."

Nolita turned and stomped out of the kitchen, while Serpentine stared at her aunt.

"You want to say something, too?" Regina asked irritably.

"No," Serpentine mumbled.

"Your mother just gets me so riled up."

Serpentine glanced at the door. "She says things without thinking about other people's feelings. She does it to me so often, sometimes I wonder if she cares at all."

Regina attached her hand to her hip. "Now what would make you say something crazy like that?"

Serpentine pulled a spoon out of the silverware drawer. "You know she's always picking at me. It gets on my nerves."

"She picks at me, too, as *you* just saw, and at your father, and LaJune. That's just her way. The more she picks at you, the more she loves you."

Serpentine shot her aunt a look of skepticism.

Regina continued, "I've known your mama all my life and you've just got to learn how to sift through her words; take what you want and toss the rest aside."

"I guess you're right," Serpentine mumbled. "But it's hard."

"You can't let folks stick you into their boxes and that includes your mama," Regina warned. "You've got to love yourself, Serpentine, in order for anybody else to love you. If you know who you are, you won't have to apologize to nobody for being you."

Regina kissed Serpentine on the cheek.

"You really gonna marry Pee Jay?"

"I might. Maybe I'll have that big church wedding me and Samuel never got around to. How do you feel about that?"

"I'll be your maid of honor."

"Thanks, baby. I'd like that," Regina said with a hug. "Now, I'd better go rescue the potential groom from your mama."

Nutty Professor

Last night I rented the video of Eddie Murphy's movie The Nutty Professor *again. Too bad most people dismissed that movie as a comedy, because it was so much more. I remember the first time I saw it. I sat in that dark movie theater with my sister LaJune on one side and my cousin Tevan on the other, totally paralyzed.*

When Klump realized that the comedian, whose show involved humiliating people in the audience, was moving in his direction, there was a look of terror on his face that I know too well.

Klump tried to get away, but he knocked over a tray and brought the comedian's attention directly to him. I know his heart stopped because mine did. The music rose as the comedian focused his attack on Klump's enormous size. At that moment, Klump's pain was my pain, his embarrassment was my embarrassment, and his anger was my anger.

A couple of scenes later Klump was at home watching Richard Simmons and stuffing half-gallons of ice cream and jars of M&M's into his mouth. I hate the fact that that's what everybody thinks we do, sit around and eat mounds of ice cream, cookies, and candy.

I can't say I don't eat, or even that I don't like to eat, but what I eat does somehow affect me differently. It's a downright dirty shame that scientists can put a robot on Mars to pick up rocks, but they can't figure out how to help people struggling with weight issues.

The saddest part of the movie was when Klump fell asleep and he dreamed that he couldn't stop gaining weight. He became a Godzilla-like monster storming the streets and terrorizing normal people. He saw himself as a monster. He believed that something was wrong with him.

In the end, when Klump told everybody that he finally understood that life was about being happy with yourself no matter what size you are, I cried. I remember wondering, as the lights came up and the credits rolled, how many people actually got it.

☙❧ ☙❧ ☙❧

Serpentine wandered through the grocery store trying to decide what she wanted to eat for dinner. She had another group therapy session tomorrow, but her mind was still fastened on the first one, when she had wished that the pounds would drop off effortlessly. Perry was right—she didn't want to work hard anymore.

Over the past twenty-five years she'd been on every diet imaginable: yogurt, astronaut's, Dr. Atkins', banana-and-milk, Opti-Fast, grapefruit, Dr. Stillman's, Weight Watchers, Jenny Craig, Olympic, high-fat, low-fat, Boston Police, Richard Simmons, drinking man's, starvation, liquid, vegetarian, fruit, rice, carbohydrate, and so many others that their names had faded away. And none of that hard work had proved worthy in the long haul. She wasn't alone; millions of people were stumbling down the same path, searching for an answer.

As she pushed the basket down each aisle, reading the product names, it suddenly struck her that there was a lot of fat-free food available. There were fat-free chocolate chip cookies and barbe-cued potato chips, nonfat caramel corn and mocha fudge ice cream, 99 percent fat-free lunch meat and 90 percent fat-free hamburger. She had been eating a lot of this fat-free stuff, but her weight was going up, instead of down. Something was wrong.

By buying into this fat-free scam, she was like a lonely woman who'd let a fast-talking hustler into her life. She pulled a small notebook from her purse and started jotting down notes. Maybe there was a story in this—a special report on weight loss.

The next day, when she pitched the idea to Evan, to her amazement, he immediately saw its potential and told her to run with it. WXYZ ran the series at a time when everybody else was praising fat-free food as the miracle cure-all for obesity.

The first segment of her "Fat-Free Farce" series introduced the basic principles of fat-free eating. Serpentine did extensive library and Internet research, then conducted interviews with nutritionists and other experts. She explained what foods to stay away from—those high in fat, such as french fries, potato chips, oils, butter, salad dressing, and whole milk.

In her second "Fat-Free" report, Serpentine gave tips for low-fat eating, such as removing the fat and skin from meats; baking and broiling rather than frying; using fewer saturated fats and more monounsaturated fats, like olive and canola oils. She also discussed good foods to eat, including fruits and vegetables, low-fat yogurt and skim milk, bread, rice, pasta, and beans.

Serpentine had to be delicate in pitching her third segment to Evan because she wanted to look at the media's role in fueling the fat-free fire. She knew she had to step lightly because some of the fat-free food companies she wanted to talk about sponsored the newscast and other shows on WXYZ.

She led the third report with information about unrealistic media images of women created by airbrushing and silicone implants. Then she talked about the media's unkind treatment of actresses such as Alicia Silverstone from the hit movie *Clueless*. When Silverstone gained a few noticeable pounds between her movie release and the Academy Awards ceremony, the tabloids ridiculed her with headlines about her upcoming role: "Batman and Fatgirl" and "Look Out, Batman, Here Comes Buttgirl!"

Fascinated by a study that suggested that black women seemed to accept their fuller bodies more easily than white women, Serpentine interviewed a focus group of black and white women about their diets. She found that both relied heavily on fat-free foods: black women used it most often to lose weight, while white women used them more to keep the weight off.

What she also uncovered was that some black women who said they accepted themselves demonstrated the opposite. One participant bragged that she didn't worry about what people said, then cried all through *The Nutty Professor* video when the group watched it. Another participant qualified her acceptance, saying she refused to wear anything sleeveless because she didn't like the flab on her arms; otherwise she was content with her larger-sized body.

For the fourth segment, Serpentine assembled a research crew for a road trip to Madison, Wisconsin, including Marleen as executive producer and a new photographer named Damon. They spent Saturday afternoon at the University of Wisconsin, meeting with researchers who had examined the link between media images and eating disorders. Serpentine set up interviews with several participants in the study, as well as Dr. Rebecca Daily, who conducted it.

She noticed on the way to Madison that there was some kind of tension between Damon and Marleen, but blew it off. As the day wore on, however, the tension got thicker until it couldn't be ignored. Finally, when Marleen slammed a door in Damon's face, Serpentine pulled her to the side.

"What's going on with you two?" she asked.

"He's ridiculous," Marleen replied, then caught herself. "It's nothing, I'm sorry, I'll try to control my temper."

"I hope so, because this is the only shot we have at getting these interviews, and I don't need any mistakes," Serpentine warned.

Less than an hour later, Serpentine found herself rushing down the hall toward familiar voices raised in an argument. When she rounded the corner, moving through a crowd of students, she saw Marleen smack Damon's face. In return, he forcefully grabbed Marleen, pushing her up against the wall.

"What the hell is wrong with you two?" Serpentine shouted, pulling them apart. "Would somebody please tell me what this is about?"

"I'm a man and I'm going to be treated like a man!" Damon shouted at Marleen.

Serpentine turned to her best friend. "What is he talking about?"

"He's an asshole who can't deal with a woman in charge. Every time I ask him to get a specific shot he gives me lip," Marleen explained.

Damon set the camera down on the floor. "She needs to ask for the shots like a professional, not bark orders at me like I'm her indentured servant," he replied.

Serpentine took a deep breath. "Look, I really don't give a damn what the problem is, but you two must stop this immediately! We've got another hour and then we have to hit the road and get back. It's already starting to rain," she screeched, then stormed away.

"*Man,* my ass," she heard Marleen mumble as she followed.

Once Serpentine got the interview with Dr. Daily in the can she felt much better. They discussed, in detail, the connection between eating disorders like obesity, anorexia, and bulimia, and the impact of unreal images that bombard women on television, in movies, and in magazine advertisements. Dr. Daily's study gave her much of the confirmation she needed to demonstrate how problematic the media's obsession with thinness as a norm could be, especially for teenagers.

On the ride home, the rain was pouring down. Serpentine pampered her headache by popping four Tylenol, and falling asleep on the back seat of the van. Marleen stretched out on the middle seat, while Damon drove. But thirty minutes later, Serpentine woke up when Marleen nudged her shoulder.

"Serpentine," Marleen whispered.

"Huh? What?" Serpentine asked, sitting up quickly.

Marleen shook her head. "Something's wrong with Damon," she said. "He's driving too fast and the road's really slick."

Serpentine leaned forward and scanned the road. It was pitch black and the rain was falling in thick sheets.

She could barely see ten feet in front of her, yet the speedometer read seventy miles an hour. Serpentine moved up to the seat behind Damon.

"Damon, I want you to pull the van over," she instructed calmly.

Damon didn't respond. He just kept his foot on the gas pedal and stared straight ahead.

Serpentine added some force to her second request. "Did you hear me, Damon? I said slow down and pull the van over!"

"I can't," Damon replied in a quiet tone that made Serpentine's heart race.

"What do you mean you can't? This is an order, not a request!"

"I'm in control," Damon told her, and tightened his grip on the steering wheel. "I'm sick of women questioning my ability."

"You're not making sense, Damon."

Marleen whispered in her ear, "I think he wants us to acknowledge that he's in charge."

Serpentine pushed her away. "Be quiet, girl, I know that."

A blue-and-white sign announcing gas and food at the next exit flew by, and Serpentine got an idea. "Okay, look, Damon, you can continue driving, but at least stop at this next exit and let me go to the toilet," she pleaded.

Damon hesitated, but he finally slowed down and followed the exit ramp off the highway. When he stopped in the gas station lot, Marleen and Serpentine both hopped out of the van. Serpentine made her way around to the driver's side window and tapped on it. Damon locked his door.

"What the hell did you do to him, Marleen?" Serpentine asked as they hustled into the gas station and out of the rain.

Marleen gave Serpentine a curious look. "I didn't do nothing to him," she said. "We went out a few weeks ago and he couldn't get it up. He's been acting stupid ever since."

"Why didn't you tell me that shit earlier?" Serpentine asked. "We could have brought a different photographer."

Marleen shrugged. "I thought we would work it out. Serpentine, you've got to do something, because I'm not getting back in the van with that fool."

"We'll have to figure something out when I get back. I really do have to go to the toilet, *bad,*" Serpentine said, hurrying toward the back.

Marleen waited at the front entrance until Serpentine returned. "Okay, now let's see if we can get this man out of the driver's seat," Serpentine said.

"He's gone," Marleen replied.

"Gone where? What do you mean?" Serpentine asked in a

panic, looking out in the parking lot for the van. She sighed with relief when she saw the van sitting in the same spot.

"I don't know. He got out of the van and walked over that way." Marleen pointed.

"Are the keys inside?" Serpentine asked, rushing out the door.

"I wasn't going out there by myself," Marleen replied, then followed.

Serpentine stepped up on the running board and peeked inside. No keys in the ignition.

"Here they are on the passenger seat," Marleen said from the other side.

"Thank God." Serpentine got into the van.

Marleen jumped in on the other side.

"Where do you think he went?" Serpentine asked.

"I don't know, but we should leave before he comes back."

"I'm going to try to find him," Serpentine said, opening the door.

"Don't, Serpentine, let's just get away from here," Marleen pleaded.

"Lock the doors. I'll be right back."

Serpentine walked around the building and had a guy check the restroom, but there was no sign of Damon. They waited another twenty minutes before they headed back to the city.

"I've been thinking," Marleen said as they drove into the city limits.

"It's about time," Serpentine spat out.

"Seriously. We could have been killed by that nut and it would have been my fault," Marleen continued.

"I done told you about playing with these crazy men, Marleen. It may seem exciting, but you're not a teenager anymore, and times have changed. There are some really sick people out there."

"I don't know why I can't find a nice guy."

"You don't pick nice guys, Marleen. You pick assholes, then act surprised when they show you their behinds."

"You talk like I do it on purpose," Marleen defended herself.

"A couple of months ago you were dating that carpenter. Granted a simple guy, but he would've done anything for you,

Marleen, and what happened? You dumped him for that archi-
tect who treated you like shit."

"I'm just trying to find my pot of gold at the end of the rain-
bow," Marleen protested.

Serpentine laughed and shook her head. "You're probably too
late and somebody's already got it."

Damon didn't show up at work to get his pink slip, so Serpentine
never did find out how he got home. Weeks later Marleen heard
that Damon was back down south, where his family lived, in rehab.

The final segment of Serpentine's special report hit the industry
hard, justifying its title, "Fat-Free Farce." The segment started
with close-up shots of fat-free foods on grocery shelves, and then
Serpentine walked into the camera shot and began her introduction.

"What does fat-free really mean?" she asked. "We're eating fat-
free foods the way we're told, yet we keep getting bigger. What's
going on?"

The report then cut to an interview with a local nutritionist, Dr.
Gerard Caius, who explained that the fat was usually replaced by
sugar, which meant additional problems for those who thought
they were on the right track to losing weight.

"Check the labels," Serpentine continued in her stand-up.
"Stay away from low-fat foods where the fat has been replaced by
sugar, corn syrup, or fructose. Such alternative forms of sweeten-
ing can be just as bad as the fat."

The report cut to comments from two Chicago State University
roommates who swore by fat-free foods. Footage of their dorm
room showed an extensive line-up of fat-free foods along their
shelves and packed in their small refrigerator.

Serpentine edited in a poignant statement from the medium-
built freshman: "I don't feel as guilty when I eat fat-free snacks. I
can eat as much as I want, because the fat, which is the problem,
is gone."

She ended the last segment in front of the dormitory. "Most of
us have been on diets at some time or another and when we hear
about each new miracle we raise our hopes up to the sky and cast

our doubts into the wind. Unfortunately, this new fat-free miracle is not the answer, at least not by itself. 'Fat-free' doesn't mean calorie-free. As a matter of fact, if you compare the labels, you will find that there is very little difference between a fat-free and regular Oreo cookie. The experts maintain that the key to weight loss is still consistent exercise with moderate food intake. For WXYZ in Chicago, I'm Serpentine Williamson."

Just Say Thank You

I accepted a compliment for the first time today and it was an invigorating experience. A woman at work told me she envied my "natural beauty." I was about to respond but my fire took control, saying: Don't sabotage it.

I laughed because that was exactly what I was about to do. I was going to say: "Most people have their own special beauty." Or I may have flat out denied it by saying: "You've got to be kidding, with the luggage I'm carrying under these eyes."

Instead, I followed my fire and absorbed all that positivity into my soul. I simply said, "Thank you."

I do have a natural beauty. My mother, my sister, and especially my aunt Regina were also blessed. We all have smooth brown skin and enticing smiles with curvy bodies of various sizes. We could easily cut ten years off our ages and get away with it.

I felt empowered like never before at that moment because I just said: Thank you.

ೞ ೞ ೞ

Just as Evan had said, Mitsy, the weekend anchor, had announced her pregnancy and her decision to leave the station. Serpentine was nervous, but determined to convince Cameron Marshall that she was the right choice for the anchor position. She selected her navy blue zip-front suit for the interview because it was slenderizing.

When she entered the WXYZ building, she took the long way around to Marshall's office, because she didn't want to risk running into Evan. The last thing she needed was his negativity bringing her down. She wished she could have lost a few pounds before the interview, but she'd just have to work with what she had.

She stopped outside Marshall's door and waited. She could hear voices inside laughing. It was ten o'clock, time for her appointment, so she knocked. In a few minutes the door opened and Trina stepped out with a big plastic grin on her face.

"Oh, Serpentine, go on in, he's expecting you," she said, then practically skipped down the hall.

Serpentine entered the spacious room and quickly glanced around. She wasn't surprised that Marshall played golf, but she was surprised to see two basketball trophies on a shelf by the window. She also noticed right away the 5 × 7 picture of a blue-eyed baby that sat on his desk.

"Ms. Williamson, good to see you." Marshall stood, shook her hand, and waved her to a chair.

Serpentine tried to look confident despite the small stream of fear that trickled through her soul.

"Thank you, Mr. Marshall," she said, sitting down. "Is this your grandbaby?" She pointed to the photo.

"No, that's my son, Justin," Marshall answered stiffly.

"Oh, oh, he's a doll," Serpentine stammered.

"Thanks." Marshall nodded, then continued. "You're one of our top candidates for this position, Ms. Williamson, but I have to be honest, the competition is steep."

"I realize that, but no one has worked as hard as I have for WXYZ, and, to be direct, sir, no one is as good for this position as I am."

"I like your confidence, Ms. Williamson. As you know, we are hoping to move someone from inside the company into the position rather than hire from the outside, so you have an advantage there. Can I call you Serpentine?" he asked.

"Sure."

Marshall smiled and folded his arms across his chest.

"We need to talk briefly about the focus-group report. I understand from Evan that you were not very happy with it," he said.

Serpentine hesitated. "Well, I do disagree with Mr. Wilson's viewpoint. There were too few people and their comments were vague and conflicting."

"And, what about your personal criticisms? How should we deal with them?" he asked.

Serpentine looked down at the floor, took a deep breath, then looked directly at him. "Personally, I don't think those criticisms mean very much when you look at the big picture," she said.

Marshall didn't speak right away. He unfolded his arms and picked up a paper clip off his desk. "You are an excellent reporter, Serpentine. What we have to determine is whether or not you would bring the same excellence to this anchor position."

At that moment, Serpentine decided to throw her major fear out there to see how he would deal with it. "We should be honest, Mr. Marshall, I'm not a little cutesy size eight, but I can do this job as well as anyone, if not better. My interviewing skills are thorough, my writing skills are excellent, and my presentational style is impressive."

Marshall's facial expression didn't change. He cocked his head sideways and studied her. "I know that, Serpentine. But there are other considerations in hiring the best person for this spot. As an anchor you won't do much interviewing and writing; the whole focus will be on your presentation. Your weight is an important part of that presentation."

"Do you know what discrimination is, Mr. Marshall?" Serpentine asked.

"Excuse me?" Mr. Marshall mumbled.

"Discrimination is bias and all bias comes from the same root: the belief that everybody has to look, sound, and act the same."

Marshall seemed at a loss for words. "I guess you're entitled to your own opinion," he said finally. "Is there anything else you'd like to discuss about the position itself?"

"I'd like to know how much this focus-group report will figure into the decision," Serpentine pressed, refusing to let him shake and shimmy on her dime.

Mr. Marshall narrowed his eyes and leaned forward with a pompous seriousness. "It will figure in a lot, Serpentine," he said. "We hired that firm to help us increase our ratings, we paid them big money, and we would be stupid not to take their recommendations seriously."

Serpentine stood up abruptly. "Well, then, I won't waste any more of your time," she said, walking to the door. "But, you know what, Mr. Marshall?" she added, standing in the doorway. "No matter how you dress it up, shit stinks!"

Serpentine regretted her words the instant she walked out the door. She knew she had blown it. She took note of how she felt, at that moment, and noticed that she didn't feel bad. She had told the truth and there wasn't anything wrong with that. She chuckled. Marshall had gotten tongue-tied when she stood up for herself. She was glad that she didn't accept his business-as-usual garbage. Doc was right, she was changing. Before she would have fallen apart as soon as he confirmed that her weight was a problem, but now, she refused to allow such a load to break her down. Instead she would carry it differently.

Serpentine was guest speaker at Mount Glory that afternoon for a youth program called Teen Talk. She decided this was another chance to put her new philosophy into motion. There were a hundred impressionable young minds waiting when she walked into the sanctuary. She looked around the room and thought again about her meeting with Mr. Marshall that morning. She was taking control of her life and she wanted to let these kids know that they could do the same.

After a brief introduction from Sister Washington, Serpentine walked up to the podium and set her outline on the subject of success on the lectern in front of her.

"Unfortunately, in this brief workshop I'm probably not going to tell you anything new or exciting," she said, nervously shifting her feet in her new navy pumps. They pinched her toes mercilessly.

She continued. "Success is probably a little bit of luck, some of God's guiding hand, but mostly under your own control. What you need first is a clear understanding of what success means to you."

Several girls near the back of the room were talking and giggling, so Serpentine decided to get them involved.

"Excuse me, ladies," she said. "Can you tell me what success means to you?"

The first girl, obviously the leader, lifted her head, responding in a high-pitched voice. "When I make a million dollars, then I'll be successful," she said, and followed it with a high-five from her partner.

"Okay," Serpentine continued. "Success is different for everybody. What about the rest of your homegirls, do they have a goal for success?"

Her buddy shouted out in a much deeper voice: "I want the same, a million dollars." They slapped palms again.

"Do you plan to share her million or do you want your own?" Serpentine asked calmly, waiting for a response. Working with the Upward Bound program in college had taught her one thing about teenagers: You can't back down if you want them to listen to you.

The rest of the group aggravated the conflict with a long "Ohhhh."

The deep-voiced girl copped an attitude. "I want my own million, what you think?" She rolled her eyes.

Serpentine didn't let up. "Well, how do you plan to get your million?"

"I got skills," High-pitched spat back with the intense anger that Serpentine knew resided in this generation.

She grew worried that she might not reach them. The crossing rails were down, the lights were flashing, but the train was nowhere in sight. She decided to shift direction and let things calm down for a while.

"What I'm trying to get everyone to recognize is how success works. You have to be very clear about what you want and how you plan to get it. For example, there are success fantasies and success realities. My success fantasy is to become a renowned television personality like Barbara Walters or Oprah Winfrey, but my success reality is to live a happy, comfortable life that includes a peaceful family, financial security, and spiritual contentment."

A homeboy from the fifth row raised his hand, and Serpentine acknowledged him. "Do you have to have a success fantasy?" he asked.

"No, of course not," Serpentine replied. "But most people do. It is very important that you be honest when you decide on your success goals, and realistic."

The group in the back started to ignore her again and they got louder with each exchange.

"For example, having a million dollars is a great fantasy, but is it realistic?" She threw the question out to the group in back. She didn't want the girls to feel she was picking on them, but she wanted their attention.

"No!" a few of the kids shouted.

"That's true, it may not be realistic."

"How the hell do you know what's realistic for me?" the leader's high-pitched voice shouted.

"You're right. I don't know," Serpentine replied quickly. "But to think about making a million dollars is somewhat overwhelming. If you separate it into pieces it seems more reasonable. For example, you could start with ten thousand, then add another ten and another ten. And, eventually, you would get there."

"When my rap group blows up, we gonna bring home phat millions every month. None of that 'ten thousand here and there' crap. You better recognize," the leader retorted.

Serpentine met the challenge. "I hope you're right," she said. "And I promise when your group does take off, I'll be one of the first people to buy your CD. What's the name of the group?"

"Kuumuba—that means creativity in Swahili," the girl answered with pride.

"I want everybody to keep a lookout for Kuumuba. We need to support our sisters in their musical endeavor."

Serpentine saw a smirk, and then the girl's nod of approval. She had saved face in front of her peers.

Serpentine moved on. "Success is about believing. It's obvious that this young lady believes in her dream and therefore has an excellent chance of achieving it."

The speech continued for another thirty minutes, as Serpentine explained techniques for effective communication, time management, goal setting, and positive self-concept.

Serpentine's excitement level finally began to drop. She wanted to get to a phone and call Marleen to see what rumors she'd heard concerning the anchor position. So she cut her wrap-up down to fifteen minutes, leaving time for a few questions.

"In conclusion, remember you are what you believe," she told them. "If you believe you're a hoochie, hottie, bitch, or hoe, you'll probably be one. If you don't, you probably won't."

"Those women who show their bodies and dance all nasty in videos are hoochies. That's a bad self-concept, right?" a chubby girl in the front row threw out.

"That's not true. They're just acting, and getting paid, stupid," Deep Voice shouted before Serpentine could respond.

"Well, I wouldn't act like that," the chubby girl continued.

"That's 'cause don't nobody wanna see your big ass up there in no video," High-pitched added.

"I wouldn't do it no matter how I looked," the larger girl said defensively. "And you can kiss this here big ass, bitch!"

The smaller girl jumped up from her seat and acted as if she were coming up front to take action, but two of her friends grabbed her and held her in place.

"Wait a minute, please," Serpentine said, hurrying down into the aisle. "This is exactly what I've been talking about. The self is learned. It's shaped and developed by your experience and knowledge." She turned to the smaller girl in back. "What makes you think this young lady couldn't be in a video if she wanted to?"

" 'Cause she don't look like none of those women that be up there," the girl said with arrogance.

Serpentine unconsciously put her hand on her hip. "So my next question is, who makes the decision that she can't be in a video, and why do we have to accept that decision?"

The leader sat with a puzzled look on her face, then spoke: "I guess you can do what you want if you got the money, but who gonna watch her fat ass dance?"

Suddenly both girls were up and pushing toward each other again with Serpentine in the middle.

"I'll kick your skinny ass down the hall, you keep talking," the chubby girl warned.

"Listen to you two!" Serpentine shouted, and the room got quiet. "You're calling each other names and ready to fight not because of what you believe, but because of what the media tells you to believe!"

"Whatever!" the leader shot back.

Serpentine felt like she was in the middle of a war, or at least some sort of skirmish, and she wasn't sure if her side was winning or losing. "If I were making a music video and this young lady had talent, I could put her in my video if I wanted to."

The buddy spoke up with her deeper voice. "And ain't nobody gonna watch it, 'cause don't nobody want to see her up there shaking that flab."

Many of the kids in the room laughed.

"Be careful whose ideas you allow into your head," Serpentine warned. "Who has the right to say what's beautiful and what's not?"

The buddy hesitated, then added, "No disrespect or anything, Ms. Williamson, but I wouldn't be considered beautiful enough for those videos either. My skin is too dark and my nose is too big. That's just the way it is."

What was left of Serpentine's energy fizzled out with that simple comment. This child was only about thirteen or fourteen years old and she already believed she wasn't beautiful.

"Well, I don't know about you, but I refuse to accept that idea," Serpentine persisted.

"Nobody is going to tell me I'm not beautiful, because I know better. And you should know it, too!"

Serpentine was relieved to get Sister Washington's signal that her time was up.

"None of you have to accept it!" she concluded. "None of you! But what happens if you believe you don't have the power to change things? Then you're right and you won't be able to change anything."

As the group gave her a lackluster round of applause, Serpentine hurried out into the hallway. She nodded and smiled at several girls, then stooped at the water fountain and slurped cool liquid into her mouth. That was exactly how she'd started out, twenty-five years ago. She didn't believe in herself, she didn't care, she didn't think she had the power to change things. Her heart ached when she thought about another generation of young black girls suffering in the same way. She froze when she heard the two familiar voices coming closer.

"You going to the Usher concert next week?" asked the high-pitched voice of the smaller girl.

"I wouldn't miss a concert with Usher. He know he too fine," the deeper voice replied.

"True dat," High-pitched agreed.

They came right up behind Serpentine, and the deep voice spoke: "Ms. Williamson, I wouldn't have said anything out loud in there, but I get tired of those video hoes, too. The men are always fully dressed and the women are running around with strings stuck up they butts."

"Girl, you don't know what you talkin' about. If I had the chance I'd be one of them hoes in a minute. They makin' big money and gettin' recognized. And ain't nothin' wrong with showin' off your body if it's nice," the girl with the high-pitched voice explained.

Serpentine stepped away from the water fountain and wiped her mouth. "Just learn to love yourselves. That's my message," she told them earnestly.

"Look for my group to blow up," High-pitched said as they walked away.

Serpentine shook her head as she stood and listened to the voices trail off down the hall. The last exchange made her sick to her stomach.

"What you wearin' to the concert?" Deep Voice asked just as they reached the front doors.

"I'm goin' anorexic this week, girl. I gotta get four or five pounds off so I can fit these thunder thighs into my sister's black leather miniskirt," High-pitched answered.

Neither one was bigger than a size ten. Serpentine watched until they vanished around the corner, then she went into the rest room to scream.

Seashells

Coming to this spa was the best idea I've had in a long time. It's good to be away from Chicago and have time to think. The sun, the beach, and the ocean make me feel lighthearted again. I actually had fun this afternoon picking up seashells from the sand. I kept six shells that I'm going to take back home because each one reminds me of someone I love.

The first is delicate and fan shaped on the outside, molded to a smooth solid surface underneath. It represents my mother, Nolita, who seems gentle at first, but eventually shows her true outspoken self in a ritual we call "Oooops Upside Your Head."

There's another that's tiny and white, with fragile ridges. It reflects the only person in my life who could exude such purity and innocence, my niece, Micah.

The next is a narrow shell with deep grooves along the sides and a long, sculptured curve in the middle. I got it to remind me that good guys are out there and I just have to look at my cousin Tevan for proof.

The mixed texture of a brown, well-worn seashell where soft and smooth areas blend with rough and lumpy ones represents my father, Kendrick.

Shades of pale yellow and hot pink streak the sides of another shell, colors that are a metaphor for my sister. LaJune is pale yellow leather clogs in church on Sunday morning and hot-pink, six-inch heels in a popular nightspot on Saturday night.

Finally, my aunt Regina's seashell is a bulky spiral cone with a bright, glossy finish. Her wide shoulders over ample hips are attached to big, pretty legs. It's a body that serves as an appropriate container for her exuberant spirit.

I've always tried to have an open mind and appreciate rather than judge the differences in the people around me. But when we look at people who are not like us through a limited scope it's easy to see ugly. In this society we don't like ugly and we judge it accordingly.

Serpentine had been listening to Dr. Greeley drone on and on about emotional stress for almost an hour, and her bathtub and scented candles were calling. When he finally stopped talking, she nodded, stood up, and inched her way to the door.

"Oh, Serpentine," Dr. Greeley added as the door swung open and freedom beckoned.

He walked over to his desk and looked down at a piece of paper as if he were reading something. "There is a question that you need to answer," he said, hesitating.

"Yes?" Serpentine spoke, just to nudge him a little.

"This is not a question that you have to answer for me or anyone else, but you should answer it for yourself." He looked up over his gold-rimmed glasses and flashed something her grandmother would have called a shitty grin.

"We've established that you love yourself. Now the next step is for you to determine how much." As Dr. Greeley let the words slide over his thin pink lips, he threw his right hand upward in a grand sweeping gesture.

Serpentine waited to see if there was more, but now he stood quietly, shifting from one foot to the other, as if the moment had passed and it was he who couldn't wait for Serpentine to get out of his office.

"Okay, I will," she said, then listened to the door shut behind her and the click of her shoes along the shiny tile floor. The elevator door dinged and opened just as she stepped in front of it. Serpentine was relieved when the doors were safely closed and she was alone inside. The elevator only stopped once, on the third floor, before it got her down to the lobby.

Serpentine hustled out into the hot noon air. Standing slightly bent, she thought about her initial response to Dr. Greeley's question.

"How can you question my love for myself?" That was the first thing that flashed into her head, but she shoved it back down. Her love for herself was not the problem: that fire had always burned intensely. It was her love for this life that needed help. That fire was weak and chaotic, burning only sporadically.

The push of the early May wind moved with Serpentine down the street until a sign in a large plate-glass window beckoned, promising change. A knot formed in the center of her stomach as she read the black-and-yellow letters. "How much do you love yourself? Enough to be pampered at a spa?"

In that moment Serpentine knew her guiding fire was at work. Sometimes it was a vivid blaze lighting her way. Other times it was a smoldering ember that allowed her to choose her own path. She followed the fire inside the double glass doors.

There were two women working: the older one was on the telephone confirming a trip to Bermuda for a long-standing client. The younger one finished pouring herself a cup of lemonade and motioned for Serpentine to sit down next to a paper-cluttered desk. She poured a second cup of lemonade and brought it to her.

"I'm Millie," she said, extending her right hand.

"Hi, I'm Serpentine," she replied, touching the extended fingers.

"What can I do for you?"

Serpentine turned and pointed to the sign. "I'd like to know more about spas," she explained, then took a small sip of the lemonade. "How expensive are they?"

Millie pulled out a folder full of brochures and handed it to Serpentine. "There are so many to choose from, I know we can find one in your price range," she said, confidently.

Serpentine listened to Millie's well-prepared spiel while she searched through the brochures, hoping the fire would lead the way.

"Are you interested in going to the mountains, or to a beach?" Millie asked.

"A beach, definitely."

"How long do you want to stay?"

"Three or four days over a weekend."

"Roommate or single?"

"Roommate."

"Vegetarian or meat?"

"Meat. No, either one. I'll try the vegetarian thing."

The woman clicked several keys on her computer, printed out two pages of information, and handed them to Serpentine.

"Here are three possible spas for you to look at. I think this one, Sunshine Spa in Fort Lauderdale, is your best choice."

Serpentine searched until she found the Sunshine Spa brochure in her pile and set the rest of the stack on the desk. As she studied the pictures of tall palm trees, a long, white, sandy beach, soothing massage treatments, and the blue ocean water, her guiding fire took control. She reached into her billfold and pulled out her Visa card to purchase two tickets.

During the twenty-minute ride from the airport to the spa that Friday afternoon, Serpentine and LaJune sat quietly, in awe of the luscious greenery all around. As Serpentine immersed herself in the pungent blue of the sky, tears came to her eyes unannounced and unexplained.

Every now and then Carlos, the van driver, would throw out an informative tidbit about Fort Lauderdale. He told them about how the Tequesta Indians founded the area in the 1800s; how the city had spent $670 million to build Fort Lauderdale into a showplace; how students invaded the city each year during spring break, causing chaos; and he even offered a few hurricane readiness tips, because it was the beginning of the storm season.

The white minivan pulled up to the spa's front door. The place was just what Serpentine had hoped for. A large white oval awning protected the entrance with dusty pink bricks for the walls. The building actually looked a little like a renovated motor lodge off any rural two-lane highway in America.

Inside, the lobby's cool southwestern motif provided a welcome contrast to the heat outside. In the center of the lobby sat a beige wicker couch-and-chair ensemble with beige, blue, and mauve flowered cushions. A gift shop was off to one side of the room and the service desk flanked the other.

Their room on the third floor was designed like most hotel rooms, nothing special, until they stepped out onto the patio and took in the view. The vast blue ocean spread into the horizon framed between tall palm trees and an isolated cabana.

"I'm glad you talked me into coming, Serpentine. I miss Micah, but I needed a break," LaJune said, following the words with a big hug. "I hope Mama's doing okay with her."

"Girl, please. They're fine. This is something we need to do often. Take better care of ourselves," Serpentine replied, returning her embrace.

They immediately replaced their blue jeans and T-shirts with swimsuits and terry cloth cover-ups. Gray courtesy towels sat on a shelf in the hallway. They each grabbed one and set out for the white sand.

Serpentine spotted a couple of empty chaise lounges and led LaJune over to them. "Anybody sitting here?" she asked the older white woman stretched out nearby.

"No. No. Sit down. Relax," the woman responded, looking up over her Carrera sunglasses. "Just get here?"

"Yeah. This is so pretty. I can't believe it's real," Serpentine replied as she sat down and surveyed the beach.

LaJune took the chair next to Serpentine, first covering it with her towel, then lying back carefully to keep the towel in place.

"I come all the time," the woman told them from under her huge brown-and-orange straw hat. "Every three or four months for at least a week or two. I figure that's the least my lying, cheating-ass husband can do for me."

Serpentine and LaJune looked at each other and tried to repress their smiles.

"Wow, thank you for sharing!" was what immediately came to Serpentine's mind, but she didn't dare say it.

"He thought he was gonna leave me with three kids and a lifetime of disappointment. No way!" the woman continued.

Serpentine looked over at LaJune, who was scrutinizing their emotionally stressed acquaintance. She probably had a lot of money. Several large, gaudy diamond rings were positioned on each hand, and her perfectly manicured fingers and toes were obviously the norm.

"I ignored the fact that he had a chippie on the side for who knows how long. I had the house and the money, so all they were getting was sex and believe me, they weren't getting much."

Serpentine closed her eyes, held back a chuckle, and prayed for a silence that didn't come.

"Then the man lost his mind. He actually tried to leave me for one of my girlfriends! Can you believe that?"

Serpentine and LaJune shook their heads, not knowing exactly how else to respond.

"The scheming bitch used to always say, 'Dottie, you got a good husband.' If any of your girlfriends ever tells you that shit, watch her closely."

Serpentine took a deep breath. The last thing she needed was to listen to somebody else's drama. She cautiously eyed the woman, whose head twisted back and forth like an agitated chicken's.

"I don't really need his money. Daddy left me in good shape, but it's the principle. The son of a bitch owes me!"

Serpentine glanced at the woman's oversized, multicolored beach towel that covered only part of her body, and noticed big sunburned legs that continued roasting.

"The tramp left him as soon as she realized I wasn't going to give him an easy divorce. She wasn't serious. Saw a stupid old man and tried to get her hands on his money, my money!"

Serpentine and LaJune finally excused themselves from the whiny voice and ran out into the ocean.

"Lord, why wouldn't that woman stop talking?" Serpentine moaned as she gingerly stepped into the water, then immediately relaxed in the tepid Atlantic.

"Sometimes when you're in one of your moods, you sound just like that woman," LaJune told her.

"That's not true," Serpentine protested, lifting her finger up to her mouth to taste the gritty, salty liquid.

LaJune stood and braced herself against the rushing force of incoming waves that splashed against her body. "I swear, you just saw yourself when you're talking about Carlin, Mama, the job, even Dr. Greeley, sometimes."

Serpentine was taken aback when she recognized the truth in LaJune's words. She walked forward carefully, avoiding the rocks, seaweed, and jellyfish. "Well, if that's the case, you don't have to worry about it happening anymore," she vowed.

Serpentine continued out toward the horizon, the briny water inching its way up to her waist, her chest, and then her neck. She took a long look around at the kids playing in the sand, lovers walking hand in hand, and sailboats drifting effortlessly out at sea.

She closed her eyes, held her breath, lifted her feet off the ocean bottom, and allowed the wonderful liquid warmth to completely absorb her.

Breathing a loud sigh of relief when she didn't see her new buddy, Dottie, on the beach the next morning, Serpentine claimed the first empty chaise lounge.

She laid down and soaked up as much sun as possible through the SPF 45 sunblock that she'd rubbed everywhere she could reach. There was a beautiful blue sky, soft, drifting white clouds, and a breeze that made the heat tolerable.

She took a deep cleansing breath and focused on the long stretch of beach as far as she could see. Her eyes stopped to follow a tiny sandpiper as it searched for edible tidbits; its twiglike legs scissored mechanically across the sand. She only had two hours before she was supposed to meet LaJune at yoga class, so she assimilated her spirit into the peace and calm all around her.

At ten o'clock, just as yoga class started, Serpentine took her place beside LaJune.

"Stretching is nothing to get bent out of shape about," joked Vian, the buff young trainer. He lifted his muscular arms, reaching toward the ceiling.

"First, reach up as far as you can. Stretch those triceps. Alternate left, then right," he added. "Slowly, reach, pull; reach, pull; reach, pull."

As Serpentine followed his directions, she could feel her muscles straining. Physical and spiritual energy spread throughout her body.

"Now, place your left hand behind your head, and with your right hand, pull your left elbow inward," Vian continued. "Your arms should almost create a box above your head."

Serpentine and LaJune looked at each other and smiled. Serpentine loved how each movement seemed to chase away the stress and anxiety. The soothing, synchronized flow in her twists and turns made her feel alive again.

Twelve women and two men spent the thirty-minute session stretching their triceps, quadriceps, neck, hamstrings, calves, shoulders, and back. As a bonus, Vian showed them several deep-breathing techniques, and for the last ten minutes they combined deep breathing and stretching until Serpentine found herself in a totally relaxed state of mind.

After class it was time for lunch. Since Sunshine Spa was vegetarian, the mainstay of lunch each day was a huge salad bar with homemade dressings and an exotic soup. For breakfast there was fruit, lots of organically grown fruit, and only fruit: watermelon, grapes, bananas, mangoes, oranges, grapefruit, strawberries, apples, pineapple, papaya, and more.

Chef Antonio managed to create some interesting vegetarian dinners. Scribbled on the menu board for dinner Saturday night was a walnut pesto mousse with black-bean pâté inside a zucchini tortuga mold. Serpentine could barely say it, let alone eat it, so she placed a special order for a baked sweet potato and salad to make sure she had something to fill up on.

The highlight on Sunday was Serpentine's reflexology massage. When the tiny Asian masseuse first led her into the small, darkened room, she sensed something wonderful was about to happen. The woman motioned toward Serpentine's clothes and left the room. Serpentine undressed and lay across the long padded table on a warmed cotton blanket.

The masseuse returned with two hot towels wrapped around a small rubber pillow; she placed the bundle under Serpentine's neck and head. The tiny fingers were surprisingly powerful as they slowly rubbed heated oil into the bottom of Serpentine's feet in a smooth, rotating motion. The masseuse pulled and twisted each toe until Serpentine felt the stress-relieving sensations all the way up into her back, shoulders, and neck.

Serpentine moaned out loud. Life had to be about "self" if it was going to be good. She couldn't believe it had taken forty years for her to understand that. She'd been taught to listen, support, and cooperate. She'd gotten lost inside other people's dreams. She wanted everybody to like her, to care about her, to love her, so she had made everything good for everybody else and forgotten herself.

The masseuse focused her mystical powers on Serpentine's left wrist, pressing forcefully. Then she continued those same movements on the right side. This was an experience of ecstasy that Serpentine hadn't had in eons. It ranked right up there with a second or third orgasm, which she also hadn't had in a long time. As she relaxed and enjoyed the soothing tropical rhythms, Serpentine couldn't remember the last time she'd felt pampered like this. She couldn't remember the last time she'd been this happy.

Monday morning came much too quickly and LaJune and Serpentine caught the ten o'clock van to the airport. As they sat and watched the same luscious greenery fly by, they couldn't help but ear-hustle the conversation going on behind them.

A dark-haired fifty-year-old grandmother from Boston was talking to a redheaded forty-something new mother from New York. The redhead was telling her companion about the baby shower a friend had thrown for her earlier in the year.

"Anyway, she offers to give me this shower and then says I can only invite ten people because her apartment is small."

"What did you do?" the Bostonian asked with a chuckle.

"I had to pick ten friends. Which of course didn't make my other ten friends, who couldn't come, very happy."

"Why didn't you just move the shower somewhere else?" Bostonian asked.

"I didn't want to hurt her feelings. She's my brother's wife, and she was so excited about doing this for me," the New Yorker explained.

"So what happened?" was Bostonian's next question.

"What could I do? I apologized to my left-out friends, who later gave me a second shower." She popped a stick of gum in her mouth. "But that's not the end of it. When I got to the apartment, I was pissed. She had invited her sister and sister-in-law. I'm not friends with them. I've only met her sister once, and I didn't know the sister-in-law at all."

"But they brought gifts, right?"

"That's not the point. These two women were *huge* and they ate like starving vultures. I swear, I could've invited my other ten friends and they wouldn't have taken up any more space or eaten any more food."

Serpentine cut her eyes in that direction as both women laughed.

When the van pulled up to the airline terminal, Serpentine and LaJune hopped out.

"Can you believe how ungrateful and two-faced that woman was, June?" Serpentine asked, adjusting the wheels on her suitcase.

LaJune draped her garment bag over her shoulder, following Serpentine inside. "I was just thinking about that. Nobody had to do anything for her tacky ass."

"And how much nerve did it take for her to talk about somebody else's size?" Serpentine continued.

"Instead of pictures, the photographer probably took posters at her wedding," LaJune joked, then hesitated, remembering Serpentine's aversion to fat jokes.

Serpentine chuckled. "That was kind of funny," she said.

LaJune was surprised. She eyed her sister carefully. "You're not going to fuss at me for that joke?" she asked.

"I'm through fussing, June," Serpentine answered. "Fussing is like sitting in a rocking chair. You can only move back and forth in the same spot."

Aqua Aerobics

I am an aqua-aerobics goddess! It's the most miraculous feeling to be in water again. The weight is literally gone. Your body moves with fluidity. You feel light and energized. You can bend, stretch, twist, and jump like never before.

I'd forgotten how much I loved to swim as a child. I stopped going swimming because when I became a teenager I needed to look good for the boys and the water would mess up my hair. Next there was the issue of showing my body in a swimsuit in public once I gained weight.

It's crazy that you don't want to swim because people will see your body, but you need to swim to get your body in shape. Kinda like not wearing a seat belt because it will wrinkle your clothes, but if you got in an accident, wrinkled clothes would be the least of your worries.

When Serpentine first learned that her "Fat-Free Farce" series had been nominated for an award from the Midwest Broadcasters Association, she didn't believe it. She tried not to think negatively, but she had never won anything before. Depending on her luck was like depending on a cheap HMO.

She found herself getting more and more excited as the banquet day rolled around. It was a prestigious nomination and if she won, it would be the highlight of her professional career. This nomination meant that she was finally being acknowledged for her talent and dedication, and at the risk of sounding cocky, it was an honor she deserved.

That Saturday morning before the event, two UPS boxes with catalog-ordered outfits sat open on her bed. She had sent for a sequined silk skirt set from Brownstone Studio primarily because of the loose flow. The catalog called the color claret, but it looked like burgundy to her. From her Roaman's catalog she'd ordered an ivory tank dress with a matching cover-up leather-and-lace embroidered swing jacket.

She hadn't tried either ensemble on yet. Serpentine hated trying on catalog clothes because they never looked as good on her as they did on the thin models. Once, she sat down and wrote a letter to a catalog company complaining that it was false advertising. Ten days later she received a form letter and a gift certificate for 10 percent off her next purchase.

Serpentine planned to wear whichever outfit looked better and send the other one back. The ivory suit was very nice. She wished it came in some color besides ivory because the pale shade didn't do much for her mahogany skin tone or her larger shape. But the flare of the jacket helped camouflage her lost waistline and the straight skirt highlighted her big, shapely legs. On a scale of one to ten the suit got a solid seven and a half.

The burgundy outfit won hands down. It was the bomb! When Serpentine slipped the jewel-necked top over her head and pulled up the elastic waistband of the hand-beaded skirt, she grinned. It hung just right. It was classy and flattering, a twelve on her one-to-ten scale. Serpentine checked the label to make a note of the brand name. She would look for more clothes from a designer who had this kind of vision.

She had called on her old standby, cousin Tevan, to escort her. He arrived right on time. They met Marleen at the banquet, where she was already sipping drinks and mingling. As Serpentine stood surveying the room, she felt lighter. She hadn't lost any physical weight during her weekend at the spa, but mentally and spiritually she felt more alive than she'd been in a long time.

"You two ladies look very beautiful tonight," Tevan said as the three of them sat down at their assigned table.

"You got that right," Serpentine said, "I look damn good tonight!"

"Excuse you. *We* look damn good!" Marleen corrected her.

"Neither one of you can compete with me," Tevan bragged in an exaggerated tone.

Serpentine laughed. "You're so full of it," she told him with a smile.

Marleen chuckled. "Some people have delusions of adequacy."

Tevan leaned forward in his chair and flirted. "If you'd give me a chance, you'd see just how good my delusions can be."

"I have to admit you're wearing me down. Another ten or twenty years and I might give you a chance," Marleen replied.

Tevan winked at her and she blushed.

"It's a shame you have the opportunity to drink from this fountain of love and you'd rather die of thirst out in the wilderness," he added.

While the two of them bantered back and forth, Serpentine picked over her baked chicken and pasta dinner.

She tuned out the continuing soap opera that unraveled next to her, occasionally nodding her head, and smiling in their direction.

She thought about how the "Fat-Free" series had been her obsession for weeks and now her work was paying off. No other story had taken on that kind of significance in her life. The series had brought her face to face with her own personal struggle, and she realized if she didn't confront it, weight would always be her Achilles' heel.

"Good evening," the master of ceremonies suddenly said into the microphone. "Welcome to the Twentieth Annual Midwest Broadcasters Association Awards Banquet. We will honor the best of the best tonight. It's a fairly long program, so I will simply say good luck to all of our nominees and turn the podium over to the lovely star of stage and screen, Rachel Adams."

Too excited to pay attention to anything but her own category, Serpentine tuned out the next fifteen minutes. Only when Tevan nudged her did she snap out of her trance to watch a fellow Chicago reporter, Winston Blue, walk up to the stage to accept his award for best news documentary. Everybody clapped.

"I want to thank the many staff members, friends, and associates who helped me create my documentary, 'Loaded Language: The Other Way to Get Shot.' It's such a crucial journalistic issue today, when large numbers of people believe what they see and hear." Blue held the gold-and-black plaque high in the air and continued: "If we change one simple word, like the President is in town to *sell* his health-care package, it can make a significant difference in how our audience connects with that topic. Someone trying to sell you something is very different from someone who's trying to present or explain something to you."

Serpentine suddenly panicked. Blue sounded so prepared up there, and she hadn't even thought about what she would say if she won. She imagined herself onstage looking like a fool. She pulled a red pen from her purse and scribbled a few notes onto her napkin.

"The next category is investigative reporting," said the emcee.

"We have some excellent nominations this year: Janice Thomas from WGN with 'These Changing Times,' Randy Martin at WBBT for 'Who Is Black and Who Is Not,' and WXYZ reporter Serpentine Williamson for 'Fat-Free Farce.' "

Serpentine held her breath. She almost didn't want to win. She wished the evening were over, so she could go home without humiliating herself.

Adams, the presenter, opened the envelope and hesitated. "Serpentine Williamson for 'Fat-Free Farce'!"

The audience applauded and cheered as Serpentine slowly rose and walked toward the podium in a daze. Her mind went blank when she stepped in front of the microphone. She took the shiny plaque and flung her mouth open.

"I'm shocked and, of course, excited," she said nervously. "I hope I don't sound like an idiot up here, but I want to thank everyone at the station who believed in the story. It was chancy to challenge the fat-free industry at a time when everybody was touting fat-free food as the new miracle. My news director, Evan Wilson, and my executive producer, Marleen Bishop, especially deserve thanks because they supported me and that made all the difference in the world."

Once Serpentine stepped down from the stage and made her way back to her seat, she had no idea what she had said or done in the previous five minutes. Everyone at her table congratulated her, but as the evening continued, Serpentine dropped in and out of a trance. She stared at the gold-plated plaque, with a journalist's pad and pen etched into it, until Tevan squeezed her hand.

"You ready to go?" he asked softly.

Serpentine looked around and saw that the room was clearing out.

"Nice work, Serpentine," Allison Payne told her. Serpentine smiled and said thanks. She wanted to say how much she admired Allison, as an anchor for WGN's nine o'clock newscast, but the words got stuck in her throat.

"Good job, Serpentine," Trina mumbled with jealousy in her voice.

"Serpentine," Mr. Marshall belted out behind her.

Serpentine turned around, smiling. She stiffened when she saw Evan standing next to Mr. Marshall.

Marshall shook her hand briskly. "Well done, well done. This is the first MBA we've won at WXYZ. We're proud of you, right, Evan?"

Evan shuffled in place and nodded. "I'll see you on Monday," he said with a phony grin. "Bright and early. Congratulations!"

"I want you to come see me this week so we can talk again about the anchor position," Marshall added. "Call my secretary and make an appointment."

"I will," Serpentine replied as Marshall and Evan left to greet the head of a rival network.

"Ohhhh. They're really backtracking now, aren't they?" Marleen teased.

"Girl, I'm through tripping. I let go and let God." Serpentine beamed.

"Well, congrats anyway; no one deserved it more," Marleen told her and gave her a big hug. Then she teased Tevan with a light good-bye kiss on his lips.

As Tevan drove Serpentine home, she held on to her award and relived the emcee's announcement in her head. They pulled up in front of her house but she wasn't ready to go inside, especially not alone.

"You want to come in for some coffee or champagne?" she asked. "I guess I just don't want the evening to end right now."

"Sure, let's celebrate your big night some more."

They got out of the car and walked up the front steps.

"Did I really sound okay when I accepted this?" she asked for the third time, holding up her award.

"You were much better than okay, especially after the anchor from WLUV got up there with that," Tevan puckered his lips and raised his voice several octaves, " 'I want to thank all the beautiful people.' "

Serpentine cracked up. "You need to stop, Tevan," she told him. "She's not a bad person when you get to know her. Just a little high-strung."

Once his laughter subsided, Tevan straightened up his face. "That's one woman I wouldn't want to get to know. Everything about her was fake from her personality to her weave."

Serpentine slipped her key in the lock, opened the door, and stepped inside. Tevan followed.

"Thank God, I'm finally getting some recognition. It's been a long time coming." Serpentine spoke out loud, more to herself than to Tevan as she got the champagne out of the refrigerator. "Thanks again for stepping in like you always do, cuz. You're my hero."

Tevan dropped down onto the couch. "My pleasure."

Serpentine popped open the bottle and filled two glasses. She had purposely put it in the refrigerator just in case she won. She handed Tevan his glass, and kicked off her shoes.

"A toast to your brilliance," Tevan said, raising his glass.

"To my brilliance, and to your wonderfulness," Serpentine added, grinning from ear to ear.

They clanked their glasses together, then Serpentine stared at Tevan for a minute. "You are a wonderful man, Tevan. Why can't you keep a woman?"

Tevan fell backward on the couch. "Damn! Where did that come from?" he asked.

"I just wonder about you sometime," she explained. "You seem like the perfect guy for somebody, yet nobody's around."

"Well, how do you know that I can't keep them? It could be them who can't keep me," Tevan complained.

"Either way, you know what I mean."

"The truth is, I've been waiting for the woman of my dreams to call."

"Well, give it up, my brother, if you're talking about Marleen. She would make you miserable, and she'll probably never call."

"How much you want to bet?"

Serpentine took another sip of the champagne. "Twenty dollars."

"Give it up," Tevan said, holding out his hand.

"What?"

"Guess where I'm going when I leave your house tonight."

Serpentine snorted. "Don't even tell me that!"

"She called a couple of weeks ago and we've spent almost every night together. I'm definitely not miserable."

"I can't believe you two were playing all coy with each other tonight at the banquet."

Tevan emptied his glass with one last gulp. "As a matter of fact, I need to go, because my baby is waiting right now," he added.

Serpentine stood up and followed him to the door. "I guess it had to happen eventually, the way you two have always flirted with each other."

"You can be the maid of honor at our wedding."

"We'll see," Serpentine teased.

Tevan stepped outside. "You gonna be okay?" he asked.

"I'm gonna be fine," Serpentine replied. "Tell me one more time before you go that my acceptance speech was okay."

"You were marrrrrrvellllous," Tevan said with a wink, then shut the door.

Superwoman Sucks

I hate to make feminists mad, but I think women got a messed-up deal. Since we've been liberated not only are we expected to work just like a man, if not harder, but then we're supposed to come home and wash, cook, clean, take care of kids, plus knock boots! What's even crazier is that many of us are so brainwashed that we actually try to stuff ourselves into that impossible mold.

Women, especially black women, are sick and dying in large numbers. High blood pressure, diabetes, stress, AIDS, heart attacks, and strokes are rampant, but we still keep trying to play superwoman. It's not fair for us to have to bring home the bacon, fry it up in the pan, eat very little of it, and of course, let him think he's "the man."

Serpentine walked into the old brick gymnasium with trepidation. She had left Lincoln High more than twenty-five years ago and really didn't know if she wanted to see any of those people again. But LaJune missed Kansas City and her high school friends. She wanted to go, so she begged and pleaded until Serpentine agreed just to shut her up.

Serpentine's black sweater-and-skirt set, size 20, fit nicely. The major reason was her new exercise routine.

Four days a week, one hour a day for the last month, Serpentine had been consistently walking, swimming, or participating in an aqua aerobics class. Her focus was not on losing weight, but on feeling better. She took leisurely strolls around her neighborhood, in the mall, or at the recreation center down the street. She scheduled her exercise sessions on her calendar under "Spiritual Rejuvenation" and treated it as if it were the most important meeting of the day.

Serpentine walked over to the sign-up table and stood in line behind a short black man who sported a perfectly round, bald head.

"Just write your name on this tag, Weldon," cooed the lady behind the table. "Can I help you?" she added as Weldon stepped aside, and Serpentine moved forward.

"I'm Serpentine Williamson."

Weldon turned. "Hey, Serpentine! How are you?"

"Hi, Weldon, I'm fine. How about you?"

The greeter looked through several pages. "Here you are," she said, handing Serpentine a blank name tag. "Your sister is LaJune, right?" the woman asked, handing Serpentine a school coffee mug. "Is LaJune here?"

"Yeah, where is that foxy sister of yours?" Weldon drooled.

"She's over there." Serpentine pointed across the room, where LaJune was already talking to other classmates.

Weldon rushed over to where LaJune stood and pulled her out on the dance floor.

"June was our class president," the lady said with pride.

"I've heard the story many times," Serpentine replied.

The lady turned up her nose. "LaJune was so much better than that Ann Mitchell. Ann had an ugly attitude, if you ask me."

LaJune stepped up behind Serpentine. "You better tell Weldon Jones to leave me alone," she warned.

Serpentine giggled. "But he loves you, Junie. I thought you wanted to see these folks?"

"Hey, LaJune!" the greeter shrieked behind the table.

LaJune reached across the table and they hugged. "Hi, Kerry," she said in what Serpentine noticed was her less-than-genuine voice. "You look good, girl."

"I was just asking your sister about you, wasn't I?"

"Yes, she definitely was," Serpentine agreed.

"I heard you had a beautiful new baby. Where are the pictures?" Kerry asked, hustling around the table.

LaJune whipped out the mini photo album from her beige purse and handed it to Kerry.

"She's just gorgeous!" Kerry squealed. "How old is she?"

Serpentine shot LaJune a curious look.

"Three months," LaJune answered, then mouthed the words "Be good" at Serpentine.

Kerry closed the book. "She's just adorable, June."

"Thanks, I still got this belly and these hips she endowed me with," LaJune joked.

"Girl, don't worry about it; you can lose that with a little willpower. I've had three girls. Here they are," Kerry said, pulling several snapshots from under a pile of papers and grinning.

LaJune took the pictures, scanned them, smiling. "They're precious."

"Excuse me, I'd like to register, please," a deep, familiar voice spoke from behind them.

Serpentine recognized the voice immediately. She turned

around to see Carlin standing there. She looked up past his broad shoulders and into his face.

A few moments of awkward silence passed as Serpentine stepped to the side and LaJune returned Kerry's pictures. Serpentine held her breath. She was afraid he might show up. She had hoped for more time to prepare. His hair looked grayer and thinner than before, but his face was the same. Reminding her that she missed those passionate eyes that had courted her and those sensuous lips that had loved her.

Carlin finally broke the silence. "You know I have to get a big hug, don't you?" he told Serpentine.

She barely returned his embrace.

"Can we talk a minute?" he asked, making puppy-dog eyes at her.

Serpentine walked slowly, almost afraid to follow him over to a private corner. She wasn't sure what she might say or do.

"So, how are you?" he asked in a sullen tone.

Serpentine picked at her thumb nervously. "Fine."

"I'm sorry things didn't work out," he said, leaning against the wall. "But I want you to know I do miss you."

"I'm sorry, Carlin," Serpentine replied. "But it was your choice to be with somebody else."

"I wish you would have talked to me about the tape," he said. "I could have explained."

"Explained what? It was pretty clear to me," Serpentine shot back.

"If you would just try to understand my side."

Serpentine cut him off. "It was just too much drama for me, Carlin. I don't need that mess in my life."

"I don't love Shalay, Serpentine. I love you. I wish women could understand that for men sex is not love."

"Oh, really?" Serpentine smirked.

"Sex and love are two entirely different things and if women could understand that they wouldn't go off the deep end for nothing."

"Look, Carlin, you don't have to explain anything to me. As far as I'm concerned, it's not an issue anymore. I've moved on."

"I was hoping to see you tonight. That's why I came. If you gave me another chance, I know I could make it up to you."

Serpentine laughed softly. "You know, that's exactly what you said when we saw each other at the club that night."

"We were great together, Serpentine."

"I'm great all by myself, Carlin." She turned toward the door.

"I hope you'll at least accept my apology. I am truly sorry," he called behind her.

Serpentine spun around. "Well, at least we agree on something, because you are definitely sorry, Carlin! Excuse me, I need some air," she said, strutting out the front door.

As she watched the dark sky, full of stars, Serpentine inhaled big gulps of the warm night air. As LaJune joined her on the bench, beside the tiger mascot, she counted silently in her head.

"Are you okay?" LaJune asked.

"Yeah, I guess."

"You said you didn't know if you could handle seeing him again, but you did good," LaJune reassured her.

Serpentine rolled her eyes. "I don't even know why I came here tonight. This place wasn't a place of happiness for me."

"You came because I asked you to," LaJune reminded her.

"And I'm much more important than Carlin or those other folks, right?"

"Right," Serpentine agreed.

"You also owed me a big one for that shopping trip, remember?"

Serpentine sneered. "I can't believe that sorry look he had on his face. I wanted to scratch those hound-dog eyes out."

"No need to get violent; you put him in his place."

Serpentine chuckled and put her arm around her sister's shoulders. "I told you this was a bad idea. Why did I have to see him first thing? June, I don't think I can go back in there."

"There's no reason not to go back in now. You've already solved the problem. Come on, I'll hold your hand."

They stood up and headed for the entrance arm in arm.

"Can you believe Kelly, grinning and cheesing all up in my face? She used to talk about me bad in school," LaJune complained.

"Give him a hug. Ain't that a bitch!" Serpentine fussed.

They stopped just outside the double doors.

"Okay, let's relax and release," LaJune said, sounding like their yoga instructor at the spa.

"We're going back inside and have some real fun!"

As Serpentine and LaJune walked into the drafty gymnasium, Serpentine made sure to hold her head up high. LaJune spotted a mutual friend across the room and pulled Serpentine over toward him.

"Hey, Dale, what's up!" LaJune said, throwing her arms around his neck.

"Junie, my love. You look fabulous!" Dale screeched, hugging her tightly.

"Hi, Dale," Serpentine followed, with a hug too.

"Do me a huge favor, Dale. Dance with my sister so she can loosen up and have some fun," LaJune said.

"No problem," Dale replied, grabbing Serpentine's hand. "How 'bout a dance, girl? Come on and show me what you got."

Serpentine shook her head. "Not right now, Dale. Thanks, but I'm not ready."

LaJune bumped her shoulder into Serpentine's. "Go on, girl. Don't sit around and sulk. He's watching."

Serpentine glanced over at Carlin, then strolled out to the dance floor with Dale. She tried to keep a straight face when Dale started to swing his hips, but somehow kept missing the beat.

"I forgot you were the one black man in the world without rhythm," she told him, rocking back and forth.

"I'm not the only one," he replied. "My roommate is worse."

Serpentine laughed and shook her head as Johnny Taylor sang "Move it in, move it out, disco lady."

LaJune soon joined them on the dance floor. She was teasing poor Weldon Jones, who'd been her boyfriend for a short time in high school until Parren came along.

"You sure I can't steal you away from Parren?" Weldon asked for the tenth time.

Serpentine and LaJune smirked at each other.

"Is that a wedding band on your finger, Weldon?" Serpentine asked.

Weldon slurred his words as if the drinking were catching up with him. "We're separated."

"Can't you think of something more original? That's the line all married men use," LaJune teased.

Weldon stumbled, then caught himself. "It's the truth! I thought women wanted the truth!"

"Weldon, you wouldn't know the truth if it bit you in the ass," LaJune huffed. "That's the reason we ain't together today."

"Damn, June, you're getting bad as Mama," Serpentine told her as the record ended.

"Say oooops upside your head, say oooops upside your head!" they chimed in unison, and smacked their palms high in the air.

Weldon frowned and hustled over to a new potential candidate for his tired rap. Serpentine and LaJune laughed all the way back to their table.

"Girl, Weldon is still a trip, ain't he?" LaJune asked, taking a sip of punch from her glass.

"I remember when you loooooved you some Weldon Jones," Serpentine joked.

"I was crazy back then, wasn't I?"

"We were both crazy back then."

Grace Jones's song "Pull Up to the Bumper" ended and the disc jockey got on the microphone to welcome everyone to the Multi-class Reunion. "It's great to see this big turnout. Help yourself to food and drink, and don't forget to sign your name on the banner that will hang in the gymnasium until the next reunion."

The Commodores began singing "Just to Be Close to You" and the disc jockey continued. "This next song goes out to Serpentine from Carlin, who says he'll always love you."

Serpentine glanced over at the corner where Carlin had been sulking, but he was gone. She got chills when she heard his deep voice beside her.

"How about one last dance?" he asked.

Serpentine's first mistake was to stare into his soft brown eyes. Her second mistake was to follow him out onto the dance floor.

Her third mistake was to allow him to hold her in his arms for that one last time.

"I love you, Serpentine. I swear I do," he whispered in her ear.

Serpentine's heart stopped beating when he tightened his hold. She wanted to believe him. She wanted to love him again.

"Please give me another chance," he begged, sliding his hand down her back and across her behind.

As Carlin rubbed hard against her, Serpentine thought she would lose her mind. This was the one man who understood her so completely, and it felt good to be in his arms again.

"I've missed you too, Carlin," she finally confessed. "But it just wouldn't work."

"I'll do anything to get you back, Serpentine," he pleaded. "Tell me what I can do."

Serpentine hesitated, then allowed the fire to take control. She seductively licked his right ear and whispered: "Follow me."

Then she led Carlin out into the hallway, where they stopped to kiss passionately next to the familiar tan lockers. They moved further down the hall, until Carlin twisted the doorknob of the teachers' lounge and the door swung open.

He pulled Serpentine inside, sliding his tongue down between her bulging breasts, and gently rubbing her lower back.

"Do you really love me, Carlin?" Serpentine asked as she unzipped his pants.

"I'm gonna show you just how much I love you, girl," he responded.

Serpentine maneuvered her black sweater skirt up over her hips. Carlin kissed her softly on her neck, sparking that familiar desire.

"I love kissing you, and I'm going to do it a lot," he said.

"So, stop talking and do it," she replied, sensually returning his kisses.

When Carlin pulled her closer to him, Serpentine didn't resist. She wanted Carlin badly, and at that moment, she didn't care about anything else.

Standing up against the wall, she gently guided him into her waiting shrine. "Oh, Carlin," she moaned softly as the heat from their bodies magnified with a constant pulsating motion and the ultimate climax lifted her higher.

When it was over, they stood silently for a moment in each other's arms. She stroked the back of his head tenderly.

"Things will be different this time, Serpentine," Carlin promised, tugging at his pants.

"Different how, Carlin?" Serpentine asked, pulling her skirt back down.

Carlin grinned. "We're going to make sweet love, just like this, for eternity, baby. I promise!"

Serpentine stopped straightening her pantyhose and looked deep into his brown eyes. "Oh, I'm sorry," she said softly. "You thought this was love. No, Carlin, sweetheart, this was just sex. And believe me, I do know the difference!"

With that Serpentine stepped out of the lounge, slamming the door behind her.

She stopped in the women's bathroom, splashed cold water on her face, then started searching for LaJune.

It was time to go home.

Hallelujah!

I know now that this struggle is not about my weight. It's about my faith. It's about my love. I wasn't just trying to get attention when I attempted suicide. I truly wanted to die. But apparently God had other plans, because I'm still here. I'm still in this screwed-up world, wanting love and needing understanding.

I know there are many women out there who feel the same way I do and have struggled the same way I have. We share similar experiences, pray similar prayers, and dream similar dreams.

I finally have a plan for the rest of my life.

While I wait to get into heaven above through my love for God, I'm going to try and find a little heaven here on earth through a love for myself. I'm going to figure out what makes me happy and healthy, and embrace those things. I'm going to start counting my blessings instead of my calories. I'm going to learn to love all of me.

Hallelujah!

෨ ෨ ෨

When Serpentine entered Dr. Greeley's office for the last time she was amazed at how comfortable the place had become. The cozy layout of two chairs and a couch in the center of the room was perfect.

The desk and file cabinets were tucked in a corner to make them unobtrusive. She also liked the fact that Dr. Greeley used two lamps to light the room with a low level of brightness, rather than using the fluorescent lights in the ceiling.

"You seem to have things pretty well under control now, Serpentine," Dr. Greeley told her after they'd both sat down and gotten cozy.

Serpentine nodded and smiled. For the past couple of months that had been her main function. She was ready to move on with her life. She was through focusing on the failures of yesterday or the worries of tomorrow. She would just be thankful for today. Serpentine was now concentrating on living instead of dying, and she was amazed at the difference it made in her life.

"Tell me about something that you used to see as negative, but now consider positive," Dr. Greeley asked, as if testing her.

Serpentine smiled broadly. "That's an easy one: my habit of checking and double-checking things. Carlin used to get upset when I checked to make sure he had the tickets to an event. He saw it as me not trusting him to take care of business. And LaJune often gets annoyed with me when I recheck the baby's diaper bag to make sure everything we need is in there. Even at work, when I check and recheck facts, it slows me down and my news director sometimes gets irritated. But my habit of checking and rechecking is a necessary part of my peace of mind. It helps me to minimize potential problems in my life, and that's good."

"Do you have peace of mind now?"

Serpentine beamed. "Most of the time," she replied. "I understand the key is looking for solutions to problems right away rather than rehashing the problem itself over and over."

"What about handling your emotions?"

"I still feel sad sometimes," Serpentine admitted.

Dr. Greeley leaned forward. "Once you have the solution, you can move past the sadness. That's your goal."

"But you also said that feeling sad can be a good thing," Serpentine reminded him.

"That's right. When a sad feeling is appropriate, you should allow yourself to feel sad. But pay attention to how long you let it linger."

Serpentine brushed her new braided extensions out of her eyes and leaned back against the couch. "I used to think something was wrong with me because I would go to a sad movie just to cry."

"Getting it out of your system is a much better remedy than holding it in."

"So how do I know when to stop?"

Dr. Greeley sat up straight in his chair. "That depends on why you're sad. Give yourself a specific time limit; an hour a day, not more than a week. At the end of the time limit, stop. Do something to change, something to make yourself feel good again."

"I just finished a great report at work that made me feel good. It's about a group of people who are using God to help them with weight issues."

Dr. Greeley lifted his eyebrows.

"I know this may sound crazy, Doc, but I truly believe I'm getting messages from God now," she told him.

"How so?" Dr. Greeley asked, setting his pad and pencil down.

"I'm not sure I can explain it, but there are passages in the Bible that deal with weight issues, and several of them have touched me.

"Can you give me an example?"

Serpentine flipped open her notebook. "Romans, chapter 14, verse 17. It says, 'For the kingdom of God is not meat and drink; but righteousness, and peace, and joy in the Holy Ghost.' Peace and joy is what I've been looking for all along," she explained excitedly.

Dr. Greeley smiled and nodded.

"Romans, chapter 14, verse 3 says, 'Let not him that eateth despise him that eateth not: and let not him which eateth not judge him that eateth: for God hath received him.' "

"And what does that mean to you?"

"It means people shouldn't judge each other the way they do and God's acceptance is all we need. You know, the crazy thing is that I was just as guilty of judging myself as the people I blamed all around me."

"Excellent, Serpentine. As you continue to focus on 'self,' you'll also discover that it's not the trials and tribulations that occur in your life that matter, it's how you allow those trials and tribulations to affect you."

Serpentine nodded. "I know that now."

Dr. Greeley wrote a couple of last notes on his pad. "Those sound like wonderful messages to concentrate on, Serpentine."

"There's one more passage in First Samuel, chapter 16, verse 7. 'The Lord seeth not as man seeth; for man looketh on the outward appearance, but the Lord looketh on the heart.' God made me, Doc, and He loves all of me."

"Well, it seems like you are ready to move on." Dr. Greeley pronounced her freedom with a grand gesture.

As Serpentine got up from that worn brown couch for what she knew was the last time, she felt a sense of newness. She picked up her red swing coat and slung it over her left arm, then grabbed her black purse and slipped it onto her right shoulder.

"You take good care of yourself, Serpentine," he offered in closure.

Serpentine smiled. "I plan to," she replied.

As she rode down in the elevator, she rubbed the back of her neck and pitied Dr. Greeley for a minute. What a terrible job! To have to sit and listen to her shit twice a week, not to mention his other clients, and of course he probably had his own shit he was dealing with every day.

She walked out onto the sidewalk and scrutinized the passing bodies on the street. Two men in off-the-rack suits talking about their latest business venture.

A woman in a blue two-piece dress with matching leather pumps, adjusting a silk scarf around her neck.

A young child and her mother stopping to pick up a raggedy stuffed animal. Everybody was hustling from corner to corner, building to building, trying, as best they could, to deal with their own shit.

Serpentine watched as the street light changed from yellow to red to green, then back to yellow again. She took a sweeping glance at the congested traffic and sighed. "Bumper-to-bumper shit."

The church sanctuary seemed more spacious when she stepped inside that evening. This was the last practice for Glory before the city's annual competition. She had just gotten into the room when Regina and Pee Jay marched down the aisle, followed by a solemn Reverend Middleton. The look on their faces caused everyone to stop what they were doing.

Regina motioned for the group's attention, and they quieted immediately like second-graders in a well-ordered classroom. "We have some bad news," Regina started. "They're going to keep Chevon in the hospital. She has gallstones and her surgery is scheduled for Monday."

Heads lowered and moans could be heard as Reverend Middleton stepped forward.

"I know you're all concerned, but we just left our sister in very good spirits. She wants us to remember her in our prayers and win another title at the Gospel Music Fest tomorrow."

Nodding heads and clapping hands mingled with shouts of "Amen!" "I'm going to let you get on with your rehearsal," the Reverend added, quickly leaving the room.

"Who's gonna take Chevon's solo? 'In the Spirit' is one of our best songs," Sister Washington asked from the back row.

"That's a good question," Regina replied. "I actually thought about it for a while on the way over here, and the person whose voice is closest in range and pitch to Chevon's is

Serpentine." Regina glanced only briefly at her niece as she spoke. "If Serpentine took the song we wouldn't have to change it at all."

Serpentine dropped her head and focused on the scuffed floor. Her aunt had been trying to get her to solo for so long, but she just couldn't do it. She rocked back and forth nervously wanting to say yes, but needing to say no. She wasn't ready, and she didn't appreciate being put on the spot in front of everybody like this.

"Serpentine, we are really in a jam here," Regina pleaded. "I wouldn't ask if the Festival weren't tomorrow."

Other choir members began to coax and cajole, but Serpentine stopped listening. She didn't say anything for fear that her heart might literally burst. She endured their pleas as long as she could. "I'm sorry, but I can't," she finally said, blinking back tears. Serpentine rushed down from the risers and raced out the hand-carved doors.

She drove past the Du Sable Museum on Clark Street, made a U-turn, and parked. Home was the first place Regina would look, so she hurried inside, hoping time and distance could dull the pain. She wandered through the various galleries admiring the African art, wood carvings, drums, and masks. For a little while they seemed to soothe her battered soul.

She looked at photographs of the late mayor Harold Washington, then a sculpture of Du Sable himself caught her attention. Even though she'd been in the museum several times, she had never read the information plaque before. Du Sable was a black man. His full name was Jean Baptiste Pointe Du Sable. Historians suggested that he lived on the edge of the Chicago River as early as 1770. At a time when traders were often dishonest and suspicious, it was widely known that Du Sable was a man of good character.

Her final stop was an exhibit on slavery where artifacts, drawings, and paintings showed the sad nature of African-American life. The horsehair whips and rusted metal shackles reminded Serpentine of something her father always said. "Take life as you find it, but try not to leave it that way." She thought for a moment and thanked God that that's exactly what her ancestors had done.

When the radio announcer said the Fifteenth Annual Gospel Music Fest was under way at Grant Park, Serpentine stepped on the gas. Even though she wouldn't be onstage with the choir, she wanted to be in the audience to cheer them on. She was a half hour late and had missed a couple of performances, but she was sure as last year's winner, Glory would perform at the end.

Serpentine entered the park and found a spot along the edge of the crowd. She maneuvered herself into a position next to the railing, then focused her attention on the stage, where a young soloist was singing the second verse of "He's All Right." The contralto voice covered a broad range, moving from high to low with a smooth, heavenly flow. When the choir began to clap, the audience joined in. Some stood up with arms raised, while others swayed left, then right. Serpentine sighed deeply. This group was going to be hard to beat, but if anybody could do it, Glory could.

Fifteen minutes later, a group of gospel rappers finished their final selection, and the emcee used the microphone to keep the gospel train running. Serpentine had just shifted her head to get a better view when she felt a tap on her shoulder.

She turned around and found herself face-to-face with Regina.

"Why aren't you behind the stage with everybody else?" Regina asked.

Serpentine's voice cracked nervously. "I got here late, so I'm just going to watch."

"Nonsense. The choir needs everybody in place to win," Regina told her curtly.

"I really don't want to sing tonight, Aunt Regina, I just want to watch from here. Okay?" Serpentine asked, like a timid child.

"No, it's not okay, Serpentine," Regina answered in a slightly raised voice. "Your problems are never going to go away if you keep God on the outside."

Serpentine's body grew tense as she stood her ground. "I'm asking for some space right now, and I think God understands that," she said in a steady tone.

Regina stepped toward her. "Space for what, Serpentine? To run and hide because you're not who other people think you should be?"

Serpentine glanced at the stage and prayed for her aunt to go away. She didn't want to have this discussion right now.

"You've got to take control, Serpentine. Can't nothing change, if you don't take control."

Serpentine struggled to stop the tears. "You're absolutely right," she said in a voice so serious that Regina paused. "And I'm taking control of this moment. God is not on the outside, Aunt Regina, he's right here with me," she said, touching her chest. "Even though I'm not singing with Glory tonight, I'll be cheering and praying for their victory. That's all I can offer and I think— no, I know—God would agree that it's enough."

Regina stepped back with surprise and beamed. She tilted her head sideways and shouted: "Well, amen!" Then gave her niece a warm hug, and marched away to join Glory backstage.

Serpentine stood in the same spot for a long time. She felt sad that she couldn't sing to please her aunt and the rest of the choir, but she also felt happy, because she knew it was more important to please herself. She picked up her feet and rocked with the Chicago Mass Choir, soaking in the tremendous spiritual power that drifted through the warm breeze.

When Glory finally walked out onto the stage, beads of sweat appeared on Serpentine's forehead and the pit of her stomach cramped with anxiety. Regina stood in the center of the group with her back to the audience. She raised her arms and the pianist began.

Glory started by singing "He's My God." Serpentine noticed right away how the spotlights seemed to catch the green-and-orange in each robe and spread the vibrant colors across the stage. They sang, "An On-Time God" in perfect harmony, and the audience went wild when the entire choir two-stepped in unison. Their final selection, "In the Spirit," was awesome. Serpentine looked around and saw very few dry eyes as Pee Jay, of all people, did a wonderful job of replacing Sister Chevon as the soloist.

Once Glory left the stage, the emcee introduced the judges.

Serpentine only recognized one of them by name, a disc jockey named Floyd Evans, who had the good sistahs moaning during his late-afternoon drive show. He stood up in his WGOD T-shirt and took a bow.

The envelope was passed to the emcee, who wasted more time with idle chatter. He finally opened the envelope and slid the piece of paper out, but somehow let go, and it floated down to the floor.

"I know y'all been waiting to hear who the winner is, but you're just gonna have to wait a little longer," he teased, stooping to pick up the paper. "I still need to thank all the folks who worked hard to put this event together."

Serpentine dropped her head and groaned while he mentioned everybody he could think of, including his mother. Finally, just as she was about to give up, she heard the words she'd been waiting for."

"The winner of this year's Fifteenth Annual Chicago Gospel Music Fest, for the second year in a row, is Glory from Mount Glory Baptist Church!"

The audience grew loud with cheers, stomps, claps, and whistles as Glory made its way back onstage. When Regina accepted the trophy, Serpentine released a special smile that struggled through tears.

After slipping through the moving crowd as fast as she could, Serpentine rushed home. That night she snuggled under the comforter and thought about how hard it had been to tune into messages from heaven, when her life was full of earthly static. She quickly slipped off into a deep and restful sleep.

Serpentine dreamed for the first time since she'd left the hospital, but it wasn't the spider dream. This time she saw herself standing on the third riser at Mount Glory Baptist. It must have been Sunday, because the pews were full of parishioners waiting for the Holy Ghost to appear. Her aunt Regina stood before them, swinging her body from side to side, and the choir followed her lead.

With her arms raised high in the air, Serpentine could feel the powerful fire moving inside her again. Her mouth opened wide and she sang loud enough for the Lord to hear. Her choir robe swayed with the rhythm, and her battered heart beat with the melody.

When the pianist started to play the next song, Aunt Regina turned the page in front of her, lifted her head, and motioned for Serpentine to step forward. Serpentine took a tiny step, then another one, then another. She soon found herself positioned center stage in front of the microphone, looking nervously out across the congregation. The pianist pounded out Serpentine's favorite, "I'll Take You There," and on cue she closed her eyes, opened her mouth, and sang. Her alto voice poured forth like a swollen dam overflowing. She was singing not because she had the answer, but because she had a song.

ABOUT THE AUTHOR

Venise Berry is an associate professor of journalism and mass communications at the University of Iowa. She is the author of *So Good,* a Blackboard bestseller and an alternate selection of the Literary Guild. She lives in Coralville, Iowa.

Look for Venise Berry's

new novel

Colored Sugar Water

coming in January 2002

from Dutton.